I0762003

BORDER OF BONES

KINGDOM OF CHAINS BOOK THREE

TANYA BIRD

PROLOGUE

Salty winds howled across the bow as the ship carved its way through steel-grey waters. Tolly's knuckles whitened against the railing, his fingers numb from cold. Belowdecks, he could hear the passengers moaning and bringing up the small amounts of food they had brought with them. Smallpox had pursued them across the Irish Sea despite every effort to escape it.

'God save us,' the old woman said a few feet away, her breath exiting her like a ghostly mist.

Tolly fixed his gaze on the horizon where the Welsh coastline would appear. A prayer passed his lips, a plea for deliverance from disease and death aboard a floating prison. He tugged up the hood of his dead father's cloak to protect his ears from the piercing cold. The wood beneath his feet felt like ice seeping through the soles of his shoes.

The old woman coughed, prompting him to shuffle further away.

She laughed at that, her weather-worn face creasing. 'I don't blame you. That sickness respects neither young nor brave.'

Tolly did not respond.

'Ye think we'll make it off the ship, boy?' she asked.

He glanced west, knowing that the moment the sun disappeared, the temperature would plummet. 'God willing.' He never slept at night for fear he would not wake.

The words had barely left his mouth when someone called, 'Land ahead!'

The crew began shouting to one another, and ropes creaked overhead. Tolly could just make out the silhouette of land in the east.

'It seems God wills it after all,' the woman said, letting go of the rail and retreating to a spot out of the wind.

Tolly leaned his elbows on the timber and blew warm breath into his hands as he watched the land grow bigger and the details more vivid. An hour passed before he could see the dock. It was packed with men watching the ship approach. Eventually, he could make out the wary expressions on their faces. He watched as a small boat rowed out to the ship, preventing it from docking. An uneasy feeling replaced the hunger in his belly.

'Why are we stopping?' the woman asked, expecting him to have answers.

He glanced back at her. 'I don't know.'

The boat's occupants climbed aboard, two men holding cloths over their mouths and noses. They looked around, heard the noises below their feet. There was no sea wind strong enough to blow away the stench of death. They spoke with the captain, their voices rising and hands gesturing wildly. Then they climbed back into the boat and rowed away.

Two hours the ship remained there, the captain pacing back and forth across the deck and speaking in hushed voices with the crew. They were waiting for something. An answer or instruction of some kind.

Patience gone, the captain told the crew to dock. A minute later, the ship was moving towards the shore again. The men on the dock responded by fetching their longbows and setting the arrows alight.

Setting the arrows *alight*.

Nobody wanted them there. Who could blame them?

'Incoming!' someone shouted.

The sky was raining fire.

'Fire on deck!' shouted another.

Panic broke out like… like smallpox.

'They mean to scorch us from existence,' the old woman said, her voice shaking.

Tolly took off towards the bowsprit, smelling the smoke before he saw the flames. The visual confirmed what he already knew: the ship was on fire. Then came the rocks. When Tolly looked back at the dock, he spotted a catapult. One rock landed barely ten inches from his foot, breaking straight through the wood. He leapt back from it, his gaze travelling upwards when he noticed the sails were on fire. Then the ropes. Then the mast they were attached to. He glanced around, unsure where to go or what to do. There was no saving the ship as the flames spread from one sail to the next.

'Everyone, into the water!' the captain shouted when the barrels beside him burst into flames. 'Swim to the shore!'

That was manageable for Tolly. He was a strong swimmer. But what about the old woman? She would not survive the drop into the water, let alone make it ashore.

People were bubbling up from the lower decks now, their faces covered in blistering pox. They ran in all directions, screaming for people and at people and some to no one at all. It was simply the sound of fear exiting their bodies.

Tolly returned to his old spot on deck and looked around for the woman, but she was gone. Nowhere to be seen. He told himself that she had already jumped overboard and was on her way to the shore, because if he believed she was hiding somewhere on the boat, he might feel obligated to search for her, help her, despite being scared to death and unsure if he could even help himself.

He stepped up to the rail and looked down at the water. What if the fear rendered his arms useless? What if God willed him dead?

The heat coming from above had him shedding his cloak. The air bit at his skin through his clothes as he climbed onto the railing and stared down at the dark churning waters breaking against the side of the ship. People were jumping left and right, and Tolly flinched every time they hit the water below. Encouraged when they reappeared, he swung his legs over the railing and let go.

Down he fell, into the water. The shock of the cold stole the breath from his lungs. He resurfaced with a gasp as flames roared above him. His arms and legs still worked. Fixing his gaze on the shore, he headed towards it. He swam hard and fast until the surrounding air was pierced by the threatening hiss of arrows. But they were not aimed at the ship. They were aimed at the people in the water trying to escape it.

Then came the cries from those struck. Tolly pulled up to watch a man drown in front of him, just out of reach. He knew trying to help him would mean death. His gaze returned to the dock, to the determined faces of the archers. They were protecting their own, ensuring the plague of disease that had just arrived on their shores did not take what little they had left. But if Tolly did not make it ashore, then his brother would never find him. Cardiganshire was their meeting place. Their reunion was supposed to take place on the very dock they stood on trying to kill him.

Panic sent him swimming backwards out of reach of the arrows, but there was no getting back on the ship. A body floated by, facedown in the water. Even though he knew they were dead, instinct had him reaching for the person and flipping them over. It was the old woman, her mouth open and eyes empty. He shoved her away with a sharp intake of breath. With a surge of desperation, he swam away from the ship and out to sea, certain it would drag him down and drown him.

But he did not drown. He did not even tire at first. Fear was fuel, and he had an endless supply of it.

Only when he was so far out that no one could see him did he stop and look back. The once-proud ship was tilting, slowly sinking into the water inch by inch. Passengers and crew continued to jump overboard while others clung desperately to broken masts and burning sails. They were waving for help, but there was none. The wood creaked and groaned as it was ripped apart by the force of the sea. Shouts and cries rang out as water rushed into the lower decks, blending with the chaos.

There was no going back.

Tolly continued swimming, staying parallel to the coast.

He could make it ashore further south. He simply had to ignore the burn in his muscles and chattering teeth, the pain deep in his lungs every time he drew breath. The cold was a living thing, intent on killing him.

As he swam, images of his family flashed through his mind. His sister's pretty grey eyes. His father's eternal frown. His mother's gentle hands on his face. And the brother who would come looking for him. Ryder needed him to survive. He needed to save one person in their family after helplessly watching the others die.

Keep moving.

Tolly was not sure how long he swam for, but as the swell rose and fell, his strokes grew sluggish and his thoughts muddled. The sea was eager to claim him, drawing a defiant roar from deep in his chest. It rang out across the tumultuous water, all his remaining energy expelled with it. The salt blurred his vision as he fought to keep his head above the water's surface. So when a longship appeared in the distance, its dragon-headed prow cutting through the water, he did not trust what he was seeing. He treaded water, blinking, spitting, and swallowing.

'Mother! Look!'

It was a youthful voice, speaking in old Norse. Through the stinging salt, Tolly saw a young girl with platinum hair, parted in the middle and held in two braids, standing at the prow of the vessel. Her hand was pointed at him. A woman appeared beside her, a concerned look on her face. Her eyes were gentle as they took him in.

'What is it?' came the gruff retort of a man.

The girl looked behind her. 'A boy. He's alive.'

'We're not taking strays.'

The woman's expression softened as she looked at Tolly. 'He's just a boy. He'll drown if we leave him.'

'Death is all he'll bring aboard,' the man said as he stepped into view, peering down at Tolly. 'Likely come from the ship —full of pox.'

They argued like Tolly's parents had once. As they continued back and forth, the young girl reached for an oar and slid it across the side of the ship, extending it all the way out to Tolly. He grasped it with both hands, which was surprising given how numbed he was by cold and fatigue. A young boy stepped up beside the girl, a gosling tucked against his chest. He was a few years younger than the girl and stared down at him with open curiosity.

'Lina, get that oar back in the boat,' her father said when he saw what she was doing.

Her name was Lina.

She made a sad face at him. 'He's going to drown. We could tow him closer to shore.'

'No.'

'Farulf,' the woman said gently, touching his arm. 'Listen to your daughter. He's a *child*.'

Farulf appeared unmoved. 'He's a *stranger*.'

Lina blinked. 'What of courage in the face of strangers?'

The man's jaw worked as he looked around the boat at the other passengers, who were all waiting to see what he would say. Tolly's fate rested on his reply.

'Curse your soft hearts,' he muttered with a defeated sigh before walking off. 'Take us closer to the shore,' he instructed, 'but keep us out of shooting range.'

Lina gave Tolly a victorious smile. 'I've got you. Now hold on properly, and don't let go.'

With strength he found from God only knew where, Tolly dragged himself over the oar so that his chest lay across the blade. The girl struggled with the additional weight, so her mother stepped up to help her. Tolly wrapped his arms around the smooth timber, and his eyes sank shut. A moment later, the boat began to move.

CHAPTER 1

Waiting for an arrow to strike you was not Lina's idea of a fun time. She adjusted her grip on her shield as she scanned the green hills and rocky cliff faces around them. Behind her, longships were being dragged onto the beach. Everyone was eager to be on land after six days at sea. Glancing sideways at her brother, she noted the nervous twisting of his axe.

'Calm yourself,' she said quietly so their father would not hear. Simian received enough criticism without her drawing more attention to him.

Farulf stepped up between them and stretched out his fingers. They had fought an easterly wind to come ashore, which had aggravated his condition. 'All quiet?'

'Looks to be,' Lina said, keeping her eyes trained on their surroundings.

Simian cleared his throat. 'How far can a Chadorian defender shoot an arrow?'

Lina's mouth turned up. 'We're too far north for defenders. Attacking us would require them to venture out from behind their *walls*.'

'Wastelanders, then,' Simian said.

Lina lowered her shield a little. 'There are no wastelanders. The handful who survived the famine have since sold their souls to the Queen of Carmarthenshire.'

Farulf glanced at his daughter. 'That doesn't make them any less of a threat. Remember, there are close to a thousand soldiers in the Carmarthen Militia and only *four hundred* of us.'

'One sea warrior is the equivalent of three soldiers,' Lina said confidently, 'which means *they're* outnumbered.'

Her father chuckled lightly before turning away. 'Silly girl. Simian, give me a hand with the crates.'

The pair headed back to their longship.

An elkhound went bolting past, kicking water up at Lina. A moment later, Aife followed, howling like a dog. The ten-year-old was as wild as her older sister. Lina watched as Trinka splashed through the shallow water towards her, dark locks of hair clinging to her face thanks to the relentless ocean spray.

'Do you think it's safe for your sister to be running about the beach?' Lina asked.

Trinka looked at Aife, who was spinning in circles with her arms outstretched. 'She's not going to hurt anyone.'

'I meant safe for *her*.'

Trinka waved a hand. 'She has more knives packed into her trousers than me.' Drawing a deep breath, she rested an arm on Lina's shoulder. 'We're going to eat so much meat this summer. We'll be unrecognisable by the end.'

'You're assuming no one else is hunting here.'

The dog ran by again, spraying the pair with water. Trinka turned her face away, then looked off down the beach. 'Father says everything between here and River Teifi is ours for the taking.'

They had arrived in Llangrannog, a village in the kingdom of Cardiganshire. The kingdom was nestled between England in the north and Chadora and Carmarthenshire in the south. 'We've seen one beach. Let's not get too comfortable just yet.'

They both stared at Aife, who was now digging a large hole with the help of her dog.

'What are you doing?' Trinka asked her.

Aife continued without looking up. 'Making a trap!'

'What are you trapping?' Lina asked.

'A husband for Trinka!'

Trinka frowned. 'Whatever gets the job done, I suppose.' Then she called to her sister, 'Make sure it's nice and deep!' Her gaze returned to Lina. 'I like a *big man*.'

Lina shook her head. 'Oh, I know.'

'Incoming!' Simian shouted.

Lina and Trinka instinctively reached back for their bows, then realised that he was warning them of Olga's arrival. The goose skated across the water and landed next to Lina.

'For the love of God, boy,' Farulf scolded. 'Think before you shout. You had the entire clan arming themselves.'

Simian sheepishly adjusted his grip on the crate he was carrying. 'Sorry.'

Lina bent to pick up Olga. 'What do you think, old lady? Happy to be on land again?'

'She's happy to be anywhere but in a pot,' Trinka said,

affectionately tapping the goose's beak with her finger. 'Your father's too soft.'

'Don't let him hear you say that,' Lina whispered as she placed the goose down again. 'We should probably help.'

Farulf dispersed men left and right to check the area and set up a perimeter for their camp. When the longships were unloaded, they all made their way to the clearing amid the trees. It was out of sight of the shoreline for safety and offered some protection from the elements. Everyone got to work erecting tents and building enclosures for the small amount of livestock they had brought with them. Once the animals were secured, they made beds and built fires to cook on.

'Why is Olga not in with the rest of the livestock?' Farulf asked, taking a seat next to Simian in front of the fire.

He knew exactly why. Lina looked down at Olga, who was tucked in a loose ball on her lap. 'She's just warming up.'

Farulf gave her a tired look before diverting his attention to Simian, who was carving into a small piece of wood. 'Why aren't you out hunting?'

'I'll go shortly.' He was so engrossed in what he was doing, he did not even look up.

Farulf leaned closer. 'What is that?'

'Every detail I can recall of the seabird I spotted while coming ashore.'

Lina watched her father's expression turn from annoyed to defeated. Simian was always carving things of interest to him. Back home in Trondheim, there was a box in their house filled with such pieces. 'A puffin?' she asked.

'No.' He finally looked up. 'Its markings were different and its legs smaller.' He turned the knife in his fingers as he thought. It was clear that hunting was the last thing he wanted to do.

Lina placed Olga down on the ground and rose. The goose flapped her wings in protest and shook out her feathers. 'I'll hunt,' Lina said, going to fetch her bow and quiver. 'You take care of the fire.'

Simian looked up all hopeful. 'Are you sure?'

'I'm sure.'

Farulf changed the position of his feet. It was clear by the speed with which he moved that they were hurting. 'You won't be sitting around carving. There's firewood to collect.'

Lina went to leave.

'Don't go past the perimeter,' her father said.

'I'll only cross if our dinner does.'

He looked at her to check that she was joking. 'Very funny.'

Olga was preparing to follow her. 'Absolutely not,' Lina said to the goose. 'You are the worst hunting companion on the planet. Stay right there.'

Simian reached for Olga, and she honked in protest.

The air was already cooling as Lina went by Trinka's tent to see if she wanted to join her. Her father, Frode, said that the girls had gone to set traps.

'They left not long ago if you want to try to catch them,' he said, pointing in the direction they had gone.

'Thanks.'

He offered her a brief toothless smile before returning his attention to the fire.

Lina headed south in search of Trinka and Aife, greeting other clan members along the way. Many were out foraging for whatever food they could find close to the camp. While she did not know everyone by name, everyone knew the chieftain's daughter.

The landscape was breathtaking, with its rolling hills that stretched for miles, though sadly the meadows that would normally be populated with wildflowers in the summer resembled muddy fields. The sun occasionally peeped through the heavy cloud cover as she walked, warming her back for fleeting periods.

She trekked for half a mile before the trail she was following disappeared. After studying the ground for a moment, she found fresh tracks and followed them east.

As she moved beneath a canopy of trees, her surroundings darkened and the temperature fell. She listened for Trinka and Aife, but all she could hear were birds. The last thing she wanted to do was call out to them and send every hare in the region running for cover. But soon, she lost the tracks completely and ended up having to backtrack before eventually giving up the search.

She would be hunting solo that day.

As Lina looked around at the cloud cover seeping between the trees, she felt a sense of unease. The birds that had been vocal the entire walk had fallen quiet. That was the moment she realised she was not alone. She felt eyes upon her, watching. As much as she wanted it to be Trinka and Aife, remaining silent to avoid scaring off all the prey, her gut told her otherwise. She loaded her bow, her fingers instinctively tightening around it as she did so. When she went to walk forwards, an arrow struck the ground right where her foot was about to land. Drawing her bow, she searched the trees.

All was still.

Lina braced for another arrow, but it did not come. A

single shot was a warning. That was as far as she was allowed to go.

She flicked her gaze down to the arrow protruding from the mud, noting the peacock fletching. It seemed they were not the only ones with a perimeter in place. Her ears strained for any thread of noise as she continued to watch the trees around her but did not see a thing. Slowly, she began to back up in the direction she had just come.

'All right,' she said calmly, in case the shooter could hear her. 'I'm leaving.'

Only when she was twenty yards away from the arrow sticking out of the ground did she turn and jog away.

CHAPTER 2

Tensions were high when Tolly arrived in Lampeter that evening. The soldiers he had sent to investigate reports of sea warriors on their shores had returned with six warrior corpses, thrown over horses and transported eighteen miles back to Lampeter.

Tolly glanced sideways at his brother, who had travelled with him from the barracks to investigate the deaths. Ryder was squinting through the rain, eyes fixed on a nervous-looking Commander Ithon, who had led the assignment.

'We trained them to be more disciplined than this,' Ryder muttered, sounding every bit the defender.

Tolly nodded, his boots squelching in the mud. 'Where are they?' he called to the commander, his tone making it clear just how unhappy he was.

Ithon gestured behind him. 'They're in the house, General.'

The brothers continued straight past him, nodding a

greeting to the soldier standing guard at the door as they entered. Tolly stopped inside the doorway and looked around at the corpses. It was a bloody massacre. 'Shit.' His hands went to rest on his hips.

'I see those wastelander instincts are still sharp,' Ryder said behind him.

'Did we lose any men?' Tolly asked the commander, who had followed them to the door.

'One injured, sir. They're all accounted for.'

The smell of open wounds in a confined space had the men retreating to the outdoors once more. Tolly looked around the quiet street. There were barely a hundred people living in Lampeter due to its isolated location. Despite the Carmarthen Militia's protection extending all the way to the English border in the north, many families preferred to live south of the River Teifi, keeping within the traditional borders of Carmarthenshire.

'We should have six *prisoners,* not corpses,' Tolly said, his hard stare on Ithon.

The commander swallowed. 'We were ambushed.'

Tolly and Ryder exchanged a glance.

'So, what did you find out?' Tolly asked. 'Before the *ambush?*'

'We returned here immediately after the… incident.'

Ryder frowned. 'So, nothing?'

'Do you at least know how many warriors came ashore?' Tolly pushed.

Ithon shifted his weight. 'We did see smoke from their campfires.' He paused. 'And we know there are women among them, possibly even children.'

'What makes you say that?' Tolly asked.

'We encountered an armed woman as we were departing.'

'Another ambush?' Ryder said, clearly not buying the story.

Colour climbed the commander's neck. 'We fired a warning shot, and she left the area.'

Tolly rubbed his forehead. 'They would have figured out by now that they have men missing, which means they're going to come looking for them at some point.'

'Would be helpful to know how many warriors we're dealing with,' Ryder said, giving Ithon a pointed look. 'Or had a sense of how long they plan on staying.'

'One thing's for sure,' Tolly said. 'They won't leave without their men.' Then to the commander, 'Go to the stables and see how many horses we have at our disposal. We know the land better than they do, so darkness is our friend.'

Ryder drew a slow breath. 'Let's wait until Alveye and Hadewaye get here. They're only an hour behind us.'

Tolly agreed.

Kelton Alveye and Nixon Hadewaye made up half the unit of Chadorian defenders deployed to Carmarthenshire. They had found ways to remain in the kingdom long after the army had been formed, mostly because the other 50 percent of the unit had married Welsh brides. The only reason the Chadorian warden had agreed to let them stay was for diplomacy and intelligence purposes. Tolly would have happily accepted them as spies if it meant his brother could remain in the kingdom.

Less than an hour later, Alveye and Hadewaye rode into the village square and dismounted their horses. Alveye was easy to spot on account of his red hair and distinct height advantage, and Hadewaye simply looked happy to be there, even if it was to see corpses.

'Nice night for it,' Hadewaye said, looking up at the sky. 'How bad is the damage?'

'Bad,' Ryder said. He turned and led the way to the house.

The two defenders followed and went in, exiting a minute later.

'They are definitely dead,' Hadewaye said, wincing.

Alveye stopped in front of the others and crossed his arms. 'So, what's the plan?'

'How do you feel about the four of us taking a small trip west to see what our visitors are up to?' Tolly asked.

Alveye gave him a wary look. 'I gather this will be for observation purposes only. I don't fancy taking on a clan with only four of us.'

'They'll never know we were there.'

Hadewaye clapped his hands together. 'I'm in. It's been a while since we've visited the coast.'

'To be clear,' Ryder said, 'this is an exercise to collect intelligence, not a beach day.'

Alveye smirked at the ground.

'Let's get moving before the sun beats us there,' Tolly said.

The four men collected fresh horses from the stables, then headed west towards the abandoned village of Llangrannog. The journey took them through rolling hills and woodlands full of ancient trees. They moved slower than they would have liked due to the slippery ground and absence of light. The summer rain had been relentless.

They stopped once to rest and water their horses, then did

not stop again until they smelled the smoke from the campfires. A dog barking ahead helped them to estimate the distance.

'I'd say half a mile away,' Ryder said.

'And one dog is better than five,' Hadewaye added.

Alveye retrieved his bow. 'Hadewaye and I will go take a look.'

Tolly did not object, because they knew how to be invisible. There were no soldiers on earth with skills equal to that of defenders, and while the four men had done their best to pass those skills on to his own soldiers, there were some things that would always remain unique to them—like scaling a cliff face and swimming through water intent on killing you while equipped with only a strong heart and buoyancy.

Alveye glanced towards the camp. 'We'll signal if there's any trouble.'

'And we'll move in,' Ryder finished. Then to Tolly, he said, 'Let's split up.'

Alveye and Hadewaye disappeared into the trees, and Ryder headed off in the direction of the ridge.

Tolly made his way east, stopping a sensible distance from the camp before dismounting. He allowed his horse to graze while he watched his surroundings. The thick cloud cover made it even more difficult to see anything, so he was forced to rely on his hearing. Aside from the occasional croak of a frog or chirp of an insect, all was silent.

Minutes slipped by.

The sound of something moving over forest debris had Tolly quietly loading his bow and aiming it at the trees in front of him. He listened for signals from the others, but none came.

Leaves rustled, maybe six feet in front of him. The string of his bow went taut, then relaxed when a duck waddled out. No, not a duck. A *goose*. It stopped and stared at him in the dark. It did not look like the geese commonly found in the area, but as he was no expert on birds, he gave it no more thought than that. Ignoring it, he returned his attention to the task at hand.

That was the wrong thing to do.

The goose charged at him, taking flight and heading straight for his head. He swung his bow, but the goose managed to get past it, beating his face with its giant wings before latching on to his cheek. Swallowing down the curse words threatening to spill out, Tolly was forced to let go of his bow in order to grab hold of it. He tore the goose off his face and threw it. The bird tumbled twice along the ground, then got to its feet and ran, honking, off into the brush. Tolly wiped his cheek, eyes on the spot where it had disappeared. He had been prepared for all kinds of attacks—except that one. Bending, he reached for his bow.

'Leave it on the ground' came a female voice behind him. She spoke in English with a heavy Scandinavian accent.

Tolly froze with his arm outstretched for it. He had not heard anyone approach amid the chaos of the goose attack. He gave himself a second to consider his options, then, realising he had no intention of killing a woman—even in self-defence—he straightened, praying she would not shoot him in the back.

'Hands up,' she said, keeping her voice low.

Slowly, he raised his hands. 'Can I turn around?'

'So long as you behave.'

He turned, eyes locking with hers in the dark. While he

could not see their colour, he could see them blazing in his direction. He could just make out the sharp edge of her eyebrows, two long braids, and heart-shaped lips pressed into a determined line. She wore a strap dress and a string of beads. The two swords secured across her back and the longbow pointed at his chest confirmed his suspicions. She was a sea warrior.

'Easy,' he said, speaking in English as she had. She held his gaze with a steady ferocity that had him calculating how long it would take to draw his sword.

'You hurt her.' Her tone was thick with accusation.

He shook his head, confused, then realised she was talking about the goose.

'Geese are territorial,' she continued. 'They can be as effective as a guard dog. Did you know that?'

His eyebrows rose slightly. 'I did, actually. I just didn't know they could bite quite so hard.'

Her gaze fell briefly to his bloodied cheek. 'Their beak and tongue have serrated protrusions that act in the same way that teeth do.'

No one was going to believe him when he told this story later. 'Is that right?'

She regarded him for a moment before speaking again. 'Some of our men went missing today. You wouldn't happen to know anything about that, would you?'

Yes, he knew something about that, but the truth would do him no favours, so he responded with a fact in place of a lie. 'I just arrived here.'

Nothing changed on her face. 'Is that a peacock feather on your arrow?'

He glanced down at the ground. 'It is.'

She looked down at his uniform. 'Carmarthen Militia. You're a little far north of River Teifi, soldier.'

'And you're a little far south of Scandinavia, don't you think?'

Her head tilted slightly. 'We stand on Cardiganshire soil, which your half-blood queen has no claim to.'

Tolly did not reply, letting her lead the conversation instead. Her gaze darted left and right, clearly aware that he was not alone.

'You have something that belongs to us,' she said. 'Six members of our clan.' She observed him carefully for a reaction. 'They were watchmen, ensuring the area was safe. We're going to need them back.'

'What makes you think I know anything about that?'

'Call it a gut feeling.' She paused. 'The only reason an arrow isn't poking from your back right now is because of the courtesy shown to me earlier in the form of a warning shot.'

So this was the woman Ithon had encountered. His gaze never left hers. 'And here I thought you were holding back on account of your friends.'

She bravely lowered her bow.

'Is that wise?' he asked.

She exhaled sharply through her nose. 'We're both somewhat safe, because we each have something the other wants.'

'The only thing I want is for you to leave our shores at first light.'

'*Your* shores.' She tutted. 'Does the sad little army you belong to not have access to a map?'

'Actually, we drew new ones.'

Her teasing expression faded. 'Of course you did.'

The banter was far too easy with her, which he found

incredibly distracting. 'All right, I'll bite. What do you have that I want?'

She blinked. 'The two Chadorian defenders you sent to spy on us.'

Nothing changed on Tolly's face despite the flicker of panic in his chest. She had to be bluffing. Alveye and Hadewaye would never allow themselves to be caught and were more than capable of fighting their way to freedom if they had. But he could not ignore the confidence with which she spoke those words or the fact that there was nothing to be gained by lying. The truth would reveal itself soon enough.

'You seem surprised,' she said. 'Sea warriors know a thing or two about survival.'

It was clear she wanted an exchange. The defenders for the missing clan members. The *dead* clan members.

He only had a few moments to think through his next move. If she was telling the truth, taking her hostage would leave him with no point of contact for further negotiations. He had no choice but to agree to whatever she asked for so they could both walk away. 'Tell me what you want.'

She looked rather pleased with herself then. 'Bring the warriors to this very spot at sunrise. If you fail to do that, we'll be forced to come and get them—and you don't want that.'

'That you believe it a possibility shows how little you know of this region and the army protecting it.'

'I've no objection to people protecting their lands, but as we've already covered, this isn't your land. This is Cardiganshire.'

They stared at each other for a few beats before a whistle reached them, a warning from his brother. A very *late* warning. Ryder would come looking for him if he did not respond, and judging by the way the warrior looked nervously about, she knew it too.

Raising her bow again, she backed up a few paces. 'You have until sunrise.' With that, she turned and fled, her footsteps soundless despite the mud and debris, a running ghost.

Tolly had barely gathered his thoughts when Ryder appeared from the trees behind him with his sword in hand. He looked around before asking, 'Why didn't you answer me?' Then he noticed the weapon sitting in the mud by Tolly's feet. 'What happened?'

Tolly bent to pick up his bow. 'First, I was attacked by a goose.'

Ryder frowned.

'Then I was held at arrowpoint.'

His brother sheathed his sword and reached back for his bow. 'Which direction?'

'We're not going after her.'

'Why not?'

'Because there's more to the story.'

Ryder waited.

'She claims they're holding two defenders at their camp.' It was clear from Ryder's immediate expression that he did not believe that. 'She didn't refer to them by name.'

Ryder shook his head. 'There's no fucking way.' Then his expression changed. 'Unless they meant to be captured.'

The thought had crossed Tolly's mind. 'It would be quite the gamble.' He paused. 'She suggested a trade.'

'What do you mean?'

He drew a breath. 'The two defenders for the six clan

members we're holding.' A long silence stretched between them before he asked, 'Do we need to go in and get them?'

'Two of us against a clan of sea warriors?'

'When you put it like that…' He looked in the direction that the warrior woman had gone, brow furrowed. 'Then I guess we wait.'

CHAPTER 3

The camp was still abuzz with news of their captives when Lina returned. The fires had reduced to embers due to the rain, but people still gathered around them, discussing what they had seen and heard. A large portion of the warriors were now guarding the perimeter, not taking any chances with defenders and soldiers lurking.

The breeze carried the scent of the ocean, which was soothing to those who spent so much of their life at sea. Lina breathed it in as she went in search of her father to tell him what had happened. When she arrived at the small tent holding the two prisoners, she was surprised to find her brother standing outside in the dark. Instead of watching his surroundings, he was looking up at the sky, stargazing.

'Does Father have you guarding the defenders?' she asked, unable to keep the surprise out of her voice.

It was clear from his expression that he had not heard her arrive. 'Don't worry, Erik and Knud are *inside* the tent.' He looked over his shoulder. 'I can't believe we captured two defenders.'

After witnessing the utter disbelief on the soldier's face in the woods, she was now having difficulty believing it also. 'Any constellations visible tonight?'

'Barely a glimpse.' His disappointment was evident.

She looked around. 'Have you seen Olga?'

'I thought you took her with you.'

'I did. Then we encountered a soldier, and she took off.'

Simian's eyes widened. 'A soldier? Not a defender?'

'Carmarthen Militia.'

He sat with that information for a moment. 'Do you get the impression that they're taking the notion of allies a little far? Does Father know?'

'Know what?' came Farulf's voice. His giant frame emerged from the shadows, and he looked between them, waiting for someone to answer.

'I came upon a soldier in the woods,' Lina said, straightening. 'I've requested an exchange.'

Suspicion settled on her father's face. 'You came upon a soldier and didn't signal for help?'

'I didn't need help.'

He sighed. 'You expect me to believe that you just came upon a soldier and the pair of you had a civil conversation, no one was hurt, and you reached an agreement?'

'Oh, *he* was hurt,' she said. 'Olga bit his face. Have you seen her?'

Farulf scowled. 'I just came from our tent. She was asleep on your cot.'

'Clever girl. Knows her way around already.'

His scowl deepened. 'You should have signalled. We have no idea if we can trust the word of this man.'

'It should be a simple swap, and you can take as many warriors with you as you like.' She stepped past Simian and reached for the flap of the tent, eager to glimpse their bargaining chips. 'Six warriors for two defenders is a good deal in their eyes.' Lina drew the fabric back and stepped inside. 'If all goes well, we'll have established trust, and…' She trailed off and blinked hard, certain her eyes were deceiving her.

The defenders were not inside.

Simian walked in and froze. 'Ah…'

She punched his arm. 'Care to explain why Erik and Knud are bound and gagged before us?'

Overhearing, Farulf poked his head in to see what was going on. 'For the love of… Where are the defenders?'

Lina rushed forwards, dropped onto her knees, and removed the expertly tied gag from around Erik's mouth. Simian went to Knud and did the same.

'Where are they?' Lina asked the second Erik's gag was gone.

The warrior opened and closed his mouth a few times, stretching out his jaw. 'They escaped.'

'We can see that,' Farulf said, teeth clenched. '*How?*'

'One minute they were tied up, and then suddenly they weren't,' Erik explained. 'They drew us in here—'

'Then jumped us,' Knud finished, his ego clearly wounded.

Simian was struggling with the knot around the warrior's wrists. 'They *are* Chadorian defenders. I'm not sure why we're all pretending to be surprised.'

'We need to find them before they slaughter everyone in the camp,' Farulf said.

Simian shook his head. 'That's unlikely given they let these two live.'

The smug face of the soldier popped into Lina's mind. 'Did they say anything to you before they left?'

The two warriors exchanged a sheepish glance, and then Erik said, 'They thanked us for having them.'

'Then apologised for having to rush off,' Knud added. He swallowed. 'The redhead told us to practice our knots.'

Farulf pinched the bridge of his nose.

'They were solid knots,' Simian said in their defence. 'I watched you tie them.'

Farulf stepped all the way inside. 'They should have been secured separately so they couldn't help each other.'

'They were,' Erik said.

Lina pressed her eyes closed. 'Perhaps they meant to be caught in order to get a look inside the camp.'

Farulf appeared exhausted. 'It's possible.'

Historically, defenders were always victorious in the end. No clan had ever beaten them. The Vargr had come close when they had breached Chadora's walls years earlier, but the attempt had cost them dearly, and they had ultimately failed.

The soldier Lina had encountered had definitely been more surprised than concerned by the news. He likely knew there would be no prisoner exchange.

'Now we have no one to trade with,' Simian said. 'How are we to get our warriors back?'

Lina drew her dagger and cut through the rope around Erik's wrists.

'What I want to know is how on earth they got past *you*,'

Farulf said, his voice full of accusation. 'I'm surprised you didn't end up tied up alongside these two.'

Simian looked like a kicked dog. 'I didn't hear a thing.'

'Clearly.' Farulf crossed his arms over his enormous chest. 'Probably talking to the owls again.'

'I can assure you there were no owls.' Then Simian added quietly, 'Though I did spot some bats. There are thirteen species—'

'If you list them, I will gag you myself,' Farulf said. 'Both of you return to the tent immediately.' To Knud and Erik, he said, 'We need to track the defenders.'

'They'll be long gone by now,' Lina said. 'And we're supposed to be meeting with the Carmarthen Militia in a few hours.'

'One problem at a time.'

Seeing her father's patience was used up, Lina closed her mouth and gestured to Simian to start walking. The pair headed towards their tent. Simian's head was down, his feet practically dragging.

'You did yourself no favours by mentioning the bats,' Lina said when they were out of earshot.

He tipped his head back. 'I realised that as soon as the words left my mouth.' He sighed. 'In case everyone needed reminding of what an incompetent warrior I am, I was left to guard a tent, and inside that tent were two guards doing my job for me, and I still failed.'

Lina pressed her lips together when she felt the beginnings of a smile.

'It's not funny.'

'I know it's not.' She took a moment to compose herself. 'He's not expecting you to be some extraordinary warrior, but he's expecting competency at a minimum.' She gave his shoulder a sympathetic squeeze. 'You're the son of a chieftain.'

'Gods, I know.' He pushed her hand away. 'My arm still hurts from where you punched me before.'

Her hand fell to her side. 'Enough moping. We both know the world needs thinkers as well as fighters.' That was what their mother used to say when he was little.

'What about *over*thinkers?'

The corners of her mouth turned up. 'You mean geniuses?'

He rewarded her with a smile.

When they reached the tent, Lina found Olga still asleep on her cot, head tucked beneath her wing. She opened her eyes briefly when they entered before going back to sleep.

'You should put her in the crate before Father gets here,' Simian said, dropping down onto his bed.

'I really should.' Lina climbed beneath the blanket, careful not to disturb her, and began stroking her back. 'Though it's late, and she's so comfortable.'

Simian drew his covers up and over him, then rolled onto his side to look at her. 'I never saw a thing.'

When Lina woke the next morning, she looked from Olga straight to her father on the other side of the tent. Thankfully, he was still asleep, having returned to the tent late. She quietly rose and picked Olga up, carrying her outside with silent feet. Looking around, she saw many families were slow to rise that morning after all the excitement from the evening prior. Lina went to find Trinka, who had been on watch when she returned, keen to fill her in on what had happened overnight.

'She's checking the traps down at the beach,' Aife informed her.

'You mean the husband trap you dug?'

Aife's face filled with disappointment. 'The tide washed it away.'

'Oh.' She gave Aife's plait a playful tug. 'I'll help you dig it further away from the water next time.'

Lina headed towards the water and found Trinka at the edge of the beach, skinning hares atop a log. She looked up when she heard Lina approaching, scratching her cheek with the back of her hand and wiping blood over her face in the process.

'Two hares from five traps,' she called out.

Lina gave her an impressed look as she stopped on the other side of the log, drawing her dagger and preparing to help.

'Heard I missed all the excitement last night,' Trinka said.

'You didn't happen to capture two defenders on their way out, did you?'

'Afraid not.' She eyed Lina. 'Was your father mad?'

Nodding, Lina proceeded to tell her about the encounter with the soldier and detailed the defenders' great escape.

When she was done speaking, Trinka asked, 'Why are the men in our clan so incompetent?'

'They were holding *defenders.*'

'And *we're* sea warriors.' Trinka dropped a handful of guts into one of the pails, to be used in sausages. 'I find it odd that the soldier you encountered simply laid down his weapon when asked.'

'He did have an arrow pointed at his back at the time.' Lina set the skin aside. 'He might also be one of those rare breeds of men.'

Trinka screwed up her face. 'The breed with morals and manners?'

'It's possible.'

Trinka held the carcass up, inspecting it. 'Was this well-mannered man handsome?'

'It was dark. I could barely see him.' But that was not entirely true. There had been things she had noticed about him, like the contours of his jawline and the way his eyes glistened like black ice.

'What of his age?'

'Maybe twenty and five.'

'Married?'

'How would I possibly know that?' Lina gave her a knowing look. 'Is the husband situation within the Wolfvanir clan really that dire?'

'It's all right for you.' Trinka tossed the hare into the other pail. 'Your father will marry you off to some rich chieftain or prince.' She wiped her face again, adding more blood. 'Maybe we don't need the defenders to get our men back. Perhaps the promise of a peaceful summer will be sufficient.'

Before Lina could respond, a horn sounded, piercing the still morning. The women exchanged a concerned glance, then sheathed their bloody knives before snatching up the pails and running towards the camp.

'So much for peace,' Lina said.

They dumped the pails at Trinka's tent, and while Trinka was fetching her weapons, Lina plunged her hands into the wash pail to remove some of the blood. Trinka left hers on, the blood on her face making it look like she was ready for battle—which she always was.

Everyone was running about fetching bows, axes, and shields. The signal was not just a warning of danger but of warriors down. That meant the fighting had already begun.

Lina ran to her tent to get her bow, colliding with Simian as he hopped from the tent, attempting to wrestle his second boot on. 'Where's Father?'

He looked around with a panicked expression. 'I don't know. I just woke up.'

She pushed past him and headed straight for her weapons, grabbing her brother's at the same time. Outside, she found Trinka waiting with him, axe in hand.

'You're going to need this,' Lina said, tossing Simian's bow to him.

He caught it. 'I was coming back for that.'

The three of them jogged off towards the eastern perimeter, alongside many others. As they entered the dense part of the woods, they slowed when they caught sight of Farulf and Knud up ahead. Their weapons glinted in the early light streaming through the trees. As they got closer, Lina noticed her father's fierce expression, and her stomach dropped. He was staring at something on the ground. Or someone.

'What the hell are they looking at?' Trinka said quietly.

A few more steps and they had their answer. Lina's breath stilled when she saw corpses laid out on the ground, lifeless bodies arranged in a precise line. Their clothes were stained with blood and contained holes from where arrows or swords had pierced the fabric.

'Shit,' Trinka said on an exhale.

Lina recognised the spot where she had stood speaking

with the soldier mere hours earlier. Her vision swam as she counted the bodies. One, two, three… six. Shock turned to anger. *Six*. The dead warriors had been left for them in the agreed spot.

Simian walked over to one of the bodies and plucked what appeared to be a piece of folded parchment from the warrior's belt.

'What is that?' Farulf asked.

Simian unfolded it and ran his eyes over the words. 'A note. Written in English.' While many of them could speak English, it just so happened that he was the only member of their clan who could read it.

'Well?' Farulf barked impatiently.

Simian studied it for a long moment, then cleared his throat. 'It reads "Delivered before sundown, as promised."' His gaze fell to the corpses. 'Then it says "Here is your border."'

Trinka leaned in closer to Lina. 'So much for morals and manners.'

The ground tilted beneath Lina as she recalled her conversation with the soldier. Marching over to Simian, she snatched the note from his hand—even though she could not read one word of English—and stared hard at the letters.

'And they call us barbarians,' Simian said quietly.

Farulf remained anchored to that spot, taking in the scene before him. For a man well accustomed to violence, he seemed unsettled by it.

'Inform the families,' he told the warrior at his side. 'The rest of you carry these bodies to the camp.'

'Should we mark the border their army has put in place?' Simian asked, reaching for a stick.

Farulf stepped up to him and knocked it from his hand, his expression saying it all.

'Trinka,' he said, looking over at her, 'I want you to remain here and keep watch.'

'I can keep watch,' Simian said.

Farulf placed a hand on his shoulder. 'You read the note. Now let Trinka do what she does best.' With that, he followed the other warriors carrying the dead.

As he passed by Lina, she asked, 'What will you do now?'

He stared after the dead, then looked back at the imprints left in the muddy ground where they had lain. 'Now we establish some borders of our own.'

CHAPTER 4

Tolly and the defenders delivered the sea warriors to the agreed location, just as Tolly had promised. They left behind a unit of five watchmen to ensure their new neighbours respected the border laid out so clearly for them before returning east to Lampeter, where they found a tavern to eat in. With their stomachs full, they tried their hardest to stay awake and figure out what to do next.

'They'll only be here for the warmer months,' Hadewaye said. 'Then they'll pack up their longships and return north, back to their homes.'

The tavern maid came to clear their plates and refill their cups, drawing mumbled thank yous from the men.

'I still can't believe you allowed yourselves to get caught without telling us of your plan first,' Ryder said.

Alveye drank from his cup, then set it down with a satisfied sigh. 'The plan sort of happened in the moment. We couldn't gauge numbers without getting inside and figured we would be out before you knew we were *in*. We weren't to know you would meet a woman in the woods who would spread panic.'

Ryder's eyebrows lifted slightly. 'No one was panicking.'

'Would it kill you to worry about us occasionally?' Hadewaye asked.

'Probably.'

Tolly smirked into his drink. 'We should definitely be prepared for them to breach the border at some point. After all, sea warriors did breach Chadora's walls once, knowing exactly what awaited them on the other side.'

'That was the Vargr clan.' Hadewaye rested his elbows on the table. 'I still remember that day, horns blasting from every wall. We weren't even recruits at the time.'

'You were still in clouts,' Alveye said, drawing a faint smile from Ryder.

Hadewaye ignored the comment. 'It was a difficult period. All of Europe was starving. I suppose they were just trying to survive like the rest of us.'

Ryder stared at him from across the table. 'Weren't you living in the noble borough during the entire famine, wanting for nothing?'

That drew a chuckle from Alveye.

Before Hadewaye had a chance to defend himself, the tavern bell sounded and the door opened. An icy breeze swept through the room. Brock Tatum stepped inside and looked around, shoulders relaxing when he spotted the four of them seated in the corner.

'Look who finally decided to show up,' Alveye said, loud enough for him to hear.

Tatum made his way over to them. 'No need to stand and

bow,' he said when he reached the table. 'You know I don't like the fuss.'

Ryder dragged a stool over to the table with his foot. 'You never have to worry about us making a fuss.'

The Chadorian defender had married Queen Charlotte a few months earlier, earning him the title of King Consort of Carmarthenshire. While he really only cared about the defender and husband part, he liked to remind the others of the royal one to get a rise out of them.

'Nice of you to show up *after* we escaped our captors,' Alveye said, pouring him some ale.

Tatum took a long drink before replying. 'First, news of the warriors only reached Dinefwr Castle this morning. And second, I'm embarrassed you got caught.'

'*Conveniently* caught,' Tolly clarified.

Tatum threw his hands up. 'That's only slightly less embarrassing.'

'Only slightly?' Hadewaye said.

Tatum pinched a piece of leftover chicken from Alveye's plate. 'There's always going to be some level of embarrassment with you two.'

Alveye dragged his plate out of reach.

'So, you delivered their men back to them—dead,' Tatum said, sitting back, 'and now you're what? Sitting around trying to predict the extent of their retaliation?'

'I think I'll send for more men,' Tolly said. 'We'll use Lampeter as a base and ensure the perimeter is properly guarded.'

Tatum nodded enthusiastically. 'Yes, more men—a lot more.'

While Tolly had final say over every aspect of the

Carmarthen Militia, he valued and trusted the opinions of those seated with him. They had, after all, been at his side since before Carmarthenshire even had an army—or a queen, for that matter. All plans would be made in consultation with the people who had been with him from the beginning. Or in Ryder's case, since birth.

Tatum's knee bounced under the table. 'Rather bold move on their behalf to choose Carmarthenshire for the summer.'

The warrior's words from the night prior came to Tolly's mind. 'Technically, everything north of River Teifi is Cardiganshire.'

Everyone looked at him.

'Carmarthenshire absorbed its people after the famine,' he went on. 'While our protection extends all the way to the sea, Queen Charlotte has no claim over the land.'

Tatum shifted in his chair. 'Because Charlotte's primary concern right now is *peace*. She's just trying to keep people alive and fed. Army protection is vital for the alive part.'

'Lampeter is north of River Teifi,' Hadewaye pointed out. 'Yet every person in this village accepts Queen Charlotte as their queen.'

'These vague northern boundaries might prove problematic in the coming days and weeks,' Ryder said.

'And best not to underestimate the sea warriors' ruthlessness,' Tatum said. 'They're of the "shoot first and ask questions later" variety.'

There was a lull in the conversation, and Tolly looked over at the fireplace, surprised to find it unlit. He would have sworn he could smell smoke. It was probably coming from the kitchen or a nearby house.

He would have thought nothing more about it, but Ryder

got to his feet suddenly, with an expression on his face that Tolly had come to recognise. The other defenders clearly recognised it also, because Tatum immediately rose and headed for the door, and the rest of them followed without saying a word.

Tatum threw the door open, and they all stepped out onto the street. Tolly froze when he saw thick plumes of smoke rising into the sky at the far end of the village, darkening the horizon. The acrid scent now prickled his nostrils.

'Ensure everyone's out and send them to the river in case it spreads,' Tolly said, darting back inside to grab his bow and quiver he had left by the door.

Hadewaye and Alveye took off at a run towards the smoke.

'We'll check the perimeter,' Tatum said, gesturing for Ryder to follow him.

A distant scream had Tolly looking behind him. There, he saw more smoke rising. While he had no confirmation yet that they were under attack, every one of his senses was screaming danger at him.

Slinging his bow over his shoulder, he ran off down the street in the opposite direction of the others. Families had exited their houses and were looking around, visibly terrified. 'Everyone to the river!' he shouted at them.

Overhead, the smoke grew thicker. The further he ran, the more his vision blurred. He slowed momentarily when he saw a house on fire, then sped up again when he spotted people standing outside it. 'Is there anyone inside?'

A woman clutching her two children looked at him with a broken expression. 'It's our home.'

Many in Lampeter had lost their homes to flooding barely a year earlier.

'Go down to the river,' he told her, looking around for anything that might clue him in to what was happening. His gaze snagged on a figure slipping into the stables, a young man with distinctly foreign clothing. Tolly drew his sword and headed for the stables.

When he reached the door, he listened for a moment and thought he heard voices. Slowly, he opened the door just wide enough for him to get through and entered, hiding in the shadows as he observed a young male sea warrior bridling a horse. *His* horse. Tolly guessed the young man to be around seventeen or eighteen. While he was dressed like a warrior, he had the build of a poet. Tolly could have killed him three different ways from that distance, but something stopped him.

Then *someone.*

A woman emerged from one of the stalls, her eyes going straight to him as though sensing him there. She had fair hair with bright blue eyes, so familiar to him. It struck him that she might be the same woman he had encountered the previous night. She leapt backwards out of sight, and he heard her draw her axe. That drew the attention of the young man with his horse, who froze when he caught sight of Tolly. *Froze.* Not really the actions of a warrior.

When the woman exited the stall again, she was ready for him this time. Her axe was raised as she went to stand in front of him. It fell a few inches as recognition flashed across her face.

'You,' she breathed.

Something about the way she said it, the word laced with

betrayal, penetrated all the way to his bones. Her fiery gaze burned in his direction as she moved closer, like a feline approaching its prey.

The young man by Tolly's horse finally drew his sword. 'Should I kill him?'

'Not yet,' replied the woman, stopping six feet away from Tolly.

'You don't want to kill me,' Tolly said plainly.

A scowl settled on her face. 'Of course I do. I let you live once, and look what happened.' Her face contorted with anger. 'You killed them—all of them.'

'They were already dead.'

She laughed. 'Oh, you just found them that way?'

He blinked. 'No. I mean they were dead before last night.'

'Is that supposed to make me want to kill you less?'

Tolly was confident that he could handle the two of them and leave unscathed, but he wanted to try another approach first. 'I'm General Tolly Blackmane. If you kill me, every member of your clan will be slaughtered.' He was aware of the young man moving closer.

'Goodness,' the woman said. 'Brother, we have a *general* in our midst. I feel the sudden need to curtsy or wash his feet.'

So, the young man was her brother.

'Should we take him prisoner?' the brother asked. 'A general will give us a lot of leverage.'

Tolly glanced in his direction. 'You mean like the defenders you took as prisoners?'

The woman did not like that. 'No prisoners. Better to be rid of him and send the army into disarray.' She said this but still did not throw the axe.

Apparently feeling braver than he appeared, the young

man ran at Tolly, sword pointed in his direction and face determined. Tolly reached down for his dagger and threw it, striking his sword arm. The warrior's weapon fell to the ground with a clatter, and he roared through gritted teeth as he clutched his injured arm.

This was motivation enough to prompt his sister to finally throw the axe. It was a solid throw, but Tolly dipped sideways and heard it swoosh past his ear. She immediately drew her sword and lunged at Tolly. He darted left and caught hold of her arm, twisting it until she screamed out in pain and the sword slipped from her fingers. Drawing her closer, he pressed the blade of his sword to her neck, eyes searching hers. He waited for the fear to show, but it did not. Instead of cutting her throat like he should have, he shoved her away, hard enough to hear the air leave her lungs as she slammed into the stall door.

A whistle echoed through the smoky air. A distress signal. He needed to go, but first, he needed to deal with the two people trying to kill him.

He looked between them, his breathing heavy. It was clear the younger warrior was no longer a threat because he had surrendered to the pain. But there was still the matter of his sister. She could have reached down for her sword in an attempt to save her own life, but she did not move.

'We're taking the village,' she said without malice. Then she waited to see what he would do next.

Without saying another word, he simply left the stables.

The air was thick with smoke as Tolly jogged out onto the street, and he could see that more houses were now on fire. He spotted Alveye in the distance, directing people away from the smoke, and headed towards him.

'Talk to me,' he shouted when he was within earshot.

Alveye coughed into his fist. 'The entire west end is up in flames. We spotted some archers on the outskirts. We're outnumbered. All we can do is evacuate everyone.'

It was the right call. There were not enough of them to fight and protect civilians at the same time.

'Keep moving!' Tolly shouted, hurrying everyone along. 'Down to the river!'

He retrieved his bow and loaded it, walking backwards alongside those evacuating. As they exited the village, he watched the trees down his arrow, expecting to be shot at. But no arrows came for them.

The sound of the fast-flowing river was a welcomed one. It was normally slow moving at that time of the year, but the rain had turned it into a churning beast. Thankfully, the bridge was still intact, and Tatum and Ryder were now directing families across it.

Tolly, Hadewaye, and Alveye remained at the back, bows swinging left and right. The general's mind kept returning to the woman, replaying her words as her eyes flashed repeatedly in his head.

'I let you live once, and look what happened.'

Then some different words. Words from another time.

'I've got you. Now hold on properly, and don't let go.'

CHAPTER 5

They had not arrived in Cardiganshire planning to fight a war and take a village, but that was what they did. The murder of six of their clan members had changed everything. They took Lampeter with relative ease, the old-fashioned way—fire and smoke, archers at the ready, but they were not needed in the end. Lampeter was not a village of fighters. It was all families. The handful of soldiers and defenders available had to make a choice between saving lives and saving face. They chose lives.

The warriors watched them cross the river and let the rain take care of the fires. The flames were extinguished a few hours after they were started. Eighty percent of the village was completely untouched, which meant there were plenty of houses for the clan to occupy. If they managed to hold on to Lampeter, they would have more hunting territory than they would know what to do with.

'I want warriors all along the riverbank,' Farulf instructed, wiping sweat from his brow despite the cool conditions. 'Lina, go check on your brother.'

Nodding, Lina went to find Simian. Trinka was quick to fall into step with her, demanding all the details from her second encounter with the soldier.

'So, he's the general of the Carmarthen Militia?' Trinka said, emitting an impressed whistle. 'And he let your brother live?'

'He didn't let him live. He *threw a knife at him*.'

Trinka waved her words away. 'Trust me, if that man wanted him dead, he would be dead—as would you.' She looked towards the water. 'I think I'll head down to the river and keep watch.'

'Don't you want to see Simian?'

'What for? He has you to wipe his arse.'

Lina watched Trinka jog away, as energised as if she had just woken from a long, rejuvenating sleep, then continued on to the house where Simian was being treated. The rumours of defenders being excellent archers were not exaggerated in the slightest. They had shot a few of the warriors hiding in the trees as they exited the village. Thankfully, all had survived.

She found Simian resting alongside the rest of the wounded. His arm was bandaged, and the dagger Tolly had thrown at him sat on a wooden stool beside his chair. Frida, one of the clan's healers, was tending to an arrow wound on the far side of the room. She looked up when Lina entered.

'You fared better than your brother, I see,' she said with a warm smile.

'Surprising to no one,' Simian said quietly.

Lina walked over and kissed his forehead. 'Stop. At least he got your arm and not your throat.'

Simian opened and closed the fingers of his injured arm. 'I still have full use of my hand, so that's a positive.'

Lina picked up the dagger next to him, turning it in her hands as she admired the blade and the green-and-gold pattern along the hilt. It was expertly crafted, with no blemishes or imperfections. Her eyes narrowed on the Celtic symbol stamped into the ferrule for a moment. 'Do you know what this symbol is?'

Taking the dagger with his good hand, Simian turned the weapon slowly, studying it. 'The shamrock.' He handed it back to her. 'Or *seamróg* in the Irish language.'

'Irish? Are you sure?'

He nodded. 'The three-leaved clover is considered sacred by the Druids. They believe in the mystical power of the number three. The shamrock is a symbol of protection against malevolent forces.' His brow furrowed. 'I guess we're the malevolent force in this instance.'

Lina spun it expertly between her fingers, enjoying the weight and feel of it. 'Why would a Welsh general be carrying such a weapon do you think?'

Simian shrugged. 'Maybe it was a gift.'

'Or maybe he stole it. Wastelanders are notorious thieves.'

An amused expression settled on Simian's face. 'The way you say that, like stealing is *so* beneath you. We just stole an entire village.'

Lina slipped the dagger into her belt. 'We didn't steal it. We're borrowing it for the summer.'

He smiled and shook his head.

'So, you're fine?' she asked, running her eyes over him.

He raised his injured limb. 'Aside from the hole in my arm, yes.'

'I suppose that's one way to get out of fighting for a while.'

'I'm certain our dear father will find plenty of other things for me to do while I'm healing.'

The sound of footsteps coming at a run had everyone in the house looking towards the door and Lina reaching for her sword. Trinka appeared, spitting stray hair from her mouth before speaking. 'Gods, that was all the way down my throat. Your father has asked for you.'

Lina made a move for the door.

'Not you,' Trinka said. 'Simian.'

Stilling, Lina looked from her brother back to Trinka. 'What for?'

'The general and his guard dogs are waiting on the bridge to speak to him. He wants someone with strong English to ensure their communication is clear.'

'I speak fluent English,' Lina pointed out.

Simian stood up, testing his legs. 'Perhaps he doesn't trust your skills after your last conversation with the general ended with six dead warriors.'

'That's not my fault. You heard what the general said. They were already dead.'

'Why are you moving like you lost a leg?' Trinka asked Simian. 'Hurry up.'

He scowled in her direction. 'Forgive me for being a little wobbly after *bleeding out in the stables*.'

She rolled her eyes. 'I'll get you a horse. The temptation to push you down the hill will be too great.'

'Thank you,' Simian said, looking unsure. 'I think.'

Trinka dashed off, returning a few minutes later with a tall chestnut mare, branded *CM*, clearly belonging to the

Carmarthen Militia. It was a stunning animal, with a coat that shimmered like copper in the sunlight.

'Do you think it'll rub salt into the wound if we arrive on one of their horses?' Lina asked.

'I hope so,' Trinka replied.

With some gentle help from Trinka—in the form of nearly throwing him straight over the horse—Simian mounted the mare. She stirred, seeming unsure of the stranger upon her. Lina took hold of the reins.

'It's embarrassing enough that I'm riding there,' Simian said. 'Don't make it worse by leading me.'

Lina let go and exchanged a glance with a smirking Trinka. Then the three of them headed down to the river in silence.

They passed through the trees at the edge of the village, and as they emerged, Lina caught sight of the bridge. On one side stood the general and two defenders, and on the other were her father, Erik, and Knud.

'I can feel the tension from here,' Simian said quietly.

Farulf glanced in their direction as they neared the bridge, waiting with an impatient expression for them to reach him. Simian dismounted at the base of the bridge and did his best impression of a healthy warrior.

'I don't want anything lost in translation,' Farulf told him.

Simian nodded. 'All right.'

'Can I come too?' Lina asked.

Farulf thought for a moment. 'Only if you can keep quiet. I want calm, as I suspect their arrows can reach a lot further than ours. Understood?'

'Yes.'

Trinka waited with the horse at the foot of the bridge as

the three of them made their way to the middle, followed closely by Erik and Knud. Tolly and the two defenders met them halfway, leaving around eight feet between them. The horse let out a small whinny, and judging by the way Tolly's gaze shot to her, it appeared to be one of recognition.

'That's my horse,' he said, competing with the noise of the river. Then his gaze fell to the blade tucked in Lina's belt. 'And that's my dagger.'

'The very one you used to stab Simian here,' Lina said, her tone light.

His gaze travelled up to meet hers, and she saw something in his eyes that had not been there the last time he had looked at her. It was familiar and unnerving. He did not reply to her comment, instead turning his attention to Farulf.

'My son, Simian, speaks excellent English,' Farulf began. 'I thought it best he be here.'

'I see.' Tolly glanced at Simian. 'How's the arm?'

Simian looked down at the bandaged limb. 'Still attached —just.'

Farulf cleared his throat before speaking. 'We came to these shores with no malice or intent to harm anyone. We were deliberate in where we pulled up our oars.' He went on about how all that had changed the moment Tolly's men had taken the lives of their warriors. The actions had marked the beginning of a war he did not initiate or want but would fight anyway. Simian corrected and clarified a few of the phrases Farulf used.

'It was unfortunate that any lives were lost,' Tolly replied, 'but my men have a job to do. They protect these lands, and your arrival threatens the safety of the people who live here.

We returned your men out of politeness.' His gaze went to Lina. 'And because I promised your daughter I would.'

Lina tilted her head. 'In case it wasn't clear, I expected them to be returned *alive*.'

'As I told you earlier, they were already dead before we met.'

'They were already dead because your men *killed* them.'

'Lina,' Farulf said, a warning in his voice.

Something flashed on Tolly's face when Farulf said her name. His gaze snapped to hers, and the malice that had been in his eyes seconds earlier was gone. He stared at her for a long moment.

'On the subject of men being killed,' the fair-haired defender said behind him, 'you wouldn't happen to know where the five men who remained near your camp today are? They've not returned.'

'Dead,' Farulf replied calmly. 'Alongside our own.'

The other defender, who could have been Tolly's twin, took a step towards the chieftain, prompting Erik and Knud to do the same. Both Tolly and Farulf raised a hand to stop them.

'You can't remain in Lampeter,' Tolly said, his tone growing colder. 'If you leave now and remain within the boundary we laid out for you, we won't come after you.'

Farulf narrowed his gaze at the general. 'I didn't trust your army before they killed my people, and I certainly don't trust them now.'

'The offer won't come twice,' said the Tolly lookalike. 'I would take it.'

When Farulf did not reply straight away, Simian asked, 'Did you need me to translate?'

'No.' Farulf pointed over his shoulder without taking his eyes off Tolly. 'That's not your land.'

'You're right,' Tolly replied. 'It belongs to the terrified people behind me. They work the land and built their homes.'

Farulf gave an understanding nod. 'Perhaps you should have considered them before you rode east and began slaughtering my people.' He turned to leave.

'I know you're not some monster,' Tolly said, stopping him. 'You could have shot these people as they fled and you didn't.'

Farulf looked him straight in the eye. 'I will shoot every one of them dead if you force my hand.' He paused to let the threat settle. 'Tell them to find new homes for the summer.'

'I'll take that as a declaration of war,' Tolly replied.

Farulf gave him a deathly stare before walking away. One by one, the others followed, but Lina remained where she was.

'You need to talk some sense into your father,' Tolly told her.

A rumble of thunder rolled overhead, and out of the corner of her eye, Lina saw the mare stir and Trinka attempt to calm her. 'What makes you think he listens to me?'

He looked over at his horse, licking raindrops from his lips as it began to fall in heavy sheets. 'She doesn't like storms.'

'Horses take confidence from their riders,' Lina said. 'And they will feed off our fear.'

He brought his gaze slowly back to hers, causing her lungs to slow down. A clap of thunder sounded, and the mare reared up. Trinka quickly got her under control.

'Perhaps you should stick to geese,' Tolly said.

'Lina!' Farulf called to her.

She began backing away from him. 'If we see you or any of your men on this side of the river, we'll shoot you without hesitation.'

Tolly's lips turned up slightly. 'Don't get too comfortable.' His gaze went again to his mare before he turned away from her.

She watched the three men exit the bridge. When Tolly stepped down onto the muddy ground on the other side, he glanced back at her. Something in his expression had her turning and hurrying after her family.

CHAPTER 6

Tolly sent a unit of two hundred soldiers north to River Teifi. He needed to ensure the sea warriors did not expand their territory any more than they already had. Once he was confident the river was secure, he and Tatum borrowed some horses from a nearby farm and headed south to Dinefwr Castle. It rained for most of the twenty-mile journey, falling so hard at one point that they were forced to take cover beneath an oak tree. Robins chirped of their wet misery from their perches above.

'If you've ever wondered what birds sound like when they curse,' Tatum said, looking up, 'that's it.'

Tolly's mouth turned up. 'I'm always learning something new from you.'

As soon as the rain eased, they continued on their way, relieved when the towering stone walls of Dinefwr Castle finally appeared, a fortress woven into the fabric of the landscape. They pushed their horses faster for the last leg of the journey, slowing to a walk once they were inside the walls.

The men dismounted near the stables, handing the reins over to the waiting grooms. A few minutes later, their boots were echoing along the corridors as they headed to the throne room. The queen's primary guard, Ita, was waiting outside the room. She smiled when she first saw them, but it faded when she registered their expressions.

'Uh-oh.' She looked between them. 'I recognise bad news when I see it. What happened?'

Tatum looked past her to the closed door, then whispered, 'We sort of lost Lampeter.'

Ita blinked, visibly confused. 'What do you mean, *lost*? How does one lose a village?'

'It was taken by sea warriors,' Tolly clarified.

'How many dead?' she asked, bracing for the answer.

'All evacuated over the river.'

Ita released a breath. 'I'd lead with that.' Lowering her voice, she said to Tatum, 'She has just finished a meeting with her father.'

The defender winced. 'Noted.'

Ita opened the door and led the men inside. 'Your husband and General Tolly, Your Majesty.'

Sunlight filtered through stained-glass windows, casting hues of blue and purple across the queen as she rose from her seat with a concerned expression. 'Back so soon?' she said, looking at Tatum. Then she sniffed the air. 'Why can I smell smoke?'

Tatum walked around the table to her, taking her hand and kissing it before gesturing for her to sit. 'First thing you need to know is that everyone is safe—'

'The sea warriors have taken Lampeter,' Tolly said, taking the seat opposite her. She expected him to be direct with her.

Charlotte's face fell. 'I see.'

Tatum pinched the bridge of his nose. 'I was getting to that part.'

She patted his hand.

Tolly proceeded to tell her everything that had happened in the lead-up to Lampeter, and then Tatum told her about the conversation with the chieftain. Charlotte listened intently, glancing occasionally at Ita, who appeared on edge and ready to run off to Lampeter to take the village back solo.

'Based on those numbers,' Ita said, 'they have two hundred competent fighters at best. Our army is close to nine hundred strong now. We could have them out tomorrow.'

Charlotte raised her eyebrows. 'Probably best to think this through properly. These clans do not exist in isolation. They are known to join forces when necessary, and the last thing we want is our beaches littered with boats and dead bodies.'

Tolly nodded in agreement. 'These people know how to stay alive and aren't afraid to kill for the sake of self-preservation.'

The queen thought for a moment. 'So the question becomes, how do we drive them back without starting a war we do not want? We may be forced to tolerate their presence for a few months, but I will not tolerate people being expelled from their homes. Our disagreement on where the border falls does not change the fact that those people are under my protection.'

The woman had been born to rule. Tolly had no doubt about it. He also knew there would never be another queen quite like her. 'I do have *one* idea.'

'Go on,' Tatum said, leaning forwards in his chair.

As it had only just come to him, he took a second to think it through. 'What if we let nature do the heavy lifting for us?'

Charlotte's brow furrowed. 'Meaning?'

'There's no sign of the rain easing, and River Teifi continues to rise.'

Ita spoke up at that. '*That's* your big plan? To wait until the river floods?' Sometimes she forgot who she was speaking to.

'I thought we could help things along,' Tolly continued, ignoring the bad behaviour. 'There's the recently built water catchment north of Lampeter. It's currently at capacity, which means some overflow is expected. With some help, that overflow could be rather severe.'

'How severe?' Ita asked, clearly invested now.

'Lampeter could be underwater within hours,' Tatum said. 'The sea warriors would have no choice but to retreat to higher ground.'

Charlotte folded her hands on the table in front of her, looking sceptical. 'Have you considered the long-term consequences of this? Have we not had enough flooded homes in this kingdom?'

Tolly nodded. 'More than enough, but our options are limited.'

'What about the women and children you evacuated?' she pushed. 'Would they be in any danger?'

'There would be time for families to relocate,' Tatum said. 'The river will rise quickly but gradually. Time on both sides, resulting in fewer deaths than if we were to attack.'

'Can't we do both?' Ita asked.

Charlotte blinked slowly. 'Ita, could you please do me a favour and check that my father has departed?'

'Are you trying to get rid of me?'

Charlotte looked straight at her and replied, 'Yes.'

Ita glanced between the men, who were both suppressing smiles. 'Of course, Your Majesty.' She intentionally clipped Tolly's shoulder as she passed by him.

After the door closed, Charlotte said to Tolly, 'If this does end in a battle, I am sending her straight to you.'

Tolly gave a small nod. 'Noted.' While Ita loved her role as the queen's primary guard, she would always be a wastelander rebel at heart.

'I have made a point of never interfering with military decisions,' Charlotte continued. 'So if you feel that destroying the water catchment that I paid for is the best course of action for the kingdom, then I support you.'

Tatum sat back in his chair. 'I'm sure we could fix it after we break it.'

Charlotte looked at him. 'Sometimes I forget what a romantic you are.' Then to Tolly, 'Where will the displaced families go in the meantime? We cannot have people out in the rain.'

'The population is quite small, around 150 people. They can be dispersed between neighbouring villages for now.'

'Good.'

Rising from his chair, Tolly bowed his head. 'Thank you, Your Majesty. I'll be sure to keep you informed of our progress.'

He had been one of her biggest sceptics when she first arrived in Carmarthenshire. The idea of a princess returning to her homeland, having never set foot on Welsh soil before, had seemed ludicrous. But she had won him over one brave and selfless act at a time. Charlotte had poured her entire inheritance into Carmarthenshire while expecting nothing in return but a happy and peaceful kingdom. There was not a person in Carmarthenshire who she had not won over eventually, simply by being herself.

'I'll return to the north with the general,' Tatum said, kissing his wife's cheek as he rose. 'I intend to remain there until Carmarthenshire's borders are secure.'

Charlotte gave him a tense smile before saying to Tolly, 'Please ensure my husband returns to me in one piece, General. Finding a replacement will only add to my workload.'

Tolly caught the glint of humour in her eyes despite the absence of a smile. 'I'll do my best, Your Majesty. And if I fail, I'll bring Alveye back for you.'

'Funny,' Tatum said.

Charlotte allowed herself a small smirk as she rose from her seat. 'Take care, both of you.'

By the time the two men arrived at the River Teifi, the two hundred men Tolly had sent for had also arrived and set up camp a few miles back from the water, out of sight of the sea warriors. That evening, Tolly and the defenders, along with the commanders, convened in Tolly's recently erected tent while rain pounded the canvas. The air inside was heavy with anticipation as the men pored over the map laid out on the ground between them. Tolly traced a finger along the winding path of the river as he calculated distances.

'We could cross here on horseback,' he suggested. 'The

water is shallow, and the archers will be easier to spot. The water catchment is around two miles from this point.'

'Is it shallow enough to get a cart across?' Alveye asked. 'We're going to need some heavy-duty tools if we wish to break through the rock and clay quickly.'

'Nowhere is shallow at the moment,' Ryder pointed out. 'And the water's moving too fast to get anything other than a few sturdy horses across at best.'

'Let's send some scouts to the river at first light to evaluate,' Tatum suggested.

Hadewaye perked up. 'I'm happy to go.'

'Good.' Tolly rubbed at his eyes, which were threatening to close after too many days in the saddle and no sleep. 'Let's do that.' He looked around the tent. 'Get some sleep in the meantime. I suspect it's going to be another long day tomorrow.'

All the men filed out of the tent except Ryder.

'Everything all right?' his brother asked as soon as they were alone.

Tolly nodded. 'Just tired.'

Ryder assessed him for a moment, then quietly left.

It was not a lie, just a shortened version of the truth. The fact that he was in the middle of a conflict with the woman who saved his life all those years back was probably worth a mention, but he could hardly talk to anyone else about it when he had not processed it himself.

Aside from those keeping watch over the river, the rest of the camp settled into a restless slumber. There was no crackling of campfires to warm themselves by, as they did not want to alert the warriors to their presence. The rain kept them cold and miserable.

Tolly fell asleep to the sound of rain hitting the canvas,

then woke just before dawn. Pulling on his boots, he fetched the map from his satchel and studied it in the grey light.

When the sun touched the horizon, the soldiers slowly emerged from their tents, their breath visible in the crisp air. Tolly went to find Hadewaye, who had already saddled a horse and was preparing to head east to investigate. Ryder decided at the last minute to travel with him in case he ran into any trouble.

'He worries about me,' Hadewaye said, winking at Tolly.

Ryder glanced in his direction as he checked the girth of his saddle. 'I worry about you handing yourself over to the enemy again and having to rescue your sorry arse.'

After they had gone, Tolly returned to his tent and threw down some bread and cheese, then took a horse from the yard and rode to the river to check in with the soldiers keeping watch.

'Everything was quiet overnight, sir,' one guard informed him, speaking loudly to compete with the noise of the river.

The water had risen another three feet overnight, and the bridge they had stood on the day prior was now half submerged.

When he arrived back at the camp, he saw that Hadewaye and Ryder had returned. They were standing with Alveye and Tatum by the horses, their expressions telling.

'I gather from your faces that we can't get a cart across,' Tolly said as he joined them.

Hadewaye shook his head. 'Even the narrowest section of the river will be a challenge for the horses. Add tools and they won't stand a chance.'

A long silence stretched out as Tolly thought about their next move. 'Isn't there a log bridge further north?'

'You won't get horses across that,' Tatum pointed out.

'But you might get donkeys across,' Alveye said.

Hadewaye frowned. 'The warriors would know of it by now, surely. It'll probably be guarded.'

'We can deal with a few guards.' Tolly's gaze went north. 'We'll likely lose both bridges when the catchment opens. Whoever crosses will be stranded until the water levels drop.'

Ryder exhaled. 'I'll go.'

'If you go, we all go,' Tatum said.

Hadewaye's expression melted. 'You two.'

'Tatum should remain here,' Tolly announced.

Tatum practically flinched as those words landed. 'What?'

'You're the king consort. We can't risk it.'

Tatum crossed his arms. 'Since when have any of you cared about that title unless you're making a joke?'

'I'll take your place, and you can manage everything this side of the river in my absence.'

He was about to object, then changed his mind. 'Fine. It's about time this army had proper leadership.'

Tolly clapped him on the shoulder, then said to the others, 'We leave in one hour.'

CHAPTER 7

Lina spent the night in one of the stolen houses, sleeping in a stranger's bed, knowing the family who owned the home was likely sleeping outdoors in the rain. In the corner of the tiny bedroom she was sharing with Simian, a badly sewn doll stared accusingly at her. She had to remove it from the room.

In the morning, she made her way down to the river to relieve Trinka, who had been keeping watch overnight. Few people enjoyed night watch, but Trinka preferred it. She enjoyed seeing what the world got up to when humans were asleep.

'All quiet?' Lina asked.

Trinka nodded. 'The water has risen quite a bit.'

Looking in the direction of the bridge, Lina saw that the water was now gushing over the guardrail. Summer simply refused to arrive. Her gaze then went across the river, where aside from a few archers on the other side, there were no signs of life.

'He came by earlier to check in with his soldiers, if that's who you're searching for,' Trinka said, a knowing look on her face.

Lina rolled her eyes back to her friend. 'Part of keeping watch is *watching*.'

The expression on Trinka's face turned playful. 'I watched the general closely yesterday. He spent more time looking at you than your father.'

'No, he didn't.'

'Calling me a liar?'

'I'm calling you an exaggerator.'

Trinka stretched her arms overhead. 'So, what's the plan?'

'Father wants to relocate the rest of the clan to Lampeter as soon as possible.' His logic was sound. They were safest together. Having them split between two locations weakened them.

'I gather he'll be sending someone else to collect them.'

'Why do you say that?'

Trinka angled her head. 'It's a six-hour walk, and he limped through the last hour yesterday.' Before Lina could deny it, she added, 'And I'm not the only one who noticed.' She drew a breath and released it. 'He's getting worse.'

There was no point denying it. Not to Trinka, anyway. 'The healers have exhausted themselves trying to find plants that will bring him some relief. The things that used to help no longer do. His hands look like they've been trapped in a vise.'

'I once trapped a man's hand in a vise,' Trinka said casually. 'He stole a cod from me.'

It was not the direction Lina had been expecting the conversation to go, but that was Trinka for you.

'Never stole from me again,' she said brightly. Then her face turned serious. 'Have you eaten?'

'Ah, not yet.'

Trinka prepared to leave. 'There'll be all kinds of goodies hidden around this place. Leave it with me.' She walked away before Lina could respond.

For the next few hours, Lina remained at the river until another warrior came to relieve her. When she returned to the house, she found Simian seated by the window, poring over a book he had found. The room smelled wonderful.

'Trinka made porridge with honey,' he said without looking up. 'She left some for you.'

'Has Father eaten?'

He brought the book close to his face. 'Mm' was all he said.

After serving herself a bowl of pure comfort food, Lina looked around the room with a sense of curiosity. She began searching through cupboards and chests, feeling guilty the whole time but continuing anyway. Her fingertips brushed over the garments of a small child, likely the owner of the doll, and she found herself reflecting on Carmarthenshire's dark history. Its people would be forever changed by what was done to them in the camps built by the marcher lords after the famine. Everyone had suffered, lost loved ones, and killed others just for the chance to survive a little longer. The people left were the ones with the stomach to see the famine all the way through—no matter what.

Olga came honking into the room, interrupting her thoughts. Lina picked her up, then opened a drawer, flicking through yellowed letters. Words and pictures filled the pages, and even though she could not comprehend the words, the act of looking still felt intrusive.

As she pushed the drawer closed, Trinka strolled through the front door with a freshly slaughtered chicken slung over her shoulder. Her gaze landed on Olga. 'You might want to cover her eyes,' she said, slapping the bloodied carcass down onto the table. 'Plucked it for you and everything.'

'Thank you,' Lina said, walking over to her. 'Who needs a husband when I have you to provide and protect?'

Simian tore his gaze from the pages of his book and frowned at the chicken on the table. 'Yes, I'm sure you're going to make a wonderful husband one day.'

'I wish I could say the same about you,' Trinka said, 'but you're destined to die alone in a monastery, your remains found several days after you pass, half-eaten by cats.'

'Leave him be,' Lina said, placing Olga on the ground. 'He's injured.'

Trinka snorted. 'Are you referring to the tiny puncture wound in his arm?'

'The dagger went all the way through,' Simian said.

Trinka remained unmoved. 'I once saw a man fight with his left hand while his right arm hung on by skin alone.'

The colour drained from Simian's face. 'Did he live?'

Trinka shook her head. 'Bled out within seconds, but he kept hold of his axe.'

Lina exhaled noisily. 'Must you?'

'What? He's old enough to know the horrors of war.' She pointed to the door. 'He should be out there practising with his left hand. Our enemy won't care if he's injured.'

Simian straightened in his chair. 'Frida said I should rest until it heals.'

Trinka waved away his words. 'What would she know? I've never seen her even pick up a sword.'

'Because she's a *healer*,' Lina pointed out.

A loud crack sounded outside, followed by a crashing noise. Lina's gaze snapped to the front door as the walls rattled around them. Olga began honking, wings extended, ready to fight anything and anyone.

Trinka retrieved her axe before running out of the house. The siblings followed, Simian tripping over the goose in the doorway. Outside, everyone was heading for the river.

'Wait right there,' Lina called to Olga over her shoulder.

The goose took a few steps after her before stopping and watching them jog off.

Lina's feet slowed when the river came into view. The savage current had torn the bridge from its stumps, and she watched as it was whisked away downstream. The water had risen well over the banks and was swallowing everything in its path. An entire tree floated by.

Simian looked up at the fine mist of rain falling on them. 'It doesn't make any sense. Even if all the water in the region was funnelling to this river, that wouldn't account for this sudden rise.'

The hair on the back of Lina's neck prickled as she looked around for her father, spotting him with Knud downstream. She headed towards him.

'Saddle a horse,' he said the moment she was within earshot. 'I want you to ride upstream and check on the other bridge, along with the men guarding it.'

There was no time for questions. She took off at a jog for the stables.

'And take Simian with you!' he called after her.

Lina slowed down and gestured for her brother to join her. He said something to Trinka, then reluctantly followed.

'So much for rest,' Simian said when he caught up to her.

Entering the stables, they were greeted with nervous nickers. The horses paced in tight circles, likely sensing the danger. The scent of hay and leather was a comforting contrast to the chaos unfolding outside.

Lina's gaze settled on Tolly's horse. She went to saddle the mare, then saddled the gelding in the next stall over for her brother. Handing him the reins, she said, 'Don't fall off.'

They rode past the house so they could collect their weapons, and Lina locked Olga inside so she would not follow them.

'The water's still rising,' Simian said as they exited the village.

In a matter of minutes, it had pushed the warriors halfway up the hill.

'Could it reach the houses, do you think?'

'It's possible if it continues at this rate.'

Lina's gaze went across the river. Not a soul in sight. 'We need to move,' she said, kicking her horse into a canter.

As they rode, Lina noticed an eerie stillness had settled over the region. The landscape appeared desolate and abandoned, as if nature itself was holding its breath. The pair urged their horses forwards, kicking mud up behind them. She expected to encounter warriors from their clan, either moving inland or returning to the village, but they saw no one.

'Where's this bridge?' she asked her brother.

'I have no idea.'

The path they were following grew increasingly muddy and was obstructed with fallen branches, forcing them to veer off it every few paces. They continued for another half mile, their horses navigating the slippery terrain with caution, before Lina suddenly pulled the mare up.

'What's the matter?' Simian asked. Then he saw them. 'Dear gods…'

Ahead of them, the ground was littered with fallen warriors. Their mud-soaked bodies lay motionless amid the trees, arrows protruding from their torsos and necks. Lina stared at the scene, trying to comprehend what had transpired.

'May the gods have mercy on their souls,' Simian said beside her.

Dismounting, Lina ran to the closest body to check for signs of life, but there were none. She moved from warrior to warrior, knowing it was a fruitless task. When she reached the last man, she noticed he was bleeding from the stomach, but there was no arrow. Upon closer inspection, she saw it was a sword wound.

She rose slowly and looked back at her brother. 'They've crossed the river.'

'The soldiers?'

She nodded.

He climbed down off his gelding and went over to inspect the body. 'But how did they…?' His gaze swept the length of the river. 'I'm guessing this is where the bridge *was*.'

Lina went to speak, then closed her mouth when she felt the ground rumble beneath her feet. 'What is that?' She turned to her brother for answers, but he looked as confused as she was.

'I don't know.'

He was supposed to know. Knowing things was what he excelled at. She forgave his incompetence in all physical pursuits because he *knew things*.

Before she could express her disappointment to him, she saw the trees shift ominously in the distance, as though a strong wind had passed through them. Registering her expression, Simian followed her line of sight, and his eyes widened. The distinct crack of wood breaking rang out around them, and then the trees began moving in their direction.

'Get on your horse,' Simian said, sounding knowledgeable suddenly. 'Now!'

'What is it?'

He was already running for his gelding. 'Landslide.'

Landslide? Lina caught hold of her horse's reins just as the mare was preparing to bolt. She was up and in the saddle a second later.

'Follow me,' Simian said, digging his heels into his horse's sides. The gelding lurched forwards and took off at a gallop, clearly sensing the urgency of the situation.

Lina had every intention of following him, but the sound of roots being torn from the ground by some unseen force sent her horse skidding sideways instead. She slid from the saddle and landed with a thud on the ground, all the air expelled from her lungs. Rolling onto her back and desperately trying to inhale, she watched her brother disappear from sight. Her horse took off in another direction entirely before Lina could manage to get herself upright.

'Skítr,' she swore when she could finally breathe.

Turning her head, she saw the entire landscape being consumed by a wall of mud that was now hurtling towards her. Scrambling to her feet, she took off at a wobbly run, inhaling small amounts of air and blinking frantically as she attempted to clear her blurry vision.

'Lina!'

That was her brother calling for her, but he sounded far away. She thought he might have called her name again, but she could not quite grasp it as nature roared loudly in her ears.

Run, she told herself.

Run.

CHAPTER 8

They had planned for every scenario—except the possibility of a mudslide.

'We need to get to those rocks,' Tolly said to the defenders, nodding in the direction of a ledge. 'It's stable and high.'

'Two things we desperately need right now, given there's a *hill* coming our way,' Alveye said.

Hadewaye began dragging the donkey to make it move faster. 'I'm not dying for this thing. If it gets close, I'm calling it.'

'It's always a fucking donkey,' Ryder said, slapping the animal's rump.

Behind them, they could hear trees collapsing, carried along by a steady stream of mud. As they reached the rocks, Tolly heard a horse coming at a gallop. He whipped his head around and glimpsed his mare racing through the trees.

'Keep climbing,' he told the others, then turned and ran towards his horse.

'Leave it,' Ryder called. 'She can outrun the mud—you can't.'

Tolly continued sprinting, a stream of his brother's curses trailing behind him. He whistled to the mare, and she slowed to a trot, her attention now on him. 'Easy, girl.' He raised his hands and continued towards her with steady steps. She slowed to a walk, and a few moments later, he caught hold of her reins. As he did so, she moved to take off again, clearly spooked by what was happening, but he kept hold of her. 'Easy.'

'Great,' Ryder said, having caught up to him. He glanced in the direction of the trees. 'We have about a minute until we're buried. Can we go now?'

'Lina!' came a voice nearby.

Both men drew their swords and looked towards the source of the noise. A sea warrior flashed through the trees on horseback.

'Lina! Where are you?'

Tolly recognised the rider—Simian.

'Want me to take him out?' Ryder asked, reaching for his bow.

Tolly's hand landed on his arm, stopping him. 'There's no time.' He swung himself up into the saddle and reached for Ryder's arm, pulling him up behind him. 'Ha!'

The mare lurched forwards, and they moved at a fast canter towards the rocks where the others were waiting for them. Dismounting at the bottom of the ledge, Tolly led the mare up the difficult slope to safety.

'Between the donkey and the goddamn horse,' Ryder muttered as they reached the top.

'Is that a person?' Hadewaye asked, narrowing his gaze. 'Oh shit. It's a woman.'

Tolly stepped up next to him and searched the trees below, eventually spotting Lina running through the trees at an impressive speed.

'She's not going to make it,' Hadewaye said, eyeing the approaching mud.

'Not our problem,' Alveye pointed out.

Hadewaye brushed a hand over his short hair. 'We can't just watch her die.'

Ryder went to disagree, but then his conscience must have gotten the better of him. 'Shit.'

'Here it comes,' Alveye said.

Tolly felt his heart rise in his chest as his eyes followed Lina through the trees, the mud gaining on her. 'Up here!' he shouted, the words falling out of him before he could stop them.

She glanced their way, took exactly one second to weigh up her options, then pivoted in their direction.

'What are you doing?' Alveye asked. 'She's the reason we're stuck up here in the first place.'

Tolly went over to the donkey and fetched a length of rope. 'She's the chieftain's daughter. She's more valuable to us alive.' He was forced to speak up as the noise grew louder.

Heading back to the edge of the rock, he wrapped one end of the rope around his wrist and threw the other down. He looked from Lina to the mud, realising she was not going to make it. 'Faster!'

The panic was clear on her face as she sprinted towards the rope, arms pumping. She was around five yards away when the ten-feet-high wall of mud reached her. Realising she was about to be buried alive, she pivoted once more. The problem was, the mudslide was moving at the same speed she was, but *she* was tiring.

Unwrapping the rope from his hand, Tolly handed it to Ryder and, before he could say anything, leapt off the edge of the rocks down into the deafening noise below.

'Tolly!' His brother's voice followed him down.

Landing in a crouch directly in front of the mud, Tolly launched into a sprint after Lina, praying the rope was long enough to reach her. The mud kissed his heels and roared in his ears, threatening to trip him.

Lina looked over her shoulder, eyes wide with terror. Seeing that she was about to go under, she pressed her eyes closed and braced for impact.

'Hold on to me!' Tolly shouted as he caught her around the waist.

A heartbeat later, the mud slammed into them.

The impact was like being hit by a wave. It knocked the breath from his lungs, and he struggled to keep hold of Lina. They were thrown about, the swirling mud threatening to drag them under its suffocating embrace. The rope went taut, almost pulling Tolly's arm from its socket as he used every ounce of strength to drag himself and Lina up and out of the churning mud.

'Tree,' she said, gesturing towards a thick-trunked yew tree ahead of them.

Tolly had no choice but to let go of the rope and let the mud carry them forwards.

Lina caught hold of the trunk with one hand, fingers

locking into the grooves in the tree as she grabbed the sleeve of Tolly's uniform with the other.

'I can't hold you,' she said, her fingers slipping.

Tolly pulled a knife from his sleeve and, with a determined roar, thrust it into the tree, creating a handle for him to hold on to. It was just in time, as Lina's fingers slipped from the trunk, and he was able to catch her before she was swept away again.

One side of the tree was semi-protected, so he dragged Lina to it, placing her between himself and the trunk. The mud could not keep coming forever, even if it felt like it would.

They clung to the tree, panting, their mud-soaked bodies trembling from the effort of trying to stay alive. Their gazes shifted from the broken trees passing them by to each other, then back to the trees.

At one point, a large log crashed into the trunk they were sheltering behind, and they held their breath, praying to their different gods that the roots would hold. The log eventually found its way around, spinning sideways in the process. Tolly flattened his body against Lina's as he felt the tree brush his side before moving on. That was the moment he realised their hearts were racing in sync. She must have noticed it too, because when she looked at him the next time, her expression was different. Less afraid.

A few more minutes passed before the mud began to slow. And when it finally stopped, they were knee-deep in it with no easy way out.

'Are you going to kill me now?' Lina asked.

He could not tell if she was joking. Tugging his knife from

the tree, he held it up in front of her face. 'I still want my other one back.' When he went to sheathe the knife, he found it full of mud. He tried to step back and put some space between them but ended up falling backwards into the mud instead. Lina stared down at him for a moment before extending a hand to him. He took it.

'We should be able to get out if we use the branches,' she said, looking around.

Tolly peered around the tree to gauge how far they were from the others. He could not even see the ledge.

'You jumped,' Lina said, watching him with a curious expression. 'Why?'

He went with the lie he had told earlier. 'You're the chieftain's daughter. You're worth more to us alive.'

'So you plan on taking me prisoner?'

He looked around. 'That would require us to get out of here first.'

Her eyes moved between his, and then she turned away and began pulling branches from the surrounding mud to use for her path out of there. Tolly helped, and soon they were climbing up over the mud, taking branches from behind them and laying them in front. Occasionally, they would snap, and one of them would sink. The other would be forced to help as best they could.

'You have the better end of this deal,' Lina said. 'I'm half your weight.'

His mouth turned up. 'Does it seem like the mud is finally thinning out?'

'I think so, but I'm trying not to get my hopes up.'

Tolly dragged the branch from behind him and handed it

to her. She wiped sweat from her brow as she took it. Without looking at him, she said, 'Thank you, by the way.'

'For handing you the same branch five hundred times?'

'For jumping.' She met his gaze.

Suddenly, he was back in the sea, clinging to an oar while she towed him to shore. He gestured past her. 'All the trees are in place just over there.'

She turned and looked. 'We're almost there.'

They continued for another fifty yards, until the mud fell below the knee, then waded through it in silence. When they finally reached firm ground, they took a moment to catch their breath. The relief was short-lived, however, because something had Tolly reaching for his sword. It was a miracle he had not lost it while being thrown about in the mud.

'What's wrong?' Lina asked.

He searched the trees. 'I don't know yet.'

A moment of stillness passed, and then Lina threw herself in front of him. 'Don't shoot!'

At first, Tolly thought she was shouting at him. But then a trio of warriors emerged from the trees, their arrows trained on Tolly. It was Simian and Farulf, plus another warrior he recognised from their recent bridge encounter. That was the moment Tolly realised how skilled they were at blending into the landscape.

'Don't shoot him,' Lina repeated, arms outstretched.

Simian lowered his bow, a confused look on his face.

'Get that bow back up,' Farulf barked at him in Norse, and Simian immediately raised his bow again.

Tolly's aunt had married a Scandinavian man before the famine, and the man's limited comprehension of English and

Irish combined with his reluctance to learn had forced the family to learn Norse in order to communicate with him.

'He saved my life,' Lina said in English, no doubt for his benefit.

A heated exchange of non-English words followed, some of it too fast for Tolly to catch. It ended in Farulf shouting, 'Enough!' before taking a menacing step towards them. Tolly noticed a slight tremor in the chieftain's hands as he continued to point his arrow at him.

'Hand my sister over,' Simian demanded.

Tolly's eyebrows rose. 'She's quite capable of walking to you. I'm not holding her.'

'You're holding a sword,' Simian replied.

'That's because there are three arrows pointed at me.'

Before they could make any headway with their situation, it became a lot more complicated when Ryder, Alveye, and Hadewaye appeared behind the three warriors, each holding a loaded bow firmly aimed at them.

'Ah…' Alveye's gaze darted between the two groups. 'We're going to need you to tell us what the hell is happening right now.'

Farulf spun around at the sound of the defender's voice, the string of his bow stretching tighter still when he realised they were surrounded. His bow swung from side to side between the three defenders.

'Lina,' Tolly said, 'tell the warriors to lay down their weapons, including swords and knives, and we'll let the four of you leave.'

'We will?' Hadewaye said, unable to keep the surprise from his voice.

Simian spoke up at that. 'Why on earth would we trust

you? You killed half a dozen more of our people mere hours ago.'

So they knew about that.

'You're not going to do it because you trust him,' Ryder said, joining the conversation. 'You're going to do it because more of you will die if you refuse.'

Lina took a few slow steps towards her father. 'Father, do what they say. The clan needs you alive. They'll let us go.'

'On one condition,' Tolly said, knowing this was his only chance to negotiate. 'If we let you walk, I want your word that your clan will never set foot in Lampeter again.'

'Lampeter's underwater,' Simian said. 'Our people have already evacuated.'

Lina looked back at him. 'You'll let us leave? All of us?'

He could feel the defenders' eyes on him. 'It's not an offer I'll make again, so I suggest you all lay down your weapons and start walking. The border has not changed.'

Lina's whole demeanour shifted when he said that. Once again, they were enemies.

'If I see you, or any member of your clan, in that village again, the men will be killed on sight and the women imprisoned.' Tolly looked at Simian. 'Ensure your father understands what I'm saying.'

'I understand just fine,' Farulf said in a deep voice.

'Good,' Tolly said, a hard edge in his voice now. 'Weapons on the ground.'

Hadewaye took a few steps towards them. 'Let's get moving, people.'

The four of them began removing their weapons, and Lina her sword. They dropped them onto the ground in front of them.

'Is that everything?' Tolly asked.

Lina looked heavenwards. 'Yes.'

Not one to take chances, Ryder went to pat them all down. Lina glared at Tolly the whole time, all goodwill now lost between them. Satisfied, Ryder stepped back, giving him a nod.

Tolly sheathed his sword and ventured closer, noticing the state of Farulf's hands. His knuckles were enlarged, his fingers slightly twisted. They looked exactly like Tolly's grandmother's hands had looked in the years before her death. The inflammation had started in her feet, then spread to her hands, knees, elbows, and hips. The pain had consumed her in the end.

'Do not mistake us for the English,' Farulf said. 'We don't hesitate like they do.'

'Better get going,' Alveye said. 'You've got a decent walk ahead of you.'

'You got rather lucky with the rain,' Simian said. 'I hope you all appreciate that.'

Lina gestured for her brother to start walking and tapped her father's arm gently as she passed by him. 'Come, please.'

Farulf's heavy stare remained on Tolly for a long moment before he finally turned away and followed the others. Lina, on the other hand, did not even so much as glance in his direction, which was probably for the best. Tolly was having difficulty differentiating friend from foe when it came to her.

'I'll follow them for a few miles,' Alveye said. 'Make sure they head in the right direction.'

Hadewaye nodded. 'I'll come with you.'

That left Tolly alone with his brother, who was assessing him far too closely for his comfort.

'Something you want to say?' Tolly asked.

Ryder's gaze drifted slowly over his mud-soaked uniform before he shook his head. 'I'm going to check on our growing collection of livestock.'

Tolly watched him walk away, then pressed his eyes closed.

CHAPTER 9

A depressing pall of grey had settled in the sky as the group made their way back to the camp, tails between their legs. Lina's breath fogged before her.

'Well, that has to be the shortest triumph in the history of our clan,' she said. 'I even lost the horse.'

'To be fair,' Simian said, 'you didn't lose it. It bolted from you the first chance it got. A bit like the marriage prospect Father invited to our village to meet you last year.'

'Ouch,' Lina said, glancing at him.

Farulf's brow was deeply furrowed as he walked. 'It's a setback, not a loss. No battle was fought.'

'Speak for yourself,' Lina said, gesturing to her mud-covered clothes. 'I have never fought so hard.'

Simian let out an exaggerated breath. 'How much further?'

'We're barely halfway,' Knud said.

Lina looked over her shoulder. 'I'm sure Trinka would have collected Olga before leaving.' Then she asked her father,

'You said she remained behind to ensure everyone got out. Do you think she would check every house to be sure?'

'The people living in the next village could have heard that thing carrying on,' Farulf said. 'It was all I could hear as I left the village to search for you.'

Lina bit her lip to stop from smiling.

'I still can't believe the general jumped off a cliff to save you,' Simian said.

'Not a cliff,' Lina clarified. 'A rocky ledge.' Her mind returned to the moment she was pinned against a tree with his suffocating weight against her. There were worse ways to suffocate. She had felt oddly safe, given the circumstances. 'We're even now. He stopped me from dying, and then I stopped him from dying. Now we can go back to wishing each other dead.' Noticing her father had slowed down a little, she matched his pace. 'Are your feet hurting?'

'I'm fine,' he lied. 'Though I would feel a lot better if we were armed. What hurts is trekking through unknown terrain while defenceless.'

Knud glanced in his direction. 'I'm going ahead to ensure it's safe.'

Lina watched the warrior stride off. Better to watch him than her father, who was most certainly embarrassed by his inability to keep pace. Resilience was in their bloodline, a legacy they fought to protect.

They reached a barren landscape as the last rays of the sun dipped below the horizon, turning the sky an angry shade of crimson. Her father was starting to limp, and Lina suggested they stop and rest, but Farulf would not hear of it.

'We need to keep moving,' he grunted, his shoulders rounded.

Lina and Simian exchanged a look but did not say a word. Their steps matched in rhythm, while Farulf's were uneven. Occasionally, Lina heard his boot dragging. Frida, their healer, referred to the condition as rheumatismus and said there was no known cure. Many of the herbs she had given him to manage the pain had stopped working.

When the clan's campsite finally came into view, Farulf signalled to the warriors keeping watch so they would know it was them. When they entered the camp, they were approached by those who had remained behind and pounded with questions. The warriors who had been in Lampeter with them were still arriving in dribbles.

'Have you seen Trinka?' Lina asked one woman.

She shook her head. 'Not yet.'

Normally, Lina would have immediately gone to Trinka's tent, but she needed to tend to her father first. He headed straight for their tent, stopping for no one. Exhausted, he fell heavily onto the log in front of the unlit fire with a grimace, his breathing sounding slightly ragged.

'What can I get for you?' Lina asked, crouching in front of him and preparing to remove his boots.

'I can do it,' he said, pulling his foot from her grasp. His fingers worked clumsily at the lacings, and after an alarming amount of effort, he finally tugged the boot off.

Lina's stomach twisted at the sight of her father's grotesquely swollen foot. The skin was an angry shade of red, his big toe twisted.

'Looks worse because of the long walk,' Farulf said upon seeing her expression, pain flickering on his face. 'It'll be better in the morning.'

She highly doubted that.

Simian got to work building a fire, narrating the entire process, explaining why his fires burned through the entire night. The noise was a welcomed distraction.

Lina filled a pot with water and set it to boil over the flames. She hoped some heat would provide a small measure of relief for their father.

'No need for a fuss,' Farulf told her when she placed a soaked cloth over one foot, though his eyes closed with immediate relief. 'This sort of pampering won't harden me for the trials ahead.'

'And stubbornness won't reduce inflammation,' Lina countered. She dipped another strip of linen into the boiling water, wrung it carefully, then placed it over his other foot.

Farulf opened his eyes and looked at Lina. She noted the sadness as he leaned heavily on one arm. 'Even the mightiest sword dulls with use.'

'Which is why a blade must be cared for,' she said, offering him a weak smile.

'I'm going to find us some food,' Simian said, stepping back to admire his handiwork for a moment. 'You see the distinct colour of the flame?'

'I do,' Lina lied.

Farulf simply frowned at it.

'If you see Trinka, can you tell her I'm here?' Lina looked over at the empty crate and swallowed the lump forming in her throat.

Shortly after, Simian returned with some eggs for Lina and a bow and quiver for his father. 'Erik said to give these to you.'

'Did you see Trinka?' Lina asked.

He shook his head.

Farulf turned the bow left and right, studying the craftsmanship. He plucked an arrow from the quiver to test it out, but it slipped from his fingers as he attempted to load it. Colour flooded his cheeks. 'How am I to protect our clan when I can't even draw a bowstring?' He threw the bow aside.

Lina reached out and took hold of his hand.

'Your strength lies in your heart and mind,' Simian said. 'You'll find a way to navigate this challenge, as you always do.' His words hung in the air between the three of them.

Lina saw that the mask of their indomitable leader was gone, revealing the vulnerable man beneath.

'A leader who cannot wield his weapon cannot protect his people.' His voice was low and raw. 'Perhaps it's time to call upon the Vargr.'

She blinked and sat up straighter. 'What?'

'The Vargr?' Simian asked. 'Things aren't that bad, are they?'

Farulf shifted his weight. 'They owe us a blood debt.'

Simian nodded slowly. 'I may have been barely ten, but I remember the promise Njal made. If we should ever need help, they would come to fight at our side.'

Apprehension tugged at Lina's insides. While the Wolfvanir were known for their strength, the Vargr were known for their brutality. Calling upon them would feel like a declaration of sorts. 'Their arrival will not go unnoticed. The Carmarthen Militia clearly watches the shoreline. Should the Vargr join us, further hostilities would be inevitable.'

Farulf shifted his foot, then winced. 'The Vargr's presence would ensure our safety.'

'It's not the worst idea,' Simian said. 'At the end of

summer, we part ways and both return home with our longships full of everything we need for the winter.'

Lina was taken aback by her brother supporting the idea. 'Perhaps you're forgetting that everywhere the Vargr goes becomes a war zone.'

'That might have been true when Njal was the chieftain, but his son leads the clan now,' Farulf pointed out.

Njal had eventually been killed by defenders when he finally succeeded in breaching Chadora's walls. Lina had few memories of him, but she definitely remembered his son. 'Sture's probably worse. He was always trying to prove himself.'

'He settled considerably in his thirteenth year,' her father said.

Lina drew her knee up and leaned on it. 'Didn't his mother end up killing herself?'

'As I recall, she was dying of typhoid and opted out of her suffering,' Simian said. 'The Greeks call it euthanasia.'

'Caution is always wise when stepping into these arrangements,' Farulf said, 'but sometimes desperation carves its own path.'

Lina was not keen on that particular path. 'Why can't Knud or Erik step up until you're feeling better? Or even Frode?'

Her father gave her a long, broken stare. 'Until I'm better? You talk as though I'll heal.'

'You have good days.'

'Yes, well, those days are becoming increasingly rare.'

A long silence stretched out, interrupted by the arrival of Frode. He looked between the three of them, then over at his family's tent. 'Where is she?'

'Trinka?' Lina asked.

'Yes.'

A sinking feeling enveloped Lina. 'We've not seen her.'

Frode's face fell. 'Since when?'

'Since this morning.' She stood up. 'I thought she might have travelled with Frida.'

He shook his head. 'Frida is already here. She told me that Trinka was waiting for you to return to the village.'

Lina swallowed down her rising panic. 'We never went back to Lampeter. We were marched on by soldiers before we had the chance.'

Frode's face twitched with worry. 'She's probably still making her way here.'

'Yes. Yes, it's a long walk.' What else could Lina say to the man whose entire life was wrapped up in his daughters? But he also knew Trinka was the kind of person who would run most of the way back to camp in order to be first. More likely, she was still in the territory occupied by an army who had made it quite clear that any sea warrior found there would either be killed or taken prisoner.

Farulf rose to his feet with some difficulty. 'Let's wait until morning. She may be in hiding, and she's more than capable of taking care of herself. Give her some time. If she doesn't return by sunrise, we'll make a plan to find her.'

Lina touched Frode's arm in a comforting gesture. 'You know I won't rest until she's back with us. I swear it before every god.'

Frode nodded. 'If she doesn't return, I'll leave for Lampeter at first light. Will you take care of Aife for me?'

'I'll go to Lampeter,' she replied. '*You* must stay here with Aife.'

Farulf's brows came together in a hard, disapproving line. 'Absolutely not.'

'She's there because of *me*. And I'm the safest person to send in. The general and I have a… history now.'

It was clear by her father's expression that he was uncomfortable with said history. He rubbed his forehead with swollen fingers. 'Let us pray she returns before sunrise. If not, you and Simian will return east to search for her.'

Simian swallowed. 'To be clear, I belong to the "killed on sight" category.'

'Your knowledge of the land will be helpful,' Farulf said. 'Your sister will handle protection.'

Simian deflated upon hearing that last part.

'You're going to send the boy?' Frode asked.

'He's not a boy anymore,' Farulf said tiredly. He gestured for Frode to start walking. 'Come. There's something I wish to discuss.'

The men walked away—or limped, in Farulf's case—to have their private conversation far from the ears of the siblings.

'I keep thinking of Olga locked in that house,' Simian said once they were alone. 'She's going to be very mad.'

'She really is.'

'What do you think the soldiers will do with her?'

Lina could not bear to think about it. 'She's not the friendliest of geese.'

'She's a good weight,' Simian pointed out. 'She could feed a lot of men—'

'Shall we cook the eggs?' Lina said lightly, not letting him finish.

Simian gave her a sympathetic look. 'Sorry.'

'It's fine. I'm starving after all that walking.'

The siblings quietly fried up the eggs, leaving a portion in a covered bowl for their father. As they ate, Simian watched her.

'Don't worry about Trinka,' he said. 'Worry about the people she encounters.'

She smiled as she looked up at him. 'I know she's fine.'

'You're not worried about the Vargr idea, are you?'

Her gaze went to the fire. 'We should all be worried about that. If they come, it'll end in a bloodbath. And Father's condition is...'

'I know. I agree with you.' Simian put his empty bowl down. 'But do you want to know why I'm for it anyway?'

She looked up and waited.

'Because it's summer, and the rain hasn't stopped falling. Because we're all scarred by famine, and I live in fear of it happening again. Because the area the Carmarthen Militia have confined us to is barely enough to sustain us for the next few months, let alone provide for us for the winter. There are no crops, nothing to steal besides the few bags of porridge oats we brought with us.' He shrugged. 'This is about survival.'

Her shoulders dropped an inch. 'You really are the smart one.'

'I had to get something since you took all the bravery.'

One corner of her mouth turned up. 'Get some sleep. I've got a feeling we have another long day of walking tomorrow.'

CHAPTER 10

The following morning, Tolly and the defenders stood at the edge of the floodwaters, looking around at the damage. While the water had retreated overnight, Lampeter remained a muddied wasteland. They had aided nature in transforming it into a desolate canvas of destruction.

'At least the houses are standing,' Hadewaye said, gazing out at the swollen river. 'They just need a good sweeping out.'

Ryder scowled over his shoulder at the homes behind him. 'We achieved our aim—even if it did take a rather dark turn.'

Alveye nodded in agreement. 'Sea warriors expelled. Minimal casualties.'

Across the river, they glimpsed Tatum and a handful of soldiers. With the bridge gone, there was no way for them to cross.

'And you got your horse back,' Hadewaye said, gesturing to the mud-soaked mare tethered nearby.

'Too bad the rest of them were stolen,' Tolly said. 'Speaking of which, I should probably clean out the stables.' He stepped away from the group, then heard the squelch of boots behind him. Looking over his shoulder, he saw his brother in pursuit. 'You stay with the others. I can manage.'

Ryder caught up and fell into step with him. 'You can't avoid me forever.'

'I'm not avoiding you.'

Ryder kept pace. 'Good, because I need you to explain to me why you leapt into a mudslide yesterday to save a woman who wishes you dead.'

'Would you have preferred to watch her die?'

Ryder kept his eyes ahead. 'You *leapt into a mudslide.*'

'Yes, a mudslide *we* caused.'

His brother looked at him. 'So, I'm not missing a part of this story? You just felt guilty for our part in it. That's it?'

Tolly stopped walking, hands going to his hips. Ryder turned to him with a questioning look. It took Tolly a few seconds to select his words.

'We don't kill women. I stand by that,' he began.

Ryder crossed his arms, waiting for him to continue.

'But I owed this particular woman a… save.'

'A what?'

He swallowed. 'A save.'

Ryder quirked an eyebrow, visibly confused. 'I'm going to need you to elaborate.'

While he did not have any secrets from his brother, there were some details from his life when they were separated that Ryder simply did not know. 'I know Lina.'

An awkward silence stretched out between them before

Ryder said, 'From the forest. When she held you at arrowpoint.'

Tolly shook his head. 'We met in 1329 on the day I arrived in Wales.' He looked around, the subject making him uncomfortable. 'The ship was on fire, and I had jumped overboard. The men on the dock were shooting at the people in the water, so I swam the other way as fast as I could, until I literally couldn't swim anymore.' The details of that day were vivid in his mind, Lina's youthful face as clear as ever. He could recall the exact shade of her eyes. 'Lina spotted me in the water.' He looked towards the other defenders, who were still gathered watching the river, their expressions serious. 'And she saved my life.'

Ryder sat with this new information for some time before replying. 'You were fifteen and likely scared out of your mind. The odds of her being the same girl are slim. Maybe she just reminds you of her.'

'Her father was in that longship, too, along with her brother and mother. Farulf told her to leave me. He didn't want the trouble.' He paused. 'Lina was probably around ten. She insisted on helping me. Her mother brought Farulf round in the end, and they towed me to the shore. By the time we got there, I had recovered enough to swim from the boat to the beach. I arrived with a dagger and a block of cheese wrapped in cloth.' He sniffed. 'Lina handed me that cheese before I let go of the oar. It would be the second time she saved me. It was three days later before I found food. There were not even any mussels on the rocks. The entire coast had been stripped bare.'

His brother was silent a moment. 'Shit,' he finally

muttered. 'Say you're right and it *is* her. It doesn't change the fact that you're enemies today.'

'I know.'

Ryder shifted his weight. 'Did she indicate in any way that she recognised you?'

'She was a child, and I was a half-starved, half-drowned ship rat.' He waved a hand. 'We have more important things to focus on right now.' His gaze went over the river. 'Like how we're going to establish a defence with no army this side of the river.'

Ryder went to respond, then closed his mouth when he heard a noise. It sounded like honking. The men turned to face the house they were standing in front of.

'Is that a goose?' Ryder asked.

Tolly headed for the front door. 'Sounds like it's locked inside.'

'Careful,' his brother cautioned. 'You've barely recovered from your last goose encounter.'

Stepping up to the door, Tolly pushed it open and looked around. Despite knowing exactly why he was standing there, he was still surprised when a goose charged in his direction like a dragon. He closed the door before it reached him, then listened as the bird scratched and pummelled the wood.

Turning to Ryder, he said, 'Would you believe me if I told you that's the same goose that attacked me?'

'After the conversation we just had, yes.' He headed towards Tolly. 'This will be the easiest dinner we ever hunted.'

Tolly stepped in front of him. 'You can't kill it.'

'Why not?'

Tolly could barely believe what he was about to say. 'I think it's a pet.'

Ryder blinked. 'You're serious.'

'You of all people should understand how women can be with their pet birds.'

His brother exhaled through his nose and walked away, saying over his shoulder, 'The debt's paid. You should eat the goose.'

Tolly went to find a crate and asked Hadewaye to help him wrestle the bird inside.

'Why me?' he asked in a complaining tone.

'Because no one else will do it.'

With a heavy sigh, Hadewaye went to help.

The two men cautiously approached the feisty bird, their arms outstretched, ready to grab it if it tried to escape. The goose, however, was not about to go down without a fight. It hissed and pecked at them, its beady eyes gleaming with defiance. Hadewaye managed to grab hold of its flapping wings while Tolly held out the crate. Feathers flew in all directions, but they succeeded.

Tolly went to sweep the mud out of the stables so they would have somewhere to put their *one* horse, donkey, and goose. Meanwhile, Alveye took the horse and went to do a perimeter check while the others cleaned out the houses under the watchful eye of a *finally* silent goose.

When Tolly had finished the stables, he found Ryder standing in the middle of the road outside, looking around and listening for something. He had seen that expression many times whenever Ryder was picking up on something they were not.

Before Tolly had a chance to ask about it, his brother took off at a run, eyes fixed on something in the distance. Tolly jogged after him in an attempt to find out what was going on.

As he rounded the corner of a house, he saw a woman dash behind a chicken enclosure. She moved so fast that he had difficulty gauging if she were a local woman or an intruder.

He whistled to Hadewaye, warning him of a potential threat. The sound echoed through the empty streets.

Ryder slipped behind the chicken enclosure in pursuit of her. Tolly decided to go the other way and try to intercept her. When he appeared from the other direction, he found Ryder attempting to pin the woman down while she thrashed wildly, trying to bite him. Her eyes blazed with a feral intensity. It was clear now from her clothing that she was a sea warrior.

'For the love of Belenus,' Ryder said. 'There are two ways to do this, and this is the hard way.'

'You want me to make it easy for you?' the woman said, spitting in his face.

Tolly stepped forwards to help. She stopped fighting when she saw him, enabling Ryder to secure her properly.

'General Tolly,' she said.

He recognised her as the woman who had been holding his horse when he was on the bridge with Lina and her father. 'And you are?'

'Enjoying some rough play with this defender.' She growled at Ryder as he sat her up.

'What are you doing here?' Tolly asked.

She leaned against the chicken enclosure, watching Ryder tie her ankles. 'Waiting for your horse to return so I can steal it.'

The honesty was unexpected but welcomed. 'You don't think your clan has stolen enough?'

'No,' she said plainly. 'And I'm going to need that goose as well.'

Tolly did not quite know what to make of the woman tied up before him. She was either far too confident given the situation she found herself in or mentally unstable. What was he supposed to do with a mentally unstable intruder?

The thunderous beat of hooves broke through the silence that followed. Tolly looked around. 'Are there more of you?'

'Sometimes I hear voices,' she said, tilting her head. 'Does that count?'

Hadewaye appeared, slightly out of breath. 'It's Alveye, returning.' His eyebrows rose when he saw the woman on the ground. 'Oh. A visitor.'

'Watch her,' Tolly said to Ryder. 'Closely.'

He and Hadewaye then went to meet Alveye, stepping out onto the street at the same time the horse skidded to a halt.

'What is it?' Tolly asked.

'Two warriors approaching. A male and a female.'

'You think they're headed here?' Hadewaye asked.

Alveye dismounted. 'Most likely.'

Tolly glanced in the direction of the chicken enclosure. 'Perhaps they're looking for their friend.'

Hadewaye leaned in and said quietly, 'Do you think she was here all night?'

'Who?' Alveye asked.

'We already have one warrior with us,' Tolly said, frowning. 'An interesting variety of female.'

'We don't need any more of those, surely.'

'Shall I bridle the donkey and come with you for a look?' Hadewaye asked.

Tolly took the reins of his horse. 'I can barely believe I'm saying this, but yes, go saddle the donkey.' Then to Alveye, he said, 'You may want to go help Blackmane. I have a feeling he's going to need it.'

CHAPTER 11

Lina's senses were sharp as she treaded softly, an arrow nocked in her bow. Simian walked beside her, his shoulders slightly rounded from the effort of trying to remain invisible.

'Will you relax?' Lina said, her voice barely more than a breath against the stillness. 'We've made it this far. It's a simple exchange.'

Simian pulled the general's dagger from his belt. 'A dagger for our friend. Why does it feel like we're getting the better end of that deal?'

Her eyes went to the weapon. 'It's valuable to him. I could tell by his expression when he saw me carrying it.'

'He could just take it back after he kills us.'

She rolled her eyes. 'Where's that warrior heart of yours? You carry an axe made by our father in the foothills of Scandinavia. It's as dangerous as any weapon they carry.'

He sighed. 'Not to complain, but it's quite heavy to carry on such a long journey.'

Lina pressed her eyes closed. 'Gods help and protect us.'

Falling silent again, she listened for any signs of life. A whisper of movement on the hill to their right had her stopping. She raised her bow, drawing the string taut as she searched the veil of underbrush.

'What is it?' Simian asked.

'Shh.'

'Trinka?'

She gave him a pointed look that clearly said *quiet*.

All was still and silent—maybe too silent. She thought she could feel eyes upon her. There were only two options at that moment: run or confront their stalker.

'Maybe we should hide,' Simian said, as though reading her mind.

She shook her head, then shouted in English, 'Show yourself!' There was some exaggerated confidence in her tone. 'We mean no harm! We wish only to talk!'

There was nothing but the sound of the wind's mournful reply.

'Shall I try in Welsh?' Simian asked.

She nodded. It was worth a try.

Simian repeated what she had said in their local tongue. Still nothing.

Just as the string relaxed beneath Lina's fingers, she heard a donkey bray nearby and the string tightened once more. Seconds slipped by.

'Their soldiers can probably shoot further than you can,' Simian whispered.

She shot a glare at him. 'Thank you for that.'

A moment later, out from the shadow of a twisted willow stepped General Tolly and a defender. The correct reaction was some healthy fear. After all, Tolly had been the one who had warned them of the consequences of returning. Instead, she felt oddly relieved that he was one of the two men making their way towards them. She was confident that he would at least be willing to hear them out.

This was confirmed when recognition flashed on his face and he lowered his weapon, prompting her to do the same.

'Was I not clear yesterday?' The agitation was evident in his voice.

She raised her hands to show that she meant no harm. 'Before you get angry—'

'Too late.' He continued down the hill towards them, never taking his eyes off her. The defender followed closely. They stopped three yards away, looking between the siblings. 'Are you lost?'

Simian's eyebrows rose, clearly offended by the suggestion. 'Lost? I'm an excellent navigator.'

Tolly's gaze slid from Lina to her brother. 'Your skills are obviously lacking if you find yourselves back *here*.'

Lina recognised the defender from the day prior. He had a friendly appearance about him, and she guessed him to be around twenty.

Clearing his throat, Simian said, 'It seems our fates are weaving a tapestry more intricate than we could have imagined.'

Everyone looked at him.

'I suppose you're wondering why we're here,' Simian continued.

'Yes, do tell us,' the defender replied. 'We're dying to know.'

Lina reached for the dagger poking out of her brother's belt, and Tolly and the defender both reached for the hilts of their swords. She paused, giving them a moment to relax before continuing with deliberately slow movements. Even the wind seemed to hold its breath as she drew the weapon from its sheath and held it up.

'We wanted to return this to you.' She offered it to Tolly hilt first. 'It's beautifully crafted and looks like something you might want back.'

Tolly's expression softened a little as he stared at the dagger before him, but he did not take it. 'So, you came all this way, risking your lives, to return my dagger?'

'While we're here,' Simian said, clapping his hands together, 'we thought we might enquire about a missing clan member.'

Something flashed in Tolly's eyes that made Lina think he might know who Simian was talking about.

'She's my closest friend,' Lina said, her words measured and clear. 'Her name's Trinka.'

Tolly leaned his weight on one foot, saying nothing.

Clearing her throat, Lina added, 'Also—'

'There's more?' Tolly asked.

'I don't suppose you've seen a goose wandering about Lampeter?'

Tolly exchanged a glance with the defender, then said, 'We did find one *inside* a house.'

Lina's heart sped up. 'Oh?'

'I knew it was familiar when it charged at me—intent on ripping out my throat.'

She proceeded with care. 'I understand that you might have some hesitancy around helping us given everything that's happened—'

'Are you referring to the displaced families stranded on the other side of the river?' the defender asked. 'Or perhaps the houses you set alight while they were still inside?'

Lina threw her hands up. 'You killed six of our men and used them as a *fence*.'

Simian cleared his throat, and she drew a calming breath before trying again. 'Have you seen her?'

'Trinka?' Tolly asked.

'Yes, Trinka.'

He crossed his arms and shrugged. 'I don't know.'

Lina's eyebrows came together. 'What do you mean, you don't know?'

'We have a woman with us in Lampeter, but she wouldn't tell us her name.'

'What does she look like?'

'A female sea warrior.'

Simian spoke up then. 'Is she young and pretty but also quite violent and slightly terrifying?'

Hadewaye looked at Tolly, waiting for him to reply.

'That's a fairly accurate description of the woman currently tied up next to a chicken enclosure, yes.'

Relief flooded through Lina. The fact that Trinka was alive was enough in that moment. 'She won't appreciate being tied up.'

'Well, that's what happens when you bite people' was Tolly's reply.

'She is not the kind of woman you want as a prisoner. The best thing for your safety and sanity is to give her to us, and we'll take her back to the camp.' Lina held up the dagger again. When Tolly still did not take it, she added, 'Please.'

He stared back at her. 'If we hand her over, then we have nothing to bargain with.'

'True, but my father would look upon the gesture favourably.'

'That means nothing to me after what he did,' Tolly replied.

Simian looked between them. 'A great Scandinavian poet once said, "Desperation cares not for the boundaries drawn by men."' Then, seeing Tolly's impassive expression, he added, 'Unless they're your men and boundaries, of course.'

Tolly finally took the dagger from Lina, eyes meeting hers as he did so. He inspected it, as though checking it for damage, then tucked it into his belt.

'I also returned your mare,' Lina said.

Amusement filled Tolly's eyes. 'That's not quite how that went.' He looked past them. 'Anyone behind you?'

Simian glanced over his shoulder. 'Gods, I hope not. I'm already feeling deeply uncomfortable.'

'He's asking if there are more clan members,' Lina clarified.

'Oh.'

'It's just us,' she said. 'Everyone else is at the camp behind the… border.'

Tolly glanced at his friend, who gave the smallest nod. 'Fine. I'll take you to her, and you will both be 100 percent responsible for her behaviour from that point.'

'She'll behave with us there, I promise.'

Tolly looked doubtful. 'Hand over your weapons to Hadewaye.'

Lina's fingers tightened around her bow. 'Why?'

Tolly raised an eyebrow in place of a reply.

'It's a reasonable request,' Simian said to her. 'We can't just walk into their territory, bat our eyelashes, and get anything we want.'

She frowned. 'Who was batting their eyelashes?'

'Your brother,' the defender said, stepping up to Simian and taking his axe. 'At me.'

Apparently, there was such a thing as a defender with a sense of humour.

Lina hugged her bow close to her when Tolly reached for it. He took hold of the top, waiting for her to release it.

'This was *your* plan,' Simian said. 'Give the man your bow.'

Tolly tugged it gently from her grip. 'Your quiver and sword too.'

Begrudgingly, Lina unbuckled her weapon and handed it to Hadewaye, along with her quiver.

'You'll ride with me,' Tolly said, turning and walking off in the direction he had come from.

Hadewaye gestured for them to follow.

At the top of the hill, hidden by the trees, stood Tolly's mare and a donkey.

Simian paused when he saw it. 'Oh. Are we on the donkey?' he asked Hadewaye.

One corner of the defender's mouth lifted. 'I think we'll just walk and give the poor donkey a break.'

Tolly mounted the horse, his tall frame blocking out the sky as he extended a hand to Lina. She took it, and he pulled her onto the horse behind him.

'Hold on,' he told her.

She rolled her eyes, grateful he could not see her. 'I am holding on—with my legs.'

He nudged the mare forwards. 'Suit yourself.'

The four of them headed off towards Lampeter in silence, the steady rhythm of hoofbeats all they needed. Lina watched the landscape as they rode, once-vibrant meadows now desolate lands.

They were about a half mile into their journey when the mare stumbled, hooves sinking into the uneven ground. Lina instinctively grabbed hold of Tolly, her fingers curling around the rough fabric of his cloak. The sudden contact sent a rush of warmth to her cheeks. Tolly looked over his shoulder at her, eyes not quite reaching hers.

'Did your legs forget to hold on?' he asked in a low voice.

That did nothing to help the colour gathering in her cheeks. 'Did *you* forget how to steer?'

She let go of his cloak but could do nothing about the lack of distance between them. They were so close that she could smell his distinctly earthy scent. It blended perfectly with the leather. Only when Tolly was facing forwards again did she resume breathing properly.

Behind them, Hadewaye and Simian were discussing what cuckoos eat, chatting away like they were old friends. Normally, she would have thrown her brother a look to discourage such familiarity, but in this instance, the defender was very knowledgeable on the subject, and she knew how much her brother wished he had those kinds of people to talk to. She could not bring herself to steal the excitement from his voice. Instead, she watched the back of Tolly's head, eyes moving over his thick inky hair. At that distance, she could see it had a slight wave to it.

'Can I ask you something?' she said.

Tolly turned his head slightly and nodded.

'I've been thinking a lot about yesterday and how you rescued me from that mud.'

'What about it?'

She looked around, nervous suddenly. 'I just… I wouldn't have done that for you. I would have watched you go under and remained firmly on that ledge.'

'Still waiting for your question.'

The air between them was charged with the resonance of something *unsaid*. 'Your actions were not duty driven. I know you said that I'm more valuable to you alive, but I'm certain no one else would have gone to the lengths you did.'

He adjusted his grip on the reins. 'Sometimes it's a reflex. You would have died, and in that moment, I had a chance to prevent it.'

Her eyes returned to the back of his head. 'I guess sometimes empathy gets in the way.'

'Gets in the way of what?'

She shrugged. 'Our hate.'

He made a noise that almost resembled laughter. 'I don't hate you.'

'Why not?'

He thought for a moment. 'You have to care first in order to hate.'

She was surprised when those words landed rather hard. 'Who do you hate if not me, your enemy?'

'Plenty of people.'

She reached back to pet the mare on the rump. 'Give me the name of one person.'

He was quiet for a moment. 'I could give you names, but it's mostly faces. Lord Hodge comes to mind.'

'What did he do to make you hate him?'

'He took over these lands and enslaved its people.' He glanced over his shoulder. 'I guess that means you're halfway there.'

Her brow furrowed. 'We've no interest in enslaving anybody.'

'Good to know.'

She was silent for a few hoofbeats. 'That's why you survived, you know.'

'Because of hate?'

She nodded. 'Nothing breathes life into a person more than the all-consuming need to exterminate their enemy.'

'What about hope?'

His words piqued her curiosity. 'What were you hopeful for? Aside from the destruction of this Lord Hodge?'

He did not reply straight away. It was as if he were weighing up whether or not to answer. 'My brother was still alive somewhere.'

'The two of you were separated?'

He nodded.

'I would ask if you found him, but I already know the answer,' she said. 'The pair of you could be twins.'

'We get that a lot.'

'You have the same snakelike eyes.'

A chuckle rumbled in his chest, causing her own lips to turn up briefly. She should have ended the conversation there, but her curiosity got the better of her. 'Is the rest of your family here?'

He shifted slightly in the saddle, then pointed ahead. 'We're almost there.'

Lina looked past him to where Lampeter was now visible, framed by a mountainous backdrop. When she looked back, she saw that Simian and Hadewaye were no longer talking but were listening in on their conversation instead. She fixed her eyes ahead once more.

As they entered the village, Lina could see that it was still empty. The soldiers could not yet cross the river. They rode along the main road to the small square, where she spotted a bound, blindfolded, and muddied Trinka tied to a veranda post. She moved to jump from the horse and run to her friend, but Tolly caught her arm in a bruising grip before she could dismount. Righting her on the horse once more, he brought his face close to hers.

'Unless you want to be tied up like your friend there, I suggest you avoid any sudden movements and remain at my side.'

Her eyes moved between his before giving him a small nod.

Halting the horse, Tolly let go of her arm. 'Now you may dismount, *slowly*, and remain by the mare. Understand?'

Her gaze fell to the spot on her arm where his hand had been. 'Yes, General.'

Even though she struggled to keep the bitterness from her voice, she followed his instructions, lowering herself to the ground and remaining next to the horse. Then she heard a sound that made her entire chest lift. In the distance, a cranky goose was airing her grievances.

Olga.

CHAPTER 12

Tolly and the defenders were gathered in a circle, speaking in low voices out of earshot of the three warriors.

'So your plan is to just let them go?' Alveye asked, his face pinched with confusion. 'What sort of message does that send to the clan?'

'They came peacefully to retrieve a friend,' Hadewaye said. 'There are other ways they could have done it. I think it's the right move.'

The men looked in the direction of the three warriors once again. Trinka was still tied up, but Lina had removed her blindfold. She was staring at the men with an unyielding gaze that felt like it might sear through the flesh on their faces.

'What's the alternative?' Ryder asked.

Alveye gestured behind him. 'There's a holding cell here in Lampeter.'

Ryder's eyebrows rose slightly. 'You want to lock up *both* the chieftain's children? How do you imagine that ending?'

'At least exchange them for the horses,' Alveye replied.

'You're forgetting that there are only four of us on this side of the river at present,' Tolly said. 'We're not exactly in a sound position to negotiate.'

Alveye thought for a moment. 'Let's question the male before we release them, get as much information out of him as we can. He seems the most likely to cooperate.'

Ryder drew his knife.

'I don't think you'll need that,' Tolly said, raising a hand. He looked over at Simian, who was now inspecting a nearby plant.

Ryder sheathed the weapon. 'What about the crazy one?'

'I wouldn't bother,' Alveye said. 'I wouldn't trust a word that comes out of her mouth—even *with* the knife.'

The four men made their way back over to the warriors.

'Is this hogweed?' Simian asked, pointing to a large plant with jagged edges and clusters of white flowers at the top.

Tolly frowned at him. 'No idea.'

'It is,' Hadewaye confirmed. 'You can tell by the leaves. They're covered in those small hairs, giving it a prickly appearance.'

Ryder rubbed at his forehead.

The only reason the defender knew that was because he was courting a woman who spent every free moment she had in her garden, nurturing each plant as though it were a child. It was the longest courtship Tolly had ever borne witness to. Although the pair were clearly besotted with each other, Hadewaye was concerned about rushing her.

'Well, aren't you two just adorable,' Trinka said.

'Behave,' Lina warned.

Trinka rested her head against the wall. 'Where's the fun in that?'

'You,' Ryder said, pointing at Simian. 'With me.'

Simian's face fell. 'Why?'

'We're going to take a little walk.'

'No,' Lina said immediately, stepping in front of him.

Trinka let her head fall to one side, a playful smile on her face. 'Do you want to take me for a walk instead, defender?'

'I really don't' was Ryder's reply.

Hadewaye stepped up to check the rope around her ankles. 'I think we'll keep you nice and secured.'

'Why can't you speak to him here?' Lina asked, panic in her voice.

Tolly gestured for Ryder to take Simian away. 'Because we've done this enough times to know that people are more comfortable without an audience.'

'I don't mind an audience,' Simian said, eyes wide.

'Good,' Alveye said. 'Then I'll join you.'

Simian had no choice but to leave with the two defenders. He glanced back at Lina at one point, who was staring after him.

'If they hurt him—'

'You're in no position to be making threats,' Tolly reminded her. He gestured for her to follow. 'Let's go.'

'Where?'

'For a walk.'

Trinka leaned in his direction. 'If you put one filthy hand on her, I'll cut your arm off and beat you to death with it.'

When he met her gaze, he saw she was not bluffing. In

fact, she looked ready to chew her own arm off in order to make good on the threat.

'Let's go,' he repeated. Then to Hadewaye, he said, 'Keep a close eye on this one.'

The defender nodded while simultaneously taking a step back from Trinka.

'Don't do or say anything that will make the situation worse,' Lina told Trinka before following Tolly.

'She'll tear your balls right off if you try anything,' Trinka called after them in a breezy tone. 'And I'll display them around my neck.'

Lina pressed her eyes shut. 'So, where are we going?'

'You'll see when we get there.'

She let out a noisy breath. 'Whatever information your brother is hoping to get out of Simian, I suspect he's going to be rather disappointed.'

'Feelings like disappointment are trained out of defenders, so I wouldn't worry.'

She stretched her step to catch up to him. 'He's safe?'

'Sure. If he cooperates.'

Lina glanced over her shoulder, a worried expression on her face.

'Almost there.'

As they walked by the empty houses, Lina looked around. 'Are you going to surprise me with more corpses?'

His mouth turned up as he stopped in front of a canvas-covered crate, sitting in the shade of a house. He pulled back the fabric, and violent honking ensued. Lina's shoulders fell a full two inches with relief when she laid eyes on the goose.

'Thank the gods.'

The goose began running up and down on the spot when she recognised Lina.

'Your possessed pet, I believe,' Tolly said, throwing the canvas to one side. 'Of course, if you no longer want her, we have some ideas about what to do with her.'

Lina stepped up to the crate and dropped into a crouch before it. 'I bet you do.' Her fingers brushed over the rough-hewn wood before she lifted her gaze to Tolly. 'Thank you.'

His eyes moved between hers before breaking contact. 'I hope your crazy friend isn't going to be a problem.'

'She's not crazy. She's just... high-spirited and disconnected from her empathy.' Lina opened the crate and retrieved the goose, tucking her under her arm before rising. 'Can we go to my brother now?'

Tolly studied her for a long moment. 'How old is he?'

'Ten and seven. Why do you ask?'

'I would have guessed younger.' He reached out to pet the goose, surprised when she did not bite him. 'I thought he would be better with weapons at that age.'

She emitted a single laugh. 'You and everyone else.'

'Did your father go too easy on him?'

'No. No, my father raised him like every other warrior raises a son, but Simian...' She took a breath. 'He's smart and curious about the world, but when he fights, he fights with his mind and body, not his heart.'

Tolly nodded slowly. 'And what about you?'

'I fight with purpose. The heart, mind, and body work in unison when you do that.' Reading his expression, she added, 'We're all just trying to survive, General. Don't stand there looking morally superior. I know all about the wastelanders. You've spilled more blood on this land than any predecessor.'

He did not deny it. The Carmarthen Militia was mostly made up of men who had once cut the throats of strangers for a few coins or a small bag of grain. 'We should head back. I don't want Hadewaye alone with Trinka for too long.'

They put plenty of space between them as they headed back to the others.

'That was quick,' Trinka said, eyes on Tolly. 'I'm sure you hear that a lot.' She winked at him.

He let the comment blow past him.

Lina held up the goose. 'Look who I have.'

'She's the reason I'm tied up right now, you know,' Trinka said. 'I knew I'd never hear the end of it if I returned without her.'

Lina gave her an appreciative look.

'And I was looking for you for quite some time. I'm glad I did, though, because I was able to figure out why the village flooded.'

Lina tilted her head, brows furrowed. 'What do you mean?'

Trinka's gaze slid to Tolly. 'You didn't tell her?'

It was clear that Trinka knew about the water catchment. It was after the fact, so it should not have bothered him that it was being discussed, yet it did. Seeing the joy from being reunited with her goose melt from Lina's face bothered him.

She looked at him. 'What's she talking about?'

He shrugged. 'I'm sure she's about to tell you.'

Trinka's eyes shone with mischief. 'The general and his defenders unleashed nature's wrath upon us yesterday. The flood was but a clever ploy to wash us from the village.'

At first, Lina did not understand. 'While they might think themselves gods, they can't control the rain.'

'No,' Trinka agreed. 'But they can control the dam.'

It took Lina a moment to grasp what her friend was saying. 'What dam?'

'The one they opened, sending water and mud our way.'

The accusation in Lina's eyes sliced through Tolly like a blade. '*That's* why you saved me. You were responsible. You did it to ease your conscience.'

Tolly exchanged a glance with Hadewaye. 'Did you really think you could take over our lands and drive families from their homes without consequence? As you said, we're all just trying to survive.'

The two of them stared at each other. Then, much to Tolly's relief, Ryder and Alveye returned with Simian, who appeared to be a little shaken but unharmed.

Ryder looked from Tolly to Lina. 'Everything all right here?'

'Perfect,' Lina said, her voice cracking slightly. She looked her brother over, like she was searching for physical injury. 'Did they hurt you?'

He straightened and shook his head. 'No.'

'Get what you need?' Tolly asked his brother.

Ryder nodded.

'Then you can escort them out of Lampeter,' Tolly said. 'Ensure they actually leave this time.' His gaze went to Lina one last time. 'Don't return here again.'

She did not respond.

'Hadewaye and I will go,' Alveye said, stepping up to untie Trinka. 'One wrong move and the ropes stay in place,' he warned.

She brought her face close to his. 'Do you want to find my hidden knife, defender?'

'Absolutely not.'

She smiled at his discomfort.

Tolly had no reason to feel guilty, and yet he did. Perhaps because it had been his idea. But with the alternative being warfare, he had really done them all a favour. She had no right to look at him like he was the devil. He could not tell if he felt guilty or angry. He just knew he wanted her gone from his sight.

Thankfully, the trio were on the move moments later, walking away and leaving him to sort out his bad mood. The moment Lina disappeared from his sight, he released a large breath, his body relaxing. He had not realised how tense he had been until that moment.

When his gaze landed on his brother, he found Ryder staring at him.

'What?' The word came out abruptly.

Ryder shook his head. 'I didn't say a word.'

CHAPTER 13

The two defenders followed the trio at a distance for the first ten miles of the journey before leaving them to complete the final eight without an escort.

'Thank the gods,' Simian said, slowing his pace. 'My legs were cramping.'

'Nothing sets a good pace quite like two armed defenders breathing down your neck,' Trinka said.

Lina glanced over her shoulder. 'Just because we can't see them doesn't mean they're not there.'

'I'm surprised they didn't keep us as leverage.' Trinka glanced sideways at Lina. 'I was sure the general would keep *you*.'

She took the bait. 'Why do you say that?'

'He stared at you like you were a prime cut of mutton the whole time.'

Simian quickened his pace to catch up. 'There were some rather intense periods of observation. I must admit, the destruction of the dam wall was a clever move on their part. Quick results with zero losses on their side.'

Lina could not deny the facts.

'Still grappling with the fact that the general jumped into the moving mud to save your life,' Trinka said.

'Clearly, he felt guilty,' Lina replied. 'It's one thing to make a plan to drown an entire people and another to watch it play out before you.'

'I would have cheered through his death had it been reversed,' Trinka said.

'Perhaps the two of you knew each other in a past life,' Simian said. 'You might have even been lovers.'

Trinka snorted. 'Or you died at his hand, and now he's trying to make amends in the next life.'

Lina was going to say how ridiculous Simian sounded, then realised she had felt a strange sense of familiarity with him. 'What did you tell the defenders when they questioned you?'

'I really tried to play the role of the incompetent son who's excluded from all decision-making.'

Trinka frowned at him. 'What do you mean, *play*?'

Simian looked guiltily at his feet. 'But I had to tell them something.'

'Simian,' Lina said, waiting for him to look at her. 'What did you tell them?'

'They wanted to know if there were more of us. Naturally, they're trying to figure out if any more longships will be pulling up on their shores.'

Lina pressed her eyes closed.

'What?' Trinka said, looking between them. 'The correct response is that there are no more longships coming. And there aren't, which should have made it even easier for you to answer.'

Lina opened her eyes. 'Well, that's not necessarily true.'

Trinka's feet slowed. 'What are you talking about?'

'A conversation was had last night about potentially inviting another clan to join us for the summer,' Simian explained. 'More specifically, the Vargr.'

'Whose stupid idea was that?'

'Father's,' the siblings answered together.

Trinka appeared surprised by that. 'It's not like your father to invite trouble to the clan. While we all admire the Vargr's strength and bravery, they're a magnet for conflict.'

'Oh, we know,' Lina said.

'I think the idea is to use that reputation to keep our enemy at bay,' Simian added.

'Wait.' Trinka stopped. 'You didn't tell the defenders that the Vargr were coming to their shores, did you?'

'No.' Simian pressed his lips together. 'Though I did mention the possibility of such an invitation after Blackmane explained in great detail how they remove fingernails before producing a small instrument from his pocket and encouraging me to hold it.'

'Gods,' Trinka said, resuming walking again. 'He was just trying to scare you, and you responded by sharing the only secret we have. Where's your loyalty?'

'He's a defender,' Simian replied. 'They don't *try* to scare people—they just scare people.'

Lina exchanged a look with Trinka. 'It was probably a smart thing to mention, because the chances are that nothing will come from it, but they'll feel like they got something big out of you. They wouldn't have let you walk away without getting *something*.'

'What else did you tell him?' Trinka asked, eyeing him suspiciously.

'He just asked about some of our previous travels. No doubt trying to figure out if we're one of the many clans that have wreaked havoc on Chadora's shores.' He paused. 'He was asking about 1329 in particular, trying to gauge if we were in the region during that winter. I told him I could barely remember that far back, but it was possible. Felt like we were always at sea during the famine, up and down the coastline in search of food.'

Lina placed Olga on the ground to walk for a while. '1329? That's nearly a decade ago.'

'Was that when the Vargr breached Chadora's walls?' Trinka asked.

Simian shook his head. 'That was 1328.'

Trinka rolled her eyes. 'Close enough.'

'Well, the main thing is you kept all your fingernails,' Lina said, watching Olga. The shuffle of goose feet had been her constant companion throughout most of her life.

The trio forged ahead as the sky above grew darker. Thunder rumbled ominously, prompting Trinka to look up. 'It doesn't seem to matter how far south we travel. The rain follows.'

A biting chill took over the air, and Lina pulled up her hood before picking Olga up and tucking her into the folds of her cloak.

'Almost there,' Trinka said, squinting into the distance. 'I can see the smoke.'

Lina slowed when she saw it. This was not smoke from a

few campfires. It billowed into the sky, the acrid scent of burning wood reaching them even from that distance.

'That's coming from the beach,' Simian said. 'And looks very much like a signal fire.'

'Ha,' Trinka said. 'I guess your father wasn't bluffing about the whole Vargr thing.'

'The question now is, will they come?' Lina said, hugging Olga closer.

The three of them picked up their pace.

'I can't believe Njal's son is chieftain now,' Trinka said as they walked.

Simian sighed. 'A fact that will be repeatedly rubbed in my face, I'm sure.'

'Sture was a proper little prick,' Trinka said. 'He used to catch me by my braids when we played.'

Lina glanced in her direction. 'I remember you telling him to stop.'

'Only once, by memory,' Simian said. 'The second time, you threw him face first into the mud.'

Trinka squinted. 'He's lucky he got a warning. I don't do those anymore.'

The wind whipped at their cloaks and hair as they drew closer to the beach, bypassing the camp entirely. The sound of crashing waves grew louder, and the smoke in the air thickened. When they finally stepped out onto the sand, they heard Aife squeak. She came at a run, almost knocking Trinka down.

'Father!' Aife shouted, dragging Trinka down the beach. 'She's here!'

The relief on Frode's face, combined with the slight tremble of his lip as he opened his arms to his daughters, brought a smile to Lina's face. Through the smoke, she spotted her own father looking out at the water, his weathered face pinched against the wind.

'I'm going to let Father know we've returned,' she told Simian, placing Olga down on the sand. The goose immediately took off, honking.

'You go ahead,' he said. 'I'm going to collapse on the sand for a moment.'

Farulf glanced in their direction, looked between them, then released a breath he had probably been holding since they left. Lina walked down the beach to join him, slipping her arm through his when she reached him.

'I gather Trinka is also here?' he asked, eyes on the sea again.

'Yes.' She squeezed his arm. 'Olga's here too.'

He looked over at the goose running about the beach with her wings spread wide. 'That thing has more lives than a cat. Do I want to know how you got them both out?'

Tolly filled her mind once more. 'The general let all of us go.'

His eyebrows came together. 'Then likely followed you here.'

'He doesn't need to follow us, because he knows exactly where we are.'

His face creased with anger. 'You shouldn't trust him.'

'I don't.'

They were silent a moment before Lina asked, 'Are the Vargr even in the channel?'

'They were several days behind us. They'll pass soon enough.'

There was that sinking feeling in her stomach again. 'Are you sure about this? You barely know Sture.'

Farulf squinted against the wind. 'I know he was raised by a good man. That's all I need to know for now.' Sneaking a glance at his daughter, he added, 'Our combined numbers will ensure our safety. That I do know.'

She looked up at him, taking in his familiar features and grey-streaked beard. 'If it brings you some peace, then it can only be a good thing.' She rested her head on his arm. 'I'm going to need a new bow.'

'I see.'

'And quiver.'

'And I'm guessing arrows too?'

She nodded. 'And a sword.'

He half chuckled, half sighed. 'At least you're both alive.'

They watched the waves roll in for a moment.

'She would have loved this beach,' Lina said after a long silence.

'Your mother?'

She nodded.

'She loved any place that wasn't the inside of a boat.'

A smile spread across Lina's face. 'True. She was a sea warrior with no sea legs.' It did not matter how much time rolled by, the grief still surfaced at its leisure. But over the years, she had learned to enjoy its company. 'Simian is so much like her, don't you think?'

He glanced back at his son, who was slumped on the beach. 'He has her gentle spirit, but not her ability to keep hold of a sword. She could fight when she needed to.'

'That's all right. I'll keep hold of the sword for both of us.'

He patted her hand. 'I'm counting on it.'

CHAPTER 14

The water levels dropped, and the river slowed. Two days after the flood, the army was able to rebuild the bridge that connected the two sides. Families returned to the homes, continuing with the clean-up and calculating their losses. All their livestock and grain had been taken. Most of their possessions were water-damaged, but they were home, and they were smiling again.

Tatum was the happiest of them all once reunited with his defender family. He demanded every detail of everything that had happened during their separation. The defenders obliged. Luckily for Tolly, Ryder was more of a listener. Some of the finer details were left unsaid.

'There have been reports of heavy smoke coming from the shores of Llangrannog,' Tatum said. 'I assumed they were sending off their dead, but after the mention of a potential reunion with the Vargr, now I'm not so sure.'

'Could be a signal fire,' Tolly said.

Hadewaye looked towards the coast. 'There aren't enough corpses to justify a *three-day* fire.'

'We should take a look,' Alveye said. 'Now that we have horses.'

'The donkey was a surprisingly comfortable ride,' Hadewaye said.

Ryder shook his head as he walked away.

The group saddled horses and rode east, arriving in time to see six longships appear on the horizon. Monstrous sea dragons, their sleek black hulls slicing through choppy waters and leaving foamy trails. Their sails billowed like clouds against the ashen sky, the raven emblem proudly displayed.

They remained on the hill, out of sight of the beach, watching in silence as the lightly built longships were dragged onto the sand. The warriors manoeuvred their vessels with an ease that came with years of experience.

'I think it's safe to say it was a signal fire,' Tatum said to no one in particular.

Tolly was counting the warriors now spilling out onto the beach. There were around forty men and women per ship, plus children.

His gaze was drawn to a familiar figure walking across the sand towards the new arrivals. It was Farulf. Another well-built warrior walked out to meet him. They saluted each other, then stood conversing on the beach while some Wolfvanir warriors extinguished the fire with seawater.

'I'd estimate around 240 additional warriors,' Ryder said.

Alveye shifted in his saddle. 'Which means they officially outnumber the soldiers available in the region.'

'You could always withdraw troops from the eastern border,' Hadewaye said, trying to be helpful.

'No,' Tolly and Tatum said in unison before exchanging a glance.

The marcher lords would take full advantage of reduced protection in that region.

'I certainly wouldn't be taking any soldiers from the southern coast right now,' Hadewaye said. 'The sea warriors may very well be counting on that.'

Ryder looked at Tolly. 'You have another two hundred men you could send for.'

'It's just a precaution,' Alveye said. 'More warriors on our beaches doesn't have to equate to more conflict.' He squinted against the glare. 'I think it best that I deliver this news to the warden in person. These kinds of numbers are a threat to the entire region.'

'Less threatening to kingdoms with *sixty-feet-high walls*,' Tolly said.

Ryder swung his horse around and rode off down the hill, and the other defenders followed him one by one. Tolly remained where he was, watching the beach.

'You coming?' Hadewaye called to him.

Exhaling, Tolly slowly turned his horse and rode off down the hill. His mind remained firmly on the unsettling number of warriors gathering on their shores and the implications of such a large force.

He was dragged from his thoughts by movement in his peripheral vision. Pulling his horse up, he scanned the trees to his left, locking onto a lone figure. Even from a distance, Tolly recognised those two familiar braids and that piercing stare.

Lina.

She held a bow, nocked and drawn—and pointed directly at him.

He should have reacted to the threat, whether it be alerting the others or drawing his own weapon. Instead, he stared back at her, not moving.

After a few tense seconds, Lina slowly lowered her weapon, her gaze remaining locked with his.

Ryder stopped at the bottom of the hill and looked back. 'What is it?' His words were snatched away by the wind.

Tolly looked forwards, then nudged his horse into a walk. 'It's nothing.'

CHAPTER 15

She could not kill him. Lina could not even bring herself to injure him. There was now a history between them that felt like it was permanently in the way. Perhaps he was the reason she had happily volunteered herself as a watchman that day. Maybe she had known he would come.

When she returned to the camp that afternoon, she found the Vargr raising tents and shelters close to their own. The women were already preparing food, and the children were getting acquainted with the Wolfvanir, enjoying the novelty of new faces and games to play. The air was heavy with the scent of fish cooking over open flames as Lina made her way between the tents in search of her father. She ran into Trinka on the way, heading to a watch post.

'All quiet out there?' Trinka asked.

'Quieter than here.' Lina decided not to mention seeing Tolly, knowing it would lead to questions she had no answers for. She had followed the group for half a mile to ensure they left. Everyone had known the smoke would draw them east eventually. And she had known before she took aim at Tolly that she would never release the arrow. It was simply an imagining, a test to see how uncomfortable the idea made her.

Very, it turned out.

'Why the miserable face?' Trinka asked, then flicked her gaze to the Vargr camp. 'Not happy about our new friends?'

'We don't know these people. I'm not sure Father's thought through the food situation. It's not as if we have twice the land suddenly.'

'I'm sure we'll have it soon enough.' Trinka leaned in. 'It's the *Vargr*. They won't settle for less than what they can get.'

'That's the part that worries me.' She looked around. 'Have you seen Simian?'

Trinka shook her head. 'He's probably drawing a tree or befriending a vole.' She pointed behind her. 'I saw your father, though. He's eating with the chieftain at his campfire.' She winked. 'Good luck.'

Before going to search for her father, Lina went to see if Olga was in her crate. It was not surprising in the least that she had been locked up while the new arrivals were getting settled. She was not one for welcoming strangers.

'Hello, little lady,' Lina said as she opened the crate. 'Behave, or I'll be forced to carry you.'

Off they wandered in search of the two chieftains, greeting people along the way. Eventually, Lina spotted them. Her father was seated beside a tall warrior dressed in furs. Sture had certainly grown up since the last time she had seen him. Her mother had still been alive then. Picking Olga up, she proceeded towards them.

Farulf looked in her direction as she approached, then rose. The motion was slow despite his best effort at making it look fluid. 'There she is,' he said. 'You would remember my daughter, Lina.'

The chieftain turned to look at her, taking Lina in from head to toe as he stood up. 'I do. You were all limbs the last time we met.'

'And you were all teeth,' she replied, forcing a smile. 'Welcome to Cardiganshire.'

His gaze fell to Olga. 'There was no need to bring me a welcome gift.'

'I didn't.'

Farulf cleared his throat. 'The goose is Lina's companion.'

'I recall you had a similar pet last time I saw you,' Sture said. 'Owning livestock for company during a famine was controversial to say the least.'

'It's still controversial,' Farulf said, only half joking.

Sture looked down at the bird. 'How long do they live?'

'Up to twenty years,' Lina replied.

'Important to note that they stop laying around their fifth year,' her father said, unable to help himself.

Lina placed her down on the ground. 'As I've always said, slaughtering her won't bring more eggs for our clan.'

'It would bring a meal, though,' Sture said, staring down at her.

Nothing changed on Lina's face. If he was trying to be funny, he had failed. If he meant to make her uncomfortable, they were not there yet.

She looked him over. He was a handsome sort of man, with bright blue eyes and a symmetrical face. Similar to his father.

'Come sit with us,' Sture said, gesturing to the fire.

Lina glanced at her father, who gave her an encouraging nod. Walking over to a spare log, she lowered herself onto it, soaking up the warmth of the flames. Olga immediately settled at her feet without waiting for an invitation.

'Where's Simian?' she asked.

'He was playing games with some of the other children,' Sture answered.

She wondered if he meant to say 'other'.

'Your father was just sharing his strategy for keeping the Wolfvanir protected for the summer. I am pleased he called us here. Queen Charlotte seems to be confused about where Carmarthenshire's borders lie. The Vargr are always happy to remind people of their place.'

Lina glanced at her father, trying to read his expression. He seemed impressed by the young chieftain rather than wary of his arrogance, like she was.

The two men discussed the state of their clans, challenges they had faced since the famine, and their plans for the upcoming summer. Farulf did not mention his health, even though anyone with eyes could see it was deteriorating. The conversation was a delicate dance, a balance that had to be maintained for the sake of both clans. Lina was certain the picture Sture was painting of his recent travels was also missing some key details, but she did not dare ask questions. Being allowed to sit with them and listen *was* the privilege. Asking questions would only see her moved along.

Her father's voice was grave as he spoke of the looming threat of the Carmarthen Militia. He also brought up the scarcity of resources within the land they had been confined to and the pressing need to gather food before returning home.

'You drastically need to expand your hunting territory,' Sture said. 'We can help with that.'

Lina was unable to stay silent any longer. 'The Carmarthen Militia have been very clear about where we can and cannot hunt and the consequences if we step outside those boundaries.'

Sture had a way of looking straight through her. 'Your father will not let a pack of wasteland rebels dictate the survival of his clan.' He looked at Farulf. 'You took Lampeter on your third day here. Imagine what you can do now.'

'And they took it right back,' Lina pointed out.

'Because they could,' Sture said, resting his elbows on his knees. 'They cannot take anything from you now. They cannot dictate borders. Your clan once came to our aid in Chadorian waters, when defenders set fire to our boats. It is our turn to help you. And we can replenish our supplies while we are on land as well.'

Farulf was actually moved by that little speech and reached out to clap the chieftain on the arm. 'Your father would be proud to hear you say these things.'

The way Sture had mentioned the Wolfvanir coming to their aid in Chadorian waters made it sound like the defenders attacked them for no reason. It was interesting to Lina that there was no mention of the Vargr attacking Chadora while attempting to steal food and weapons.

'You will hunt without the threat of violence while we are here,' Sture assured him. 'The Vargr have some of the most skilled fighters in all of Europe.'

Lina fought hard not to roll her eyes. He was certainly not lacking in confidence.

'The first thing we need to do is establish some new borders of our own,' Sture said. 'Once the Carmarthen Militia get used to the fact that we are making the decisions, we will expand the borders further.'

Farulf said nothing, apparently content to let him lead the decision-making.

Lina was far less content. 'I worry you're underestimating this army. They've evolved from the days of hiding and looting for survival. The soldiers have been trained by Chadorian defenders. They will not be easily intimidated.'

His gaze slowly shifted back to hers. 'The aim is not to intimidate but to demonstrate. Perhaps you underestimate the Vargr. We are the only clan to have ever successfully breached Chadora's walls.'

Could it really be considered a success when so many warriors had been slaughtered before their feet even touched the ground? When his own father had died that day?

A look from Farulf made it clear that her contribution to the conversation had come to an end.

'Go find your brother,' he said. 'I'll see you both at our tent shortly.'

Lina picked up Olga and rose to her feet, relieved.

'Perhaps I will come and eat by your campfire tomorrow,' Sture said to Lina as she was preparing to leave. 'You can cook for me.'

She pressed her lips together to stop the threat of laughter. He actually thought she would swoon at the honour of cooking him a meal. 'Simian does more cooking than I do.'

'Lina is a fine cook,' Farulf added quickly, 'and an excellent hunter.'

One corner of Sture's mouth lifted. 'A woman after my heart.'

She doubted that. Sture had not changed much. His arrogance had simply morphed into adult form. 'Looks like I'm going fishing tomorrow.'

'We brought plenty of supplies with us,' Sture said. 'You will not starve under my watch.'

Her father looked uncomfortable for the first time since she had arrived, dropping his gaze to the fire. Sture's comment was probably a reminder that Farulf was struggling to provide for his clan at present.

'You can go to the kitchen area if you need eggs or butter,' Sture continued. 'Just tell the women I sent you, and they will give you what you need.'

Lina felt embarrassed on her father's behalf. She mumbled some version of 'Thank you' before leaving them to their plotting.

The air was heavy with smoke from all the campfires as she navigated her way through the labyrinth of tents. Lina could hear the laughter of children in the distance, their carefree voices carried to her on the breeze. She found her brother in the middle of them, playing a game with a stick and an old leather ball. His hair flopped over his forehead as he ran and laughed, oblivious to her watching him. An unexpected anger rose within her. 'Simian!'

His laughter ceased abruptly, and he looked in her direction with a raised eyebrow. Excusing himself from the game, he walked over to her. 'What's the matter?' He wiped sweat off his face, leaving a streak of dirt in its place. How was he dirtier than the children?

'What's the matter is that our father is seated with the Vargr chieftain, planning all kinds of violent acts, and you're out here playing games. You should be with them, listening and learning, not running among the children.'

She instantly hated herself when she saw his face fall.

'I was just being nice.' His voice resembled a wounded child's.

Her anger deflated as she witnessed the effect her words had on him. Reaching out, she squeezed his shoulder. 'Sorry. Long day.'

Not one to hold a grudge, he nodded and began walking with her, waving goodbye to the children, who were verbally protesting his departure. They strolled through the Vargr camp, shoulder to shoulder.

'So, you spoke with him?' Simian asked. 'Sture?'

She nodded. 'And let me tell you, he hasn't changed one bit.'

Simian threw an arm around her. 'He's changed. He's grown into his teeth, for one.'

She laughed lightly. 'It irritates me that he ended up quite handsome.'

'We don't have to be friends with the man. We can simply enjoy the benefits of his company, like sleeping a little easier at night.'

With a sigh, she dropped her head to his shoulder. 'Don't ever change.'

He drew back to look at her. 'Usually, that's all any of you want from me. Are you feeling all right?'

She straightened. 'Yes.'

'How was your watch today?' he asked. 'Could you see the longships arriving from where you were?'

'I could.' She checked her surroundings before adding, 'And I wasn't the only one.'

He gave her an intrigued look. 'Meaning?'

'Tolly was there with the defenders. I obviously wasn't close enough to hear what they were saying, but their expressions were *loud*.'

'I can imagine. Did you tell Father?'

'I didn't even tell Trinka.'

'Scandalous.'

She jabbed him playfully with her elbow. 'They were clearly there to investigate the smoke, and they got their answer.'

Simian scrunched his nose up. 'I don't feel as bad about spilling the beans now. They were going to find out one way or another.'

The smell of food cooking had Lina's stomach rumbling. She was aware of warriors watching them as they walked by. 'I've got a bad feeling about all this.'

'You have bad feelings most days about most things.'

Lina shrugged her brother's arm off her and placed Olga on the ground. The goose immediately opened her wings and went to charge at a warrior passing by from the other direction, so Lina quickly scooped her up again.

'I had a clear shot of General Tolly today,' she confessed. 'In fact, I had several. The range wouldn't have been a problem, and I could have fled in time and gotten away with it.' She swallowed. 'It would have been quite the achievement.'

Simian's eyes moved over her face. 'Your relationship with him is so fascinating to me.'

'Relationship?' she laughed.

'I stand by my theory that you were lovers in another life.' His eyes lit up when he said it.

'Stop.'

'I've read about these kinds of love stories. They keep finding each other in the next life.'

'I'm afraid it might be more tragic than that.'

He leaned in. 'How so?'

She looked cautiously around before speaking. 'I think I may…'

'You think you may what?'

Lina hesitated. '*Respect* him.'

Simian emitted a dramatic gasp that drew the attention of passers-by. Lina pinched his arm.

'I've never heard you gush over a man that way,' he whispered. 'You're surely doomed.'

She laughed and shoved him away. 'Will you go make yourself useful, please? Light a fire or something.'

Simian walked backwards for a few paces. 'Fine. I'll light the fire. Then I think I'll write some poetry. I'm feeling rather inspired suddenly.' He grinned at her before facing forwards again.

CHAPTER 16

The following morning, Lina's eyes flickered open at the sound of horses approaching. Dim light was seeping in through the canvas as she sat up to take in her surroundings. The wooden cot where her father slept was empty, the blanket still folded at the end. Farulf had always been an early riser, but he was certainly not one to fold his own blanket. Normally, Simian would tidy their space, since he was always the last to rise.

Horses pulled up mere feet from the tent. Lina glanced over at Simian, who did not so much as stir. Rising, she tugged on her boots and headed outside, emerging into rare sunlight filtering through the trees. She found a dozen or so warriors dismounting alongside Sture and her father. Her gaze narrowed on the blood splattered across Farulf's face and arm.

'Whose blood is that?' she asked, going to him. 'Are you hurt?'

Her father dropped a large, reassuring hand on her shoulder. 'I'm fine.'

'Then whose blood is it?'

He shook his head. 'At least let me sit down before you start with the questioning.'

She crossed her arms. 'You're out all night, returning covered in blood, and I can't ask questions?'

Frowning, Sture handed the reins of his horse to one of his men. 'Your father had a matter to take care of, Lina. Leave the poor man be.'

Her gaze went to him. 'And what matter would that be?'

He studied her a long moment before saying to Farulf, 'I think your daughter has forgotten herself.'

'No, I have an excellent memory.'

Sture's eyes shone with amusement. 'Go prepare your father some food. He will be hungry.' He nodded once at Farulf before walking away, his men following him.

Lina turned back to her father, annoyed. 'Anyone would think he's *my* chieftain.'

Farulf gave her a tired look. 'Calm yourself.'

'I have been perfectly calm throughout the entire conversation.' She nodded towards the gelding he was unsaddling. 'Where did all these horses come from?'

After releasing the girth, Farulf stretched out his fingers and winced. 'From the soldiers.'

'The ones you killed?'

He lifted his gaze to hers, looking more and more tired as the conversation went on. 'We had to expand our hunting territory or our being here is pointless.'

She stepped up to help him remove the saddle from the

horse's back, placing it atop a log beside their tent. 'Did you think you could quietly start a war and not tell anyone?'

'That's enough,' Farulf said. 'Sture is right. You must remember your place and trust me to lead.'

She bit her tongue.

Farulf retrieved a hare from a saddlebag and handed it to her. 'For the dinner tonight.'

'Oh, the one I'm cooking for Sture?'

He gave her a stern look. 'Yes. I need you to be an obedient daughter for once in your life. Can you manage that?'

'Of course.' She pressed her lips together hard to stop herself from saying the next part—and failed. 'Maybe I'll see if Frida has any special herbs I can add to his bowl.'

Farulf came close to her, pointing a twisted finger at her face in warning. '*Enough*.'

She dropped her gaze to her feet.

A sigh slipped from her father's lips as he lowered his hand. 'We have watchmen all along the perimeter. I need you ready to help protect this land.' He gestured towards the tent. 'And your brother.'

When he went to walk away, she asked, 'Does the general know yet? What you did to his men?'

He paused. 'I'm certain he'll know soon enough.'

'And you truly believe they're going to respect our borders after they find the dead bodies of their comrades?'

Farulf's eyebrows came together in an angry line. 'They won't have a choice. The Carmarthen Militia are outnumbered. Retaliation would be suicide.'

She could not believe that her father was following Sture so willingly down this path of violence. Without another word, she went to fetch her bow, knowing she needed to get away from him before she said something that got her into a lot of trouble.

When she entered the tent, Simian rolled over and looked at her. 'Where are you going?'

'Out.'

Her father blocked the exit with his gigantic frame. 'What are you doing?'

'I'm going to forage. I can't serve bland meat to a great chieftain, can I?' She slung her bow over her shoulder and waited for him to move.

Every muscle in Farulf's face was tense, but he eventually stepped aside. She dashed past him and went straight for the horse.

'It's not safe for you to ride around by yourself,' he said, following her.

She swung herself up onto the horse, content to ride bareback, then gathered the reins. 'The Vargr are here now to keep us safe, remember?'

His neck turned red.

Lina swung the horse around and cantered away before he could say anything else. The wind whipped through her unbraided hair as she urged the gelding faster, scanning the landscape ahead. Fields and trees stretched out before her, a patchwork of colours and shadows.

Eventually, she came upon a raven banner fluttering in the breeze. It stood tall and proud atop a gentle slope, framed by the open sky. She reined in her horse and approached with caution, spotting a Vargr watchman nearby. He frowned at her, and she backed her horse up and headed in the opposite direction.

As she walked her horse along the perimeter, she heard

hooves thundering against the ground. She moved behind some brush cover as a precaution, watching the horizon through the gaps. The sound grew louder until a lone rider came into view. She recognised the horse, then him. Tolly sat atop his mare, his cloak billowing behind him as he scanned his surroundings. She shrank down in the saddle and waited for him to pass.

That was her cue to leave.

However, her curiosity got the better of her, and she followed him instead. Kicking her horse into a slow trot, she tracked him for the next half a mile, at one point passing a watchman who warned her to steer clear of the boundary.

'There are soldiers in the area,' he explained.

Lina feigned ignorance, thanked him, then moved away from the perimeter, only to return to it once she was out of his sight. By that time, she had lost Tolly. Stopping her horse, she looked around, figuring she should probably return with some herbs to justify her rebellious outing.

'Why are you following me?' came a voice behind her.

A gasp slipped from her as she turned to see Tolly. She pressed a hand to her racing heart, annoyed at herself for being so careless.

'Lucky for you,' he said, sounding tired, 'I'm not in the habit of shooting people in the back. That's more of a clan thing.'

She turned her horse to face him properly. 'You can't be this side of the banners. There are warriors about.'

'I know.'

She regarded him for a moment. 'Are you here for revenge?'

He broke eye contact and looked around. 'I'm looking for

a missing soldier, likely dead. Judging by the state we found the others in, I suspect no prisoners were taken.'

The pity she felt for him caught her off guard. 'You shouldn't be out here by yourself.'

'Neither should you. I could have killed you three times already.'

The appropriate reaction to his words was fear, but she felt nothing even close to that. 'I could help you find him if you like.' Why she offered such a thing, she did not know. They were bigger enemies now than they had been the day prior.

'I think it's a little late to pretend you care,' he said. 'Wouldn't you agree?'

She lifted one shoulder in a shrug. 'If I don't go with you, then you'll have to worry about me alerting the guards.'

'It would be safer to kill you.'

'No, it wouldn't. The Vargr chieftain is looking for a reason to kill more of you. I'd strongly suggest you don't hand it to him so easily.'

He inhaled and looked around. 'The soldier was patrolling around here. I was looking for tracks.'

Lina turned her horse and slowly began walking it, helping him look. After a few minutes, she came upon some tracks. 'There,' she said, pointing to the ground, then looking off in the direction they continued.

Tolly walked his horse closer to see. 'Those are clearly boots. He was on horseback.'

'But his killer wasn't,' she said almost apologetically. For all she knew, she was riding the very horse he was slaughtered on.

Their gazes met briefly before they continued in silence.

Soon, they emerged into a clearing dotted with wilted flowers trying to survive the rain. Lina stopped her horse when she spotted a motionless figure on the ground. The once-green uniform was now all shades of red and brown. Tolly froze when he caught sight of it, then dismounted. He walked over to inspect the body, checking for any signs of life, even though they both knew the exercise was futile.

'What a fucking mess,' he said to himself.

Lina swallowed and slid from her horse, walking over with the intention of helping in some way. She was a few feet away when he rose suddenly and drew his sword in the same motion, pointing the tip to her neck. Her eyes bored into his, and she felt a strange feeling wash over her. It was warm and familiar. Her brother's theory came to mind, and she wondered if perhaps they had known each other in another life.

'Have we ever met before?' she asked, knowing it was an odd time to ask the question.

The sword retracted a few inches, and the hard edges of Tolly's face softened a little.

'Have we?' she asked again. 'Before all of this?'

He withdrew his sword and took a small step back, eyes returning to the corpse. It was clear by the way he had completely shut down that she was not crazy in thinking they had.

As she studied his profile, a memory surfaced. She was in the boat with her family, leaning over the edge, holding on to an oar. A half-drowned boy stared up at her from the water. Her eyes widened as she made the connection.

'It was you,' she breathed. 'In the water.' She saw Tolly's throat bob as he continued to stare down at the bloodied corpse. The memory became clearer the longer she looked at him. 'We towed you to the shore, watched you swim over the waves before collapsing on the beach.' It was a vivid scene now. 'They set fire to your ship.'

His hands went to his hips, and he leaned his weight heavily on one foot.

'We heard the entire ship was infected,' she continued. 'Father said that all we'd done was extend your misery, that it would have been kinder to let you drown.'

Still, he did not look at her.

'You were so thin and had no one to care for you.' She swallowed. 'I assumed you died.'

He finally looked at her. 'Well, I'm still here. And your father still wishes me dead.'

The burn in Lina's throat caught her off guard. 'It's not personal.'

He laughed, but it was an unfriendly sort of noise. 'No. You're all just trying to survive, isn't that right?'

The way he threw her words back at her was both clever and cruel.

'It all makes sense now,' she said, watching him closely. 'Have you known the whole time?'

He shook his head.

'When?'

His eyebrows pinched together, as if the conversation was causing him physical pain. 'When we were on the bridge. Your father used your name.'

'You remembered my name?'

He appeared genuinely taken aback by that question. 'Are you really asking me that? I'm standing here because of you.'

It was her turn to be speechless.

'And I remember your mother.' He shook his head, like he was shaking a thought away, then brushed a finger down his nose. 'You could have taken them as prisoners,' he said, tone hardening once more.

It took her a moment to return to the present. 'That didn't work out so well for us last time.' She swallowed against her thickening throat. 'We needed more land to hunt.'

He nodded slowly. 'Well, you have plenty now.'

Her eyes sank shut.

'The soldiers' blood is on my hands,' he said. 'We should have shot the Vargr as they came ashore, sent the rest of you running for your boats.'

It was clear he wanted a reaction from her. She did not give it to him.

'Perhaps I should kill you,' he said, not settling for silence. 'Tie you to your horse and send you back to your father.'

'I don't think you have it in you to kill me, even now.'

His eyes moved between hers. 'I'll have to find it in me so I can better protect my kingdom next time.'

'And ruin our long history of keeping each other alive?'

'That certainly doesn't extend past you.'

'You could have killed Simian,' she countered.

'It would be like killing a child.'

That struck a chord, which was likely why he said it. 'He can fight if he needs to.'

Tolly held her gaze. 'We'll find out soon enough.' He crouched, picking up his comrade.

Despite their bitter exchange, Lina went to help. They laid the man over the rump of Tolly's mare. She half expected him to take her horse since it was stolen.

'His name was Aneirin,' Tolly said as he tied the man to the saddle. 'He has a daughter, born last year.'

Lina took a step back.

He glanced at her briefly before mounting. His mare stepped sideways in protest of the additional weight. Then, gathering the reins, he rode away without saying another word.

CHAPTER 17

Initially, Farulf had wanted Lina to do all the preparation and cooking for the evening meal, likely wanting to prove to Sture that his daughter was capable. But when he learned the chieftain would be bringing additional guests, he insisted Simian help her.

The siblings sat by the fire in the late afternoon, making barley bread and cleaning fish. The hare their father had brought back with him that morning was stewing in the pot with onions and some herbs Simian had found earlier.

'You're very quiet,' Simian commented as he kneaded dough. 'You're not worried about the dinner, are you?'

Outside of preparing the food, Lina had thought little about the upcoming dinner. Her mind had been on Tolly all day. 'I'm worried I'll like Sture even less by the end of dinner. Does that count?'

Sitting back, Simian studied her. 'This dinner is important

to Father, so perhaps you should focus less on Sture's flaws and more on being a gracious host.'

'I can't believe you of all people are lecturing me about keeping Father happy. Perhaps if you picked up a sword occasionally, that responsibility wouldn't fall solely on me.'

Simian began tearing the dough into small portions. 'That's fair.'

Their guests arrived as the sun dipped below the horizon, their father with them. He took in the small feast laid out and gave Lina a subtle nod of approval.

'Lina,' Sture said by way of greeting. 'It looks as if you have been busy.'

'Only a little,' she said. 'Simian helped.'

Sture glanced back at the two burly warriors flanking him. 'This is Bo and Toke. They will eat with us tonight.'

Introductions were made. Bo seemed to be a man of few words, with sharp features and a keen eye. He watched Lina closely, along with the rest of the family. Toke had a kind face and a presence about him that demanded respect.

'Sit, please,' Farulf said.

The savoury aroma of stewed meat and fresh bread mingled with the smoke from the fire, creating an inviting atmosphere. As the men settled themselves, Lina poured mead into cups, feeling Sture's eyes upon her the whole time. After ensuring everyone had a drink, she went to sit down.

'Lina, come sit beside me,' Sture said, gesturing to the space between himself and Toke.

It was more of a command than an invitation, and she felt a flutter of unease as she took a seat next to him. She made a point of not looking over at Simian for fear she would see pity in his eyes.

The fire cast dancing shadows across the faces of everyone gathered around it. The men spoke about clan matters, matters Lina would normally have an opinion on but knew better than to express in that particular group. Sture only addressed her when he needed his cup refilled.

Toke was the only one who spoke directly to her. Leaning in, he said quietly, 'It can be hard to get a word in sometimes.'

He was throwing her drowning soul a lifeline, which she appreciated.

'Are we boring you, Lina?' Sture asked, eyes on her once more.

She straightened. 'Not at all.'

'Lina is used to such conversation going on around her,' Farulf said. 'It comes with being the chieftain's daughter.'

Sture nodded and drank. 'My men said they saw you riding along the boundary today. What were you doing out there?'

He really did not miss much. She was aware of her father shifting with discomfort in her peripheral vision. 'I wanted to see the new perimeter, and I thought I would collect some herbs while I was out there.'

Sture leaned forwards, resting his elbows on his knees. 'Security and cooking.' He glanced at Farulf. 'Your daughter really can do it all.'

'It will be a lucky man who marries her,' Farulf said.

That comment had her and Simian exchanging a glance.

'Do you agree, Lina?' Sture asked. 'Do you think you have a lot to offer a man?'

The conversation had her wishing the ground would open up and swallow her whole. 'I have a lot to offer my family. That's all I'm focused on right now.'

Simian spoke up at that. 'We would be lost without her.'

'That bodes well for your future husband,' Toke said.

Lina smiled in place of a response.

'A good wife at your side is certainly a blessing,' Sture said.

Farulf nodded in agreement.

'Sounds like you have thought a lot on the subject,' Simian said.

'A man must,' Sture replied. 'The person you choose will raise your children.'

Cooking and birthing. What else had she expected? He was so painfully predictable. She really should not have responded. 'It sounds as though you have thought of everything.'

An amused glint filled Sture's eyes.

'Do not forget obedience,' Bo said, speaking for the first time. He looked at Lina when he said it.

Sture nodded in agreement. 'A wife must trust her husband to lead.'

'Well, that's me done for,' Lina said humourlessly.

Her father pressed his eyes closed, and Simian took a drink to cover his smile.

'Keeping in mind that not all men are born leaders,' Toke said. 'Be careful which ones you trust.'

The change in Sture's expression suggested he did not like that comment from Toke.

'I'm inclined to agree,' Farulf said. 'That's why I would only entrust the happiness of my daughter to a strong leader.'

Sture raised his cup in response, while Lina looked down at hers.

Clapping his hands together, Simian rose. 'Shall I serve some food?'

Bo looked up at him with an amused expression. 'You serve as well as cook?'

His condescending tone had Lina pressing her teeth together. 'Better he knows how in case he can't find a wife to do it all for him.'

Farulf coughed—a warning.

'Let me serve,' Lina said, standing up. 'I need the practise.'

Simian slowly sat back down. The men resumed talking while Lina distributed plates and served them food. They all ate with hearty appetites.

When Sture's plate was empty, he held it in her direction and said, 'More stew, please.'

At least he said 'please'.

Farulf appeared happy that Sture had enjoyed her cooking enough to request seconds.

As she was spooning meat onto Sture's place, he placed his hand over hers, a gesture so intimate, it had her looking up.

'Thank you,' he said, seeming genuine.

Nodding, she sat back down to finish eating.

CHAPTER 18

Tolly dispatched another two hundred soldiers to the west of Lampeter, bringing their total defence numbers in the region to four hundred. Their aim was to ensure the sea warriors took no more land than what they had allotted themselves. While the urge to push them back was strong, Tolly knew the loss of soldiers would be unimaginable. It was better to manage their presence for a few months than step into a war they were not sure they could win.

They positioned themselves atop a hill with a stream nearby for water. The sound of stakes being hammered into the ground could be heard throughout the valley. Heavily armed men stood looking out over the sprawling landscape, watching for any movement below.

Tolly would not be taking any chances moving forwards.

When his men were settled and the camp secure, he and Ryder walked the perimeter, hammering flags into the ground that were twice the size of the warrior banners they had torn out earlier. Alveye and Hadewaye had returned to Chadora, and Tatum was expected to rejoin them the following day, while Ryder had barely left his side since the warriors had arrived on their shores.

As the brothers were working together in silence, Ryder straightened suddenly and looked off down the hill.

'What is it?' Tolly asked.

Ryder did not move. 'I think we have company.'

No sooner had he said the words than half a dozen warriors walked into view. Ryder signalled to the guards, and a moment later, archers stepped up to the perimeter. The warriors were undeterred.

As they drew closer, Tolly realised he did not recognise any of them. Their eyes gleamed with a feral intensity he had not seen in the Wolfvanir. He understood then what Lina had tried to warn him about. These men were an entirely different breed of warrior with their bushy beards and scarred faces. They moved with a confident stride and relaxed hands. He could see the runes tattooed on their arms and chests. It seemed they wanted to talk.

Tolly signalled to the archers to stand down. 'Let's hear what they have to say.'

Ryder nodded, eyes never leaving the men. 'That's far enough,' he called when they came within fifteen feet.

The men walked a few more paces before stopping. The one at the front ran his eyes over the flag Tolly had just put in the ground and let out a long whistle.

'They look expensive,' he said. Then, looking at Ryder, he added, 'You even have your very own defender.'

'Who will remove your eye if you don't make your point quickly,' Ryder said.

A faint smirk came and went on the warrior's face before he focused on Tolly, taking in his uniform. 'You must be the general we have heard so much about.'

Tolly nodded once. 'And you must be the men responsible for killing my soldiers.'

The warrior looked him over. 'Sture, chieftain of the Vargr clan.' He nodded towards the camp behind Tolly. 'Where is the other half of your army?'

Nothing changed on Tolly's face. 'I brought enough soldiers to maintain order in the region.'

Sture nodded. 'Good, good. I am sorry about your men. It is a shame they were not better at their jobs.'

Ryder shifted his weight.

'Do not get too comfortable up here on your little hill,' Sture said. 'When the food runs out, we will come looking for more.'

'I strongly advise against that,' Tolly said. 'Our tolerance won't stretch any further.'

Sture's eyebrows lifted. 'But we just got here.'

'Listen to me,' Tolly said. 'I'm going to talk slowly and clearly because you don't seem particularly bright. We value the lives of our soldiers here in Carmarthenshire, so we don't step into fights lightly, nor for the sake of our egos. I know that might be difficult for men like you to understand.' He let those words settle before continuing. 'That said, if you pass these flags before you, you will be killed. Your heads will be mounted on spikes and your bodies left on the ground to feed the wildlife. Do you or any of your halfwit comrades have questions about that?'

Sture watched him with an amused expression. 'This is a pretty spot,' he said, looking around. 'Hares aplenty, clean water.' His gaze returned to Tolly. 'You do not mind if we join you by the stream, do you?'

Tolly simply shrugged.

'I'd be pitching your tents out of shooting range if I were you,' Ryder said.

Sture's eyes moved over his uniform. 'What is the shooting range of a defender nowadays?'

'I'm happy to let you take a guess.'

Sture chuckled. 'That is a fine guard dog you have there, General. Be sure to keep him leashed.' The smile fell from his face. 'See you soon.'

Tolly exchanged a glance with his brother as the men walked away.

The following morning, hundreds of sea warriors returned to the area, raising tents amid the trees at the base of the hill. Tolly and Ryder watched them from their vantage point.

Tatum arrived in the afternoon, joining the brothers at their watch post. He took in the scene below. 'Someone care to explain to me how we lost another four miles of territory in the short time I was gone?'

They filled him in on everything that had happened during his absence. Afterwards, Tatum returned to staring, choosing his words carefully. 'At least we have a height advantage. Though it would have been better to be on a hill with boulders that we could gently push in their direction.'

Tolly's lips turned up. 'I'll keep that in mind for next time.'

'Annoying that Sture figured out our shooting range,' Ryder said.

Tatum tilted his head. 'I'd probably get close.'

Ryder gave him a doubtful look. The competitiveness between the defenders was a constant source of amusement to Tolly.

'What did the queen have to say?' he asked, moving the conversation along.

'She's not thrilled about the arrival of the Vargr, as you can imagine. She's not only concerned for the security of her kingdom but the safety of the army.' He paused to watch the movement below. 'And frankly, so am I. *Two* nights I was gone.'

Tolly inhaled a deep breath. 'Trust me when I tell you your absence wasn't a factor. There was no warning. The warriors move like ghosts.'

'I fucking hate the Vargr,' Tatum said.

'Everyone hates the Vargr,' Tolly replied. 'But I imagine they're a sore point for defenders.'

'They won't like that we're here, given we killed their last chieftain, and I'm guessing that's his son.'

'He's a proper arse,' Ryder muttered.

'No one likes an arse.'

Ryder raised an eyebrow at him.

'Unless that arse is me,' Tatum clarified. Then, resting his hands on his hips, he added, 'I think we should make a plan for the worst possible outcome and every outcome in between.'

'Agree,' Ryder said. 'You need to ensure your army is ready for whatever they throw our way.'

Tolly had been thinking the same thing. 'Let's gather the

commanders and figure out how to keep the camp and region safe.'

Ryder nodded once, then walked away to relay the order.

A few hours later, eleven men were crammed under a shelter in the centre of the camp. Every one of them bore the weight of their responsibility, exchanging concerned glances while Tolly spoke at length with input from the defenders.

With their strategies sorted, they dispersed. Tolly fetched a clean uniform and headed down to the stream for a wash. There were twenty or so soldiers bathing and collecting water when he arrived. Tolly found some space close to the boundary and took in the sight of the crystal-clear water running through an area which likely had no stream a decade ago. They never had to worry about drought but rather how to manage the oversupply.

His gaze drifted downstream, landing on two women undressing. It was Lina and Trinka, their figures silhouetted against the setting sun. Lina's long hair was out, as it had been when he saw her the day prior. He had been unable to rid his thoughts of her since.

'The only thing I leave on is the dagger strapped to my thigh,' Trinka called out.

It took Tolly a moment to realise she was talking to *him*. He had been caught red-handed looking.

'That's not good for your dagger,' he shouted back. 'I'd hate to see it corrode.'

She laughed as she removed her sark, then strode confidently into the water. The soldiers nearby fell silent, watching her. Tolly cleared his throat, and they immediately averted their gazes and returned to their tasks.

Tolly stripped down to his braies, keeping his gaze straight ahead, then down, then fixed on the half-naked men around him at one point. The problem was, while Lina was quite far away, she was close enough for him to make out her figure as she waded into the water. He was grateful that she had kept her sark on, mostly because it saved him from yelling at the soldiers glancing in her direction, but also because the garment had soaked up the water and clung to her skin. It was see-through enough to have him dashing into the chilly water.

The stream was only thigh-deep, but he crouched to have a proper wash. The cold water energised him and cleared the fog from his mind. He closed his eyes for a moment, enjoying the prickling sensation over his skin.

As he rose to exit the water, he discovered Lina had waded closer to the boundary and was watching him. At that distance, he could make out some details he could not see earlier, like the blotches of red on her cheeks from the cold and the water dripping from the ends of her hair.

The exact shape of her breasts.

He swallowed thickly, letting his gaze wander where it should not go. Though, to be fair, she was no better, her eyes raking down his bare torso. Then slightly lower. That was enough to drive him from the water and send him rushing towards his uniform. He left without looking back.

Her expression, her curiosity, the way she angled her body as though inviting his gaze to linger... his insides were a melting pot. The list of reasons why he could do her no harm was getting longer. Now he had to add beguiling. It was undeniable. Beneath the weapons, strange clothes, and tough front she put on was a woman of extraordinary beauty.

The cool air wrapped Tolly's damp skin as he dried

himself. His fingers fumbled slightly with the buttons of his tunic.

As he made his way back up the slope towards the noisy camp, he did not look back but was aware that something had shifted within him.

It was the most alive he had felt in some time.

CHAPTER 19

Lina could not stay mad at her father once she realised the amount of effort he was putting in to appear healthy in front of Sture. He finished each day exhausted, often falling asleep while sitting up after his evening meal. The performance was draining him.

Over the next week, Lina observed the extra food coming into the camp. Hunters from both clans were returning with deer, hare, fox, pheasant, and even the occasional boar. The difference the extra territory had made was undeniable. She had initially objected to moving closer to the boundary, but those objections had been ignored. If Sture deemed it necessary in order to protect their territory, then that was what they did.

The two clans fell into a rhythm of life that might have been considered normal if it were not for the enemy camp less than half a mile away. Despite this, Lina found solace in the easy routine of each day. When she was not hunting, weaving, or sewing, she liked to spend time down at the stream with Olga, watching her swim. But she made a point of going early in the day in order to avoid Tolly, who usually visited late in the afternoon. Since her encounter with him there, she had felt things. They grew inside her like a tumour. The problem was not that he was attractive but that she was *drawn* to him. Drawn to a man who had killed clan members, murdered people she cared about.

What did that say about her?

Sometimes it was impossible to avoid him. She was expected to do her part in keeping the clans safe, which included keeping watch over the boundary. Normally, such orders came from her father, but as the days slipped by, Sture began giving orders directly to the Wolfvanir—and they followed them without question. It worried Lina that people obeyed Sture the same as they would her father. The Vargr chieftain had arrived with all the confidence Farulf was lacking.

Lina was feeding Olga one morning when Sture arrived at their tent.

'Good morning,' he said, stopping in front of her.

She was crouched with some greens in her hands and looked up. 'Morning.' Dropping the food on the ground, she rose. When Olga went for the chieftain's leg instead, Lina swooped down to pick her up. 'Are you looking for my father?'

'Actually, I was looking for you. Can you keep watch over the eastern perimeter this morning?'

She glanced behind her at the tent where Farulf was still sleeping. 'I think so. I'll have to see if Father needs for me anything.'

'Is he sleeping?'

'No,' she lied. And she could tell by his face that he knew it was a lie. 'I'm sure it won't be a problem,' she added.

'Good.'

Unexpectedly, Olga stretched out her neck and latched on to his hand. Lina pulled her away, then eyed his bleeding finger. 'Sorry. She usually behaves if I'm holding her.'

He ran his thumb over the blood. 'She is lucky she has *your* arm around her. I have killed dogs for less.'

That did not surprise Lina at all. She instinctively drew the goose closer to her. 'She just doesn't know you.'

He stared at the bird for a long moment, then gave Lina a weak smile that did not reach his eyes. 'Eastern perimeter. I will send someone to relieve you in a few hours.'

She nodded, not bringing up her father again.

When he left, she went inside the tent and found Simian practising his writing beneath the light streaming in through a gap in the canvas. He glanced in her direction when she entered, then sat up when he saw her gathering weapons.

'Where are you going?' he whispered.

Lina walked over to him. 'To watch the eastern perimeter. *Sture* came by to ask me.'

Simian's brow furrowed. 'Why didn't he ask me? He only ever asks me to collect firewood.' He seemed genuinely offended.

'Finding dry wood in this weather is an art form. We must all lean into our strengths.'

'Everyone knows the most effective approach is to search for trees that are resistant to water and wood that's elevated from the ground. This includes pieces still attached to living trees, lying on branches, or standing dead—'

'Like I said, it's an art form.' Lina cut him off to spare herself further explanation. 'Tell Father where I've gone when he wakes.' She secured her quiver to her back, then her bow. 'I'm taking Olga with me.'

He nodded and returned to his writing.

Lina made her way to the eastern perimeter, Olga waddling at her side. The morning mist hung about like a ghostly shroud. She passed several warriors also on watch. They nodded a greeting as she went by. There were also plenty of soldiers on the other side, their green uniforms bleeding into the landscape. They stood tall and vigilant, their weapons gleaming menacingly.

Lina relieved one of the warriors, taking up her position in front of a gnarled old tree with skeletal branches. She scanned the horizon, observing movements in and around the enemy camp. Time seemed to stretch endlessly as she did her due, every minute feeling like five. She spent the majority of that time watching Olga foraging in the mud. Then finally, when the sun was high in the sky, a Vargr warrior arrived to take over from her. Olga lowered her head and honked in warning at the young man.

'Easy, girl,' Lina said. 'He comes in peace.' She gave the warrior an apologetic look before ushering Olga in the opposite direction. 'Let's walk off your bad mood.'

Lina strolled along the perimeter, away from the watchful eyes of warriors and soldiers, arriving at a grassy field. It was a sea of green and gold that seemed to stretch all the way to the horizon.

Olga spread her wings wide and gave a joyful honk before she took off running. Lina watched for a few moments before throwing her arms out and running after her. When she caught up to Olga, she closed her eyes and let the cool breeze wash over her, relishing in the simple freedom of that moment. Olga turned in happy circles, so Lina copied her, spinning until she was dizzy. Olga stopped and shook out her wings as Lina laughed, bending to pet her.

'Still the same silly goose girl.'

The sense of peace she felt was replaced with a prickling sensation along her spine. She stilled, feeling eyes upon her. Reaching back for an arrow, she swiftly loaded her bow as she straightened, taking aim.

Sitting on a horse at the edge of the field was Tolly. He was heavily armed and wore a serious expression. Lina looked around to ensure he was alone before lowering her bow. His gaze shifted to Olga, who watched him for a moment before losing interest and waddling away.

'Safe to approach?' Tolly called to her.

Lina shrugged. '*I* won't kill you, but I won't know what Olga will do until you get here.'

Tolly checked his surroundings before dismounting and leading his horse closer. The strange energy that Lina had felt that day at the stream returned, turning her hands clammy. She put her arrow away and positioned her bow between them like a shield.

'You're a long way from the camp,' he said.

'As are you.'

He nodded. 'Well, this is our land, so…'

She was silent a moment. 'Did you follow me here?'

'Yes and no.'

'Yes and no?'

He looked towards the camp. 'Blackmane saw you pass by. I wanted to check that you were all right.'

Olga waddled by them, ignoring Tolly entirely.

'That's progress from having my face torn open,' he said.

Lina pressed her lips together to stop from smiling. 'She likes it here. Do you mind if we walk in *your* field for a few minutes longer?'

'You really shouldn't be out here alone. It's not safe.'

She slung her bow over one shoulder and took a step towards him. 'But I'm not alone, am I?'

His eyes moved between hers as though trying to read her. And there was that feeling again.

'I'll walk with you,' he said. 'You on your side of the boundary and me on mine.'

She began strolling through the tall grass, watching Olga explore. He walked adjacent. The sun broke briefly through the clouds, but the golden light was fleeting. It was gone before she could comment on it.

'I heard you met Sture,' she said after a spell of silence. 'How did that go?'

'About as well as you would expect. The slaughter of my soldiers with no attempt to negotiate didn't help matters.'

She looked at him. 'Would you have negotiated with him on territory?'

'No.'

'Ah.'

Tolly kept walking. 'He's young for a chieftain.'

'You're young for a general.'

He nodded. 'That's true.'

She watched him for a few paces. 'How does one get from foreigner on a smallpox-infected ship to general of the Carmarthen Militia?'

'Why do you assume I'm foreign?'

She gestured towards his dagger. 'First, your accent is different. Subtle but noticeable. Second, you have a shamrock on your dagger and arrived on a ship from Ireland.'

'Strong points.' His lips twitched. 'Well, you already know the background of this army. You've rubbed our gritty history in my face.'

'Yes, but why you?'

He considered the question before replying. 'I guess I proved to be the most difficult to kill. I was here when these lands were nothing but wastelands, and I was still here when all that changed.'

'Clearly, you earned the respect of these men if they're prepared to take orders from you.'

'Having a brother who's a defender probably helps.'

She slowed her pace. 'Which leads me to my next question. How does an Irishman end up a defender in the Chadorian army?'

Tolly shrugged. 'He's also hard to kill.'

'There's more to it than that.'

'It's a long story.'

'I have time.'

He was silent as he weighed his response, then told her the brief version of how smallpox had torn through their village in Ireland. His brother had sent him to Wales to protect him, promising to join him soon.

Lina sat with that information before replying. 'You lost your entire family?'

'Everyone except Ryder. Blackmane,' he corrected.

Her expression softened. 'So, Ryder travelled to Wales, like he promised, and learned that the ship had been destroyed?'

He nodded.

'How did he find out you were alive?'

Tolly rested his hand on his weapon. 'The reunion was unexpected, to say the least, but we were brought together by a common enemy—Lord Hodge.'

'The infamous lord, whom you hated.'

'That's him.'

'The marcher lord who enslaved an entire people—except you, General Hard-To-Kill.'

A smile flickered on his face, then faded. 'My turn.'

'For what?'

'To dig for painful memories. When did your mother pass?'

Her face fell. 'How do you know she's dead?'

He gave her a sideways look.

'A year after we met,' she said quietly. 'Consumption.'

'I'm sorry.' He sounded like he meant it. 'She seemed like a kind woman.'

The kindest.

Lina looked behind her, trying to gauge how far they had walked, and somehow tripped over Olga in the process. Tolly caught her arm, stopping her from going down. She looked up, straight into those eyes which were nowhere near black up close. More of a rich brown.

She straightened, holding his gaze. Instead of letting go of her, he merely loosened his grip. The warmth from his hand burned through the sleeve of her smock. She opened her mouth to thank him, but no words came out. His gaze fell to her open mouth, his eyebrows drawing together.

'Lina!'

The sound of her father's voice sent her leaping backwards out of Tolly's grasp. Her cheeks flushed scarlet as she stumbled over Olga—again—before bending to pick her up.

'I have to go,' she said without looking at Tolly.

Her feet moved quickly towards her father. She struggled to lift her gaze to him, and when she finally did, she was met with the fury of one deceived. He looked her up and down as though checking her for signs of disease, then glared in Tolly's direction. Lina did not dare look back. She felt a lump forming in her throat, likely shame.

'Father—'

'Not a word.'

Farulf's eyes burned holes into her back as she walked on. With her head down and the goose tucked against her chest, she headed for the camp.

CHAPTER 20

By the time Lina and her father reached the camp, Farulf was limping. It had been too far for him. *She* certainly had not been expecting to walk as far as she did. Now she was forced to watch her father's once-strong gait reduced to a painful shuffle. Yet even in his weakened state, there was a steely resolve in his eyes. She was relieved when he finally lowered himself onto a log in front of the fire, wincing the entire way down. He waited for Lina to take a seat, preparing to reprimand her.

Before he could begin, Simian emerged from the tent carrying a plate of chopped herbs. He looked between the two of them. 'Everything all right?'

Neither of them answered straight away. When Lina went to speak, her father cut her off. 'I'll be doing the talking.'

She closed her mouth.

Simian awkwardly dropped the greens into the pot, then looked around, seemingly unsure what to do next.

'Sit down, Simian,' Farulf said. 'This concerns you too.'

Lina's eyebrows rose. 'It does?'

Farulf changed his position, huffing and puffing through the five-second ordeal.

'Shall I get you a hot cloth for your knees?' Lina asked.

'No.'

Simian chewed his lip, clearly not enjoying the tension. 'Did something happen during your watch?'

Farulf pinched the bridge of his nose. 'May I speak, please?'

The siblings fell silent.

Taking a calming breath, Farulf began. 'I spoke at length with Sture this morning. We were discussing the future of our clans.'

It was not the conversation Lina had been expecting to have upon returning to the camp, but she did not interrupt.

'Sture's not only a strong and capable leader, but he's also a forward thinker with the ability to adapt. These are important attributes during periods of relentless change. If we can't pivot as our environment and circumstances demand, then we perish.'

'You should have invited me along,' Simian said. 'I could have written all that was said. It's helpful to reference these conversations in the future.'

Farulf gave him a tired look. 'We prefer to rely on our memories and honour.'

'Both of which can be easily lost.'

Lina subtly shook her head at Simian to silence him, sensing their father was already at his limit for patience—thanks to her. Simian fell silent, and the chieftain looked between his two children.

'Sture has made a bold proposal, one that may shape the future of our clans for generations to come.'

A knot formed in Lina's stomach at the gravity of her father's words. She snuck a glance at Simian, who mirrored her apprehension.

Farulf looked only at Lina when he said the next part. 'He wishes to take you as his wife, and I've given my blessing. We agreed it would be best if we waited until the end of summer. It'll give you some time to get to know each other better, and I want to ensure that the two clans work well together before binding us to them in this permanent way.'

The crackling of the campfire seemed to intensify. Lina's heart had not just skipped a beat but stopped altogether. She wondered if perhaps she had misheard him.

'What?' The one-word question was all she could manage.

Her father's expression remained determined. 'As I said, he's a good man and strong leader. The match would benefit everyone.'

Everyone except her.

His words sat like a heavy stone on her chest. Simian shifted uncomfortably beside her, his silence loud. Lina struggled to process the implications of Farulf's announcement. As the silence stretched on, a whirlwind of thoughts and emotions swelled up inside her. She had always known her father would decide who she wed, but never in a million years did she think he would make such an arrangement without so much as a conversation with her first. While love was not a factor, surely compatibility was.

'You barely know him,' she said. 'Knowing his father is not knowing *him*.'

'I know you are worthy of a chieftain,' Farulf said. 'And I

know I must consider what's best for the entire clan, not just one individual.' He looked around. 'This sort of alliance with the Vargr will ensure we always have another clan to fight alongside us when the need arises.' He swallowed, perhaps guiltily. 'It's a strategic decision, one that goes beyond personal desires.' His tone remained matter-of-fact. He was speaking from a place of responsibility.

Simian reached out to touch Lina's arm, a silent gesture of support. She looked at him as she tried to gather her thoughts, then back at her father. 'I worry this decision has been made from a place of fear. You need someone to replace you someday, I understand that—'

'Enough,' Farulf said.

'There are warriors in our clan who will make fine chieftains if given some time to—'

'How much time do you think I have?' Anger crept into his tone. 'How long until I can't hold a sword at all?'

She reached out and took hold of his hand. 'We will hold it for you. That's what family does.'

'If you want to be supportive, to help like family, then this marriage is the way. This is what I ask of you. This is what I *need* from you.' He paused, allowing his words to settle. 'Do you understand?'

Lina's hand fell away. 'Please tell me this doesn't have anything to do with the general.'

Straightening, Simian looked between the two of them. 'What about the general?'

Farulf's entire demeanour changed. 'Why would you mention him?'

'Because… what you saw in the field.'

'What did you see?' Simian asked.

'Nothing,' Farulf snapped.

Feeling sick, Lina rose, a hand pressed to her stomach.

Her father looked up at her. 'Where are you going?'

'I need some air.'

'We're seated outside,' Simian helpfully pointed out. 'How much more air do you need?'

The betrayal she felt was siphoning it straight from her lungs. 'A lot more.' She stepped back from the fire. 'I told Trinka I would come find her in the afternoon.' It was a believable lie.

Simian went to stand, but she raised a hand, stopping him in his tracks. She needed to be alone.

Her father sighed. 'Lina—'

'I'll see you later.' She left. Olga was so exhausted from her full day of play and exploration that she did not even try to follow, remaining by the fire.

Lina made her way through the camp to Trinka's tent, where she found Aife, alone, cleaning a fish. She forced a smile for the girl. 'Is Trinka here?'

'No.' Aife dropped the fish into a pail of water. 'I can help you look for her if you like.'

'No, you're clearly busy.'

She touched Aife affectionately on the shoulder before leaving, heading out of the camp and making her way up the western hill that overlooked the sea. The sight was like stepping into a warm bath. The salty breeze whispered soothing words to her, the crashing waves beckoning.

Her thoughts turned to her mother, imagining what she would have said to her. There was no doubt she would have supported Farulf's decision, but she would have softened the whole situation. She would have helped Lina through it, made it less frightening and shone a light on the possibilities.

'He will be your greatest protector,' she would have said. *'You will grow to love him.'*

And those things could be true.

Lina remained on that hill for several hours, watching the sea change colour as the sun moved overhead towards the horizon. Eventually, Trinka showed up with a bottle of mead. She sat down beside Lina, looking out at the water.

'We hate it when we're stuck on that boat, then miss it when we're on land.' Opening the bottle, she handed it to Lina. 'I ran into Simian. I thought you might need this.'

Lina took it and drank, savouring the sweetness and slight burn in her mouth.

'So, your father wants you to marry Sture,' Trinka said, taking the bottle from her and swigging from it. 'You didn't think you could avoid marriage forever, did you?'

'You've managed to avoid it.'

'But I'm not the daughter of a *chieftain*.' She drank again before handing it back. 'And I'm yet to meet a man who could handle being married to me. Plus, my father needs me.'

Lina had a long drink before saying, 'That's what I thought too.'

'Your father needs you. He just needs you to marry Sture for the sake of the clan.' She took back the mead. 'You could do a lot worse than a handsome chieftain close in age with all his teeth.'

'That is a very short and tragic list of attributes.'

Trinka wrapped an arm around Lina and pulled her close, planting a noisy kiss on her cheek. 'Probably has a tiny prick, though. Those handsome types always do.'

Lina pulled away. 'Thanks for that visual.'

They each took another drink.

Trinka glanced sideways at her as she said, 'Knud said he saw you and the general out walking today. He seemed very confused by what he saw.'

Lina took another drink, then drew her knees up. 'I was out with Olga and ran into him.'

'You just ran into him?'

'Yes.'

Trinka appeared sceptical. 'Running into him isn't the issue—it's that you *remained* with him.'

'Would you believe me if I told you he's surprisingly amiable company?' Lina asked, placing the bottle down between them.

'He's also your enemy.'

The word 'enemy' did not seem to fit. 'Not really.'

'He's your father's enemy, and your future husband's enemy, which makes him *your* enemy. That's how these things work.'

She was right, of course. Lina could feel her mind blurring from the mead. 'My father caught us.'

Trinka almost spat her drink. 'What do you mean, *caught* you? Doing what?'

'Nothing happened.' She felt heat climb up her neck. 'It was just… this moment.'

A look of disgust settled on Trinka's face. 'Gods, this is worse than I thought. It reeks of feelings.'

Lina rested her chin on one knee. 'It was a fleeting, very inconvenient, and ill-timed moment.'

'I'm not liking the word "moment". It's vague and unsettling.'

A smile spread across Lina's face. 'Haven't you ever stood before a man and just had this flash of connection?'

'Do you mean lust?'

'Not necessarily.' Though there had been some of that as well.

'Because if that's the case, you could always sleep with the man, be thoroughly disappointed by the experience, then move on easily after that.'

Lina gave her friend a questioning look. 'Why must it be disappointing?'

'The bigger the build-up, the bigger the disappointment in my experience. Plus, the really handsome ones tend to be a bit lazy.'

A soft laugh escaped Lina. The mead had drained all the tension from her body, and she was enjoying the warm buzz from it. After a long silence, she said, 'I don't want to marry Sture.'

'I figured as much.'

'It's so… permanent, such an enormous piece of my life to hand over to him.'

Trinka exhaled. 'For what it's worth, I'm sorry it falls on you.' There was a pause. 'Maybe he'll change his mind once he gets to know you.'

More laughter rose in Lina.

Trinka picked up the bottle and passed it to her. 'Here. It'll all seem far more bearable when we reach the bottom.'

Taking the bottle, Lina drank.

CHAPTER 21

Tolly struggled to sleep that night. He lay awake thinking about Lina and the fury on her father's face when he had collected her. Tolly had been holding on to her at the time, *touching* her. And it had felt entirely comfortable. Good, even. Her arm had been a perfect fit for his hand, slim with a good covering of muscle. That strength had softened in his grip. Her lips had softened too. His temperature had risen as he stared at them.

He had wanted to kiss them more than he could put into words.

It would have been better if she had pulled away and rejected him instead of lingering in the moment with the same curiosity. It took her father showing up to prevent them from making a big mistake. And it would have been a mistake. Despite knowing this, Tolly could not stop thinking about what might have happened had Farulf not appeared. He wondered what the mistake would have tasted like.

The sun was barely up when he climbed from his cot the following morning and made his way down to the stream for a wash. The cool air hugged him as he crossed the dew-covered grass, greeting exhausted soldiers coming off night watch. He stopped briefly to speak to Ithon. All had been quiet overnight, but Tolly was not naive enough to think the peace would last.

He continued down the slope towards the slow-moving stream. It glistened in the grey light as he stopped at the water's edge before crouching to test the temperature. He was not sure why he did that, as it was the same temperature every day: freezing. Cupping his hands, he splashed water over his face, immediately more awake. The droplets clung to his skin. He left them there as he drank, then sat back on his heels and looked up at the trees.

The soft thud of footsteps drew his attention downstream. It was difficult to see much in the poor light, but he made out a figure approaching the water, followed by a goose.

It was Lina.

She knelt by the stream and stared at her reflection for a long time, oblivious to his presence thirty yards away. He should have alerted her. Instead, he remained still, watching her, knowing it was the wrong thing to do. Wrong for her, and wrong for him.

Lina tipped forwards suddenly, dunking her entire head into the stream. She remained underwater for some time. From that distance, he could just make out the tiny bubbles rising around her. Just as he was beginning to worry, she popped up again, throwing her head back so that her hair was out of her face.

As though finally sensing him there, her head snapped to

the side, eyes meeting his across the boundary. Her shoulders dropped when she recognised him. Getting to her feet, she walked, as if in pain, towards him. Tolly rose also, meeting her at the boundary. The goose eyed him for a few seconds before jumping into the water and swimming away. Lina's hair clung to her shoulders in heavy strands. Water dripped from it, tracing intricate paths down the curves of her frame and soaking into the fabric of her smock. Her normally bright eyes appeared more subdued.

'Did you sleep as badly as me?' he asked.

She walked right up to him, smoothing her unruly hair with trembling fingers. 'I slept fine—thanks to a large amount of mead.' She practically winced at the sound of her own voice. 'Trinka's fault.'

'Ah.' So she was hungover. 'I wish I had the luxury. A clear head is key in keeping people alive, apparently.'

'Being the humble daughter of a chieftain has its perks.'

He searched her eyes, trying to fight the urge to ask questions that were none of his business. But he lost. 'Did you get in trouble yesterday with your father?'

She drew a slow breath and looked out at the water. 'He wasn't entirely happy about the company I was keeping.'

'But you weren't punished in any way?'

Her gaze returned to him, her expression thoughtful before shaking her head. 'No, he's not like that.'

He was relieved after hearing stories over the years about female sea warriors enduring all forms of punishment from starvation to mutilation.

'I'm getting married,' she blurted suddenly, looking almost guilty. 'To Sture. At the end of the summer.'

It took a tremendous amount of effort to keep his face

neutral, even though he had no right to have an opinion on the subject. 'Congratulations.'

Colour flushed her cheeks. 'I'm not sure why I told you that.'

He was not sure either. 'He seems like… an interesting choice.'

'It worked out for my mother.' She shrugged. 'Maybe it'll work out for me.'

She sounded like she was trying to convince herself.

'Is Sture like your father?'

A laugh escaped her. 'No. No, he's quite a different breed of man. More…'

'Bloodthirsty?'

'Well, there's that.'

Tolly squinted in the camp's direction. 'Shame you couldn't choose your own husband, as I suspect you would have chosen better.'

She squeezed water from the ends of her hair, regarding him. 'Are you married?'

'I'm married to the army.'

'Any regrets?'

'Ask me in a year.'

She pressed her lips together.

'How's the head now?' he asked.

Lina brought her hand to it. 'It's pounding in time with my voice, so I should probably go eat something.'

Spotting a small leaf tangled in her hair, Tolly reached up to pull it out, then showed it to her.

'There's probably half a forest caught up in there. Motivation to comb it.'

Tolly let go of the leaf, and they both watched it flutter to the ground. 'Good luck,' he said. 'With the hair and the marriage.'

Her eyes filled with disappointment. 'Thank you.'

He went to leave, then stopped. 'How long has your father had rheumatismus?'

She swallowed. 'I don't know what you mean.'

'My grandmother's hands looked the same towards the end. She struggled to manage the pain.'

Lina checked her surroundings before replying, 'Around five years. The symptoms were mild at first. He has good weeks. He used to have good months.'

Tolly nodded. 'There's no cure. His condition will only worsen.'

She swallowed. 'I know.'

'Have you tried willow bark?'

'I've not heard of it.'

He looked past her. 'There are willow trees in the area. I suspect your brother will be able to help you locate them. Boil the bark and have your father drink it like a tea.'

She gave him a wary look. 'How do I know you're not trying to poison him? One chieftain out of your way would be helpful.'

'If I wanted to poison a chieftain, he would be my second choice.'

The corners of her eyes creased. 'It's worth a try. Thank you.'

Tolly wished they were back in the field, far away from the men guarding the perimeter. Though it was probably for the best, given the recent news of her betrothal.

'I'll see you around, General,' she said, backing away.

He nodded once in place of a reply.

As she walked away, Tolly felt a heavy weight settle in his chest. He watched her until she was gone from sight, then headed towards the camp. Halfway up the slope, he found Tatum and Ryder standing with concerned expressions. He stopped before them, bracing for questioning.

'What the hell are you doing?' Tatum asked, the concern morphing into anger.

Ryder looked down at the ground, and Tatum noticed.

'Did you know about this? The eyes across the boundary? The little chats?'

Ryder lifted his gaze. 'I'm aware of their history—'

'What history?' Tatum looked accusingly at Tolly. 'Between you and the chieftain's daughter?'

Tolly wanted to be annoyed with his brother but knew the defenders did not keep secrets from one another. 'We met some years back.'

Crossing his arms, Tatum waited for more.

With a resigned sigh, Tolly retold the story of their brief history. 'But you don't have to worry,' he said when he was finished. 'No lines will be crossed.'

'I've heard that before,' Tatum replied.

'Was it from your own mouth in reference to your *current wife*?' Ryder replied with a neutral expression.

Tatum went to object, then changed his mind. 'Touché.' He looked back at Tolly. 'But this is worse than what I did. Charlotte wasn't part of a violent clan that wished us all dead.'

'Relax,' Tolly said. 'Lina's betrothed to the Vargr chieftain.'

That got Ryder's attention. 'Since when?'

'Since yesterday, apparently.'

A look of disgust settled on Tatum's face. 'There's really no accounting for taste. Can you imagine having marital relations with that man?'

Tolly pressed his eyes closed. 'I'd really rather not.'

'I'd be staying well away from her now,' Tatum said. 'If you probe that oversized man—'

'Please use another word.'

Tatum tried again. 'If you provoke that oversized man and his behemoth friends, when we're this grossly outnumbered, it will all be over.'

An awkward silence followed.

'You're right,' Tolly said.

Tatum seemed surprised by his response. 'I am?'

'Yes. Everything you say is valid.' He glanced tiredly at Ryder before heading up the hill.

CHAPTER 22

When Lina arrived back at the camp, she found Sture and her father standing outside her tent. Bo was waiting a few yards away. Her feet slowed as she registered her father's grave expression, then stopped completely when Sture's eyes darted in her direction. The irritated look on his face turned her blood cold. She forced her feet forwards.

'Where were you?' Farulf asked, his expression matching Sture's.

'At the stream. What's going on?'

'Bo claims he saw you liaising with General Tolly.'

Lina looked over at the warrior, who stared back unapologetically. 'I was on my side of the boundary, and he was on his. What exactly is the problem?'

'The problem is that he was seen touching you,' Sture replied calmly.

She was about to deny it when she remembered the leaf he

had pulled from her hair. From a distance, that could have easily been misconstrued. 'It wasn't like that. Nothing inappropriate happened, if that's what you're implying.'

'Is there an appropriate way for him to touch you?' Sture asked, his hands twitching at his sides.

Lina could feel anger radiating off him despite his calm tone. 'There was a leaf in my hair. He picked it out—an instinct.'

'Why were you standing close enough for him to reach it?'

'We were talking.'

Sture blinked. 'About *what*?'

She could hardly say that they had been talking about him. 'I barely remember.'

He nodded slowly. 'There are consequences for fraternising with the enemy, Lina.'

Simian emerged from the tent, looking between them. 'What's going on?'

'Put Olga in her crate,' Lina said immediately.

He went to fetch the goose, looking around at everyone's faces as he did so.

'Did you share information with him?' Sture asked, his voice now laced with bitterness.

'Of course not.' She could barely believe that her father was just standing there silent while Sture accused her of being a traitor.

'Information with whom?' Simian asked, returning to them.

'This doesn't concern you,' Farulf said. 'Stay out of it.'

'This is ridiculous,' Lina said. 'I've done nothing wrong, and I don't appreciate your men spying on me either.'

'You are to be *my wife*,' Sture said. 'You will be protected accordingly. So when you meet in private with the man who seeks to kill and starve us, I am going to have something to say on the subject.'

Lina's eyes rolled without her permission. 'He's not seeking to kill or starve us. He's simply protecting the land and the people who live here.'

Clearly that was the wrong thing to say, going by her father's mortified expression.

'The man has killed *our* people,' Farulf said. 'Where's your loyalty to them?'

She went to speak, but Sture raised a hand, silencing her. 'Let us not argue but resolve this. I will accept an apology and assurances that you will not see the man again without my knowledge and permission.'

While the entire sentence was absurd, Lina was stuck on the apology part. 'Apologise for what?' She was so confused by her father's silence. 'Nothing happened.'

Sture turned to Farulf. 'Your daughter must learn respect and humility if she is to be my wife. She has been without a mother to teach these attributes, which is the only reason I will show her some grace.'

The mention of her mother took Lina from frustration to rage. 'What did you say?'

Farulf's neck turned red. 'Let me speak with my daughter in private.'

'She does not need your words. She needs your correction.' Sture's gaze returned to Lina. 'You will apologise for the shame and embarrassment you have brought to your father, and then you will kneel before me and ask my forgiveness.'

A humourless laugh escaped Lina. 'I'll do no such thing.'

Farulf went to say something, but Sture cut him off before

he could speak. 'You will ask my forgiveness for allowing another man to touch you.'

A lump formed in Lina's throat as the humiliation set in. 'If my mother were here, she would tell me to kneel before no man.'

Farulf dropped his gaze because he knew it was true.

'If you refuse, you will be confined and isolated while you are reconsidering.'

Simian's mouth fell open. 'What?'

Her father seemed so small beside the Vargr chieftain suddenly.

'Father?' Lina said, willing him to say *something*.

He rubbed his forehead. 'An apology would go a long way —even if it's delivered on your feet.'

Sture nodded. 'Very well.' Focusing once again on Lina, he waited.

She was speechless for a moment. Then, crossing her arms, she said, 'No.'

Simian's face fell. 'For God's sake, Lina. Just say you're sorry so this can be over.'

'And what would you like me to say in this apology? Sorry for *speaking*?'

Sture stepped forwards and took her by the arm, marching her away from the tent.

'Where are you taking her?' Simian called, going after them.

Farulf followed as well at a hurried shuffle. 'Sture.'

'Relax, the two of you. I am just giving Lina some time to think about her apology.'

Lina tried to pull free of his hand, but his grip only tightened. 'I don't need time to think. I politely decline.'

A bitter smile appeared on Sture's face. 'You will learn the lesson quickly, and it will stick.' He gestured to Bo, who was following behind. 'Tell Toke to fetch the pole.'

The fact that he said *the* pole instead of *a* pole had Lina worried.

Simian ran up to Sture, matching his pace. 'Release her this instant.'

'Or what?'

Simian looked back at Farulf with a pleading expression.

'No harm is to come to my daughter,' Farulf said, finally sounding like a chieftain and a father again.

Sture glanced over his shoulder. 'You think I would harm the woman I am to marry?'

'Then let me go,' Lina said, attempting to free herself a second time.

He dragged her forwards.

'Father, do something,' Simian said.

Farulf attempted to catch up but could not. 'This is a family matter.'

'You are wrong. It is a clan matter. And since you refuse to handle it, I am forced to take care of it on your behalf.'

The sound of a hammer hitting steel had Lina flinching. When they emerged from the trees out into the open, she found Toke pounding a pole into the ground. He paused when he spotted her, then looked at Sture.

'It's for the girl?' He sounded surprised.

Sture pulled Lina to a stop. 'Finish the job.'

Toke let out a frustrated breath, clearly unhappy, then tested the pole. Satisfied it would hold, he stepped back and produced some shackles.

'This is excessive,' Farulf said, finally catching up.

Simian nodded furiously in agreement.

Sture turned Lina to face him. 'Would you like to apologise before this goes any further? Or do you need more time to think about it?'

'Lina, tell him you're sorry, and we'll return to the tent,' Farulf said.

The pleading look in Simian's eyes almost had her relenting, but she stood her ground. 'I will apologise to my father later, in the privacy of our tent. But not for my actions earlier. I'll be apologising for my defiance right now.'

Farulf's posture collapsed. 'Foolish girl.'

Sture held her gaze for a long time. Then, without another word, he guided her to the pole, where he shackled her.

'Your stubbornness will be the death of me,' Farulf said.

Simian stood frozen to the spot.

'When you are ready to be humble before those who protect and provide for you, then you let Bo know.' He gestured to the blank-faced warrior standing a few feet away. 'Until then, no food or water.'

All the colour drained from Simian's face. 'You can't do that.'

'Return to your tent, Simian,' Sture said. '*Now.*'

Farulf nodded. 'Go.'

Simian gave Lina a helpless look before turning and walking slowly back in the direction they had come.

'This isn't how the Wolfvanir do things,' Farulf said once Simian was out of earshot.

'Your clan lacks discipline, and this is the result,' Sture replied.

Toke leaned his weight on one foot. 'Whatever is going on here, let her father deal with it.'

Sture ignored him. To Bo, he said, 'Anyone caught sneaking her food or water gets their own pole.'

The warrior nodded.

'My daughter's stubborn nature could see her dying of thirst before she ever utters a word,' Farulf said.

'Trust the process.' Sture clapped him on the arm as he passed. 'It never fails.' With that, he strode away.

Toke gave them both a sympathetic look before following him. Bo put some distance between himself and the pole, giving them a chance to speak in private.

Lina and Farulf stared at each other. The anger on her father's face was gone, replaced with defeat.

'I told you inviting them here was a mistake,' she said. 'And this is the man you wish me to marry? One who puts his wife in chains?'

Farulf's throat bobbed.

'You and Mother disagreed about things all the time,' she said, eyes burning. 'You would never have treated her this way.'

He rubbed tiredly at his forehead. 'You've put me in a very difficult position.'

'You've put yourself in a difficult position by giving him too much power. He was invited here to *help*.' She rattled the chains against the pole. 'Does this seem helpful to you?'

Farulf glanced in the boundary's direction. 'I'll speak with him.'

When he went to leave, she said, 'You've met him before, you know. The general. Long before all of this.'

Farulf's browed creased. 'What are you talking about?'

'Mother was still alive. We saw the smoke from the burning ship and went to investigate. He was in the middle of the sea, so close to drowning. We saved him.' She watched her father's face change as the memory returned to him. 'You wanted to leave him. You said he was trouble, but Mother wouldn't hear of it. Do you remember?'

He nodded. 'I remember. You held him on an oar all the way down the coast, then gave him the last of our cheese. I was furious. You said there was no point in saving him from drowning only to see him die of hunger.'

Lina had forgotten about the cheese. It had been wrapped in waxed cloth, and Tolly had hesitated, his desperate eyes moving between the food and the warriors watching him from the boat. She had reached a little further. *'Take it.'* His purple fingers had wrapped around it, his hand shaking from the cold.

'Thank you.' The only words he ever spoke.

He had let go of the oar then, swimming backwards away from the boat, likely fearful of being shot in the back. Lina did not blame him. Her father had told her it was a waste of cheese, and her mother had wrapped her arms around Lina and kissed the top of her hair, saying nothing at all.

'That's why he saved you,' her father said.

She swallowed. 'I know it's more convenient to hate him, but unfortunately, he's proving to be an honourable man.'

Farulf glanced briefly towards the Carmarthen Militia's camp. 'When Sture returns, tell him you're ready to apologise. Tell him whatever he needs to hear in order to put this shameful day behind us.'

A tiny piece of Lina's heart chipped away when he said that. She knew without a doubt that a few years earlier, he would have fought the entire Vargr clan before letting anyone put his daughter in shackles. He did not agree with Sture's actions. He simply knew he stood no chance against such a man. Lina was not just losing the protection of her chieftain but her father too.

'And if I refuse?' she asked.

'Then you're a fool.'

Head down, he left her chained to the pole.

CHAPTER 23

Tolly was due to meet with one of his commanders that afternoon to discuss a rotation of soldiers. As he exited his tent, he ran into his sombre-faced brother.

'What's the matter with you?'

Ryder looked around. 'There's something I think you're going to want to see.'

His curiosity piqued, Tolly followed him along the muddy paths of the camp to the boundary. There, he found a group of soldiers gathered, looking off down the hill.

'What is it?' Tolly asked as he neared them.

Ryder gestured for him to walk on and see for himself, offering no explanation.

The men moved aside to make room for him, and Tolly stepped into the gap, looking out at the clearing between the two camps. His lungs came to a sharp halt when he saw Lina shackled to a pole out in the open. She was standing up straight, staring at the trees in the distance. Even with three hundred yards between them, he could feel her defiance. Anger welled up inside him as he took in the sight. The sudden urge to charge across the boundary line and break those chains apart with his hands caught him by surprise.

'How long has she been chained up like that?' he asked, relieved he sounded calm.

Cynan, one of the soldiers on duty, answered. 'A few hours, sir. Both chieftains were present when it happened.'

He felt sick when he heard that. Her own father had been involved. Where was Simian? Trinka? The outrage from *someone*? 'Do we know why she's chained?'

'No, sir.'

Ryder stepped up behind him. 'My guess is that we weren't the only ones down at the stream earlier,' the defender said in a low voice.

Lina chose that moment to look in their direction, immediately averting her gaze when she saw him standing there. It dawned on him then how humiliated she must be feeling with them all gathered there, staring at her.

He looked around at his men. 'All right, back to your posts.' To Cynan, he said, 'I want you to inform me when she's freed. Or if anyone comes to see her. Understood?'

He nodded once. 'Yes, sir.'

It was the hardest thing in the world to turn away. He met his brother's all-knowing stare as he did so. Stepping past Ryder, he attempted to go about his day.

Tolly had several meetings that afternoon, but during each one, his mind kept drifting back to Lina. That visual of her chained up made it impossible for him to focus on anything else. He found himself constantly looking around, waiting for news and wondering how long they planned on keeping her that way.

As the sun began its descent towards the horizon, Tolly's restlessness grew. Unable to bear it any longer, he excused himself under the guise of needing to speak to someone and headed for the perimeter. His steps were swift as he made his way back there. When he arrived, he discovered that Tefor was now at that watch post. He hoped the message had been passed along and that Lina was not long gone.

'She's still there, sir,' the soldier informed him. 'Her brother showed up an hour ago. I didn't notify you because he was turned away by the guard before they had a chance to interact.'

Tolly's chest tightened when he laid eyes on her. Her shoulders were slumped with exhaustion. He could feel her weariness as if it were his own.

'Has she received any water?'

'Not a drop, sir.'

Tatum was walking by and made his way over.

'Blackmane filled me in earlier,' he said, stepping up next to Tolly and crossing his arms. 'Still there.'

'Still there.'

Tatum glanced sideways at him. 'Listen, I'm sorry if I was a bit short with you earlier. It's just that there's never been a queen more deserving of peace, yet we can't seem to grasp it. It's fleeting in this part of the world.' When Tolly said nothing, he added, 'And for what it's worth, I've not forgotten all the times you helped me keep Charlotte safe.' He brushed a finger down his nose. 'That helpless look on your face is all too familiar.'

With a sigh, Tolly looked at him. 'So, what am I supposed

to do now? If I cross the boundary, they'll consider it an act of war.'

Tatum thought for a moment. 'Maybe that's what Sture wants.'

'You think he's baiting me?'

Tatum shrugged. 'It's an interesting choice of location to make his point. Why not do it in the centre of the camp where *his* people can see?'

Before Tolly could respond, a figure caught his attention in the distance. It was Trinka, wandering along the boundary, likely returning from her watch post. She always walked fearlessly along it, staring down any soldiers she passed. A mischievous smile lit up her face when she caught sight of Tolly, and she headed towards him.

'Why the long face, General?' she said, pouting. 'Are you contemplating your death again?'

It seemed unlikely from Trinka's playful mood that she was aware of Lina's predicament.

'I wonder if you could do me a favour and practice your sarcasm on your way to help Lina.'

Trinka looked between Tatum and Tolly. 'All right, I'll *bite*. What are you talking about?'

Tolly gestured past her. 'Lina's been chained up there for most of the day.'

With a look of pure suspicion, Trinka took a few steps back from them before daring a glance over her shoulder. She froze when she spotted Lina. 'What in the…?'

In the blink of an eye, she drew her sword and pointed it straight at Tolly, prompting both Tatum and Cynan to draw their weapons as well. 'What did you do?'

Tolly never reached for his weapon. 'You think *I* did this?'

'You did something.'

'A more reasonable question is, how did you not know?'

'Not that it's any of your business, but I've been on watch all day.' She snuck another glance at Lina, her face contorting with anger. 'If I find out that you had anything to do with this, I'm coming back to finish this moment.'

'Will you spare the rest of us if we throw the general over the border?' Tatum asked.

Trinka stared hard at Tatum as she sheathed her sword, then took off at a jog towards Lina.

'I'll look away if you wish to shoot her in the back,' Tatum joked.

Tolly's eyes were fixed on Lina once again. 'Trinka may be the only person in that camp brave enough to help.'

'You mean *crazy* enough to help? You know she barks at the soldiers, right?'

Tolly did not reply, because he was watching the warrior guarding Lina, who was preparing to intercept Trinka. 'I once heard you and Alveye arguing about who could shoot the furthest. You claimed to be the stronger archer.'

Confusion flashed across Tatum's face. 'Was I drunk at the time?'

'Yes, actually.'

'Well, there you go.'

'You made Hadewaye measure the distances with his feet.'

Tatum made a face that suggested he did not remember. 'And did I win?'

'You kept trying until you eventually shot an arrow over three hundred yards.' He looked at Tatum. 'How far away is that guard, do you think?'

Tatum shook his head. 'Absolutely not.'

'How far?'

Tatum fell silent to mentally calculate. 'Maybe 280.'

'Shouldn't be a problem for you, then.'

Tatum stared hard at him for a moment. Then, with a shake of his head, he retrieved his bow. With practiced ease, he notched an arrow and drew the bowstring taut, aiming it at the guard who was approaching Trinka. Shouts erupted between Trinka and the warrior, their voices drifting up the hill to the boundary.

'I assume you'll tell me if you want me to kill someone,' Tatum muttered.

Tolly watched the growing chaos below. 'I don't want you to kill him. I just want you to be *ready* to kill him.'

Trinka was gesturing wildly as she confronted Lina's guard, her sword gleaming dangerously in the dying light. The guard, a burly man with a patchy beard, squared his shoulders defiantly, then yelled something back. He gestured for her to keep walking, physically blocking her from getting to Lina. Trinka lunged forwards and shoved the man hard with both hands. He stumbled backwards, reached for his sword, then froze when Trinka's was pressed to his neck before he could draw it.

'You stay out of my way!' she roared before slowly withdrawing her weapon. She stared hard at him as she backed away, then turned and ran over to Lina.

The string of Tatum's bow loosened. 'Thank Belenus for that.'

Tolly observed the women in tense silence. The evening sun cast fiery light on the scene as Trinka took hold of Lina's face and spoke to her. Whatever Trinka was saying seemed to breathe new life into her. Lina straightened, nodded.

After a brief exchange, Trinka ran off towards their camp, but not before making a crude gesture at the guard.

'I think the chieftains are about to get an earful,' Tatum said, lowering his weapon.

Lina glanced in Tolly's direction, then turned her body so her back was to him. He could feel her embarrassment.

Turning to Cynan, he said, 'Keep me informed.'

Tatum gave him a surprised look. 'You're leaving?'

'We're both leaving.' He gestured for Tatum to start walking. 'She needs help, not an audience.' He refused to contribute to her humiliation. 'I'll be in my tent.'

CHAPTER 24

Lina could not tell whether Trinka was mad at Sture for chaining her up or mad at her for refusing to say sorry. Perhaps both. It was not as though Trinka would have apologised in that situation.

'Has everyone lost their minds?' she had said, squeezing Lina's face with a strange blend of affection and rage. 'I'll speak with Sture and your father and end this insanity. I'll be back soon—with a key.'

She had thrust a finger in Bo's direction as she left. It was clear by the look on his face that he had a sensible amount of fear. Trinka did not do wrath by halves.

Lina waited for her to return, but when night fell over the encampment, she realised Trinka was not coming back. Her father did not come either. Nor her brother. Even the sun abandoned her.

It was obvious that if she wanted to be released, she would need to apologise. And she could have done that. She could have asked Bo to send for Sture, then put on some humble display like he wanted. But it was not just an apology. She was setting a standard for their entire marriage. If he won, it would reinforce his controlling behaviour. By standing firm, she was making it clear that her future nos were final, that she would not be intimidated and manipulated into behaving a certain way. She would sooner die of thirst or hunger than hand him that power.

So, as the moon rose high in the sky, and a new guard arrived to take over from Bo, she settled in for the night.

Towards midnight, the temperature dropped and the cold air began seeping in through her clothes. Lina knew it would only get colder, and she needed to find a way to keep warm. She moved to crouch, but before her skirt had even brushed the grass, the guard shouted, 'On your feet!'

Lina rose, every muscle in her legs protesting. Every joint ached with fatigue. Time dragged on, each passing minute feeling longer than the one before. The chill penetrated her bones, making her shiver uncontrollably. Through the trees, she could see flickering light from the campfires. She closed her eyes, imagining the warmth of the flames, then opened them when her legs wobbled. Gods, she was tired.

As the night wore on, Lina's exhaustion grew. Her vision blurred at the edges, and her arms felt as though they were made of stone. Every breath she took hurt, the air sharp in her lungs. Yet she remained standing—out of sheer stubbornness.

Finally, the sky lightened in the east, tinting the horizon pink. She lifted her heavy gaze to the crest of the hill, where she found Tolly standing at the boundary, watching her. He was a dark shadow against the growing light, but she could recognise him by silhouette now.

Instead of the shame she had experienced the day before, a surge of emotion welled up within her, threatening to come out in the form of tears. Something about his presence made her feel less alone, somewhat protected, despite the fact that he was all the way up the hill with no way to help her.

Lina summoned all her remaining strength to stay on her feet, but the night had been an endless stretch of torment, and her legs finally gave out. Her knees could no longer bear her weight. Lina collapsed to the ground, a groan escaping her parched lips as she landed.

The guard marched over, barking repeatedly at her to get up.

But she could not move.

She stared up at the guard, wanting to say things, yell back, but finding no energy for words. Instead, she closed her eyes and let the weariness wash over her. Everyone had a limit, and she had reached hers, physically and emotionally.

'On your feet!' The guard's face was so close to hers, she felt his spit hit her cheek. Then he was jabbing her arm, her shoulder. Her head. 'Get up!'

The jabs got harder. Perhaps he was simply hitting her, and she could not tell.

'I can't,' she breathed. Her head went to rest on the pole, her arms extended above her.

Then the jabbing stopped.

Unsettled by the silence that followed, Lina forced her eyes open and found the guard standing still with a shocked expression frozen on his face. Confusion clouded her mind until she noticed the arrow protruding from his neck. Blood seeped from the wound and ran down into his furs. He reached up to touch the arrow lodged in his flesh. Then slowly, he crumpled to the ground.

Lina's heart pounded against her ribcage as she scanned her surroundings with wide eyes, searching for the source of that fatal shot. If it was Trinka, she would pay with her life. But Trinka was nowhere to be seen.

Her gaze snagged on Tolly once more, and she could just make out the bow he was holding. She closed her eyes, confused. It could not have been him. He was still at the boundary, hundreds of yards away. There was no way he could shoot that far… was there? If he had, Sture would hunt him down.

As she was trying to make sense of the unfolding chaos, a loud clang rang out above her, and her arms dropped into her lap. When she looked up, her eyes widened. Tolly stood over her, his expression tense and watchful of his surroundings. Behind him, Ryder held a loaded bow as he turned in a slow circle.

'Let's go,' Tolly said, sheathing his weapon and extending a hand to her.

She should have refused to go anywhere with him. It was the ultimate betrayal to her clan and would only cause more problems. And yet she took the hand without hesitation, unsure if she could get to her feet. There was no need to worry, because he scooped her up in his arms and took off at a steady jog up the hill.

Lina felt ridiculous being carried like an invalid. However, the fact that she could not stand, let alone walk, left her with no choice. To further add to her embarrassment, she found she could not keep her head steady while he ran, so she had to rest it on his shoulder like a sleepy child.

When they neared the boundary, Lina saw a line of soldiers, all with loaded bows, pointed down the hill. As they crossed, she spotted a dead warrior lying in the grass, his throat slashed. Another reason for Sture to wage war against the Carmarthen Militia.

'It's all right,' Tolly assured her. 'No one's going to hurt you here.'

It hit her at that moment that she was safer with the enemy than she was with her own people. Her father had lost control of his clan, and the Vargr had proven untrustworthy.

'He's going to kill you,' she whispered.

His arms tightened around her. 'He'll try.'

'You don't know him.' Her gaze darted back and forth, taking in her surroundings. There were endless rows of identical tents.

He finally slowed to a walk. 'I know plenty of men just like him, and they are never as invincible as they seem.'

Another defender came jogging up to them, looking from Tolly to Ryder to Lina. 'Ah, what have I missed?'

'Tatum, we're going to need more men along the boundary,' Tolly said.

The defender—Tatum—fell into step with Tolly. 'Please tell me she wandered over the boundary of her own accord.'

'With some help,' Ryder replied.

Tatum blinked slowly. 'But killing no one, right?'

No response from either man.

'You crossed the boundary and killed the guard?' Tatum whisper-shouted at Tolly.

'Two guards,' Ryder said, throwing him into the deep end.

Tolly continued towards his tent. 'The boundary guard came for me when I killed the other guard. It was self-defence.'

Tatum's brow creased. 'Wait. You killed Lina's guard before the boundary guard?'

'Yes.'

'Did he come towards you?'

'No.' Tolly glanced sideways at him. 'Why?'

Tatum's face was pure disbelief. 'You expect me to believe that you shot an arrow over three hundred yards and hit your target?'

'That's right.'

'It was a solid shot,' Ryder said, speaking up. 'Not sure I could have made it.'

Tatum dropped back to walk with Ryder. 'You witnessed it?'

Tolly rolled his eyes over his shoulder. 'Can we focus on the boundary for now and get our measuring sticks out later?'

Tatum and Ryder fell away to deal with security, and Tolly stopped at a large tent, shouldering his way inside. He sat Lina down on the cot and reached for the waterskin next to it. 'Small sips,' he instructed, holding it to her mouth.

She watched him as she drank.

'I'll have some soup brought in,' he said when she had had enough.

Her gaze wandered around the tent, taking in her surroundings. 'It's only been a day. I won't drop dead of hunger just yet.'

'You're shivering.'

'It'll stop.'

Picking up the folded blanket at the end of the cot, he

shook it open and wrapped it around her. Then he sat beside her, elbows on his knees and eyes on the ground. 'Who chained you up?'

Of course he wanted answers.

'Sture.'

He turned his head. 'Why?'

Now it was her turn to look at the ground. 'Because I refused to apologise.'

'For what?'

For letting you pull a leaf out of my hair, and for the way I looked at you when you did.

'Because of me?'

Lina swallowed. 'He clearly overreacted.'

'And your father just let him?'

She reached for the waterskin again. 'So many questions.'

He helped her to drink, eyeing the shackles still around her wrists. He had busted the chains, but the cuffs remained very much in place.

'You didn't happen to steal the key during your heroic rescue, did you?' she asked.

'No.' Tolly got up and walked to a bag containing some belongings. He pulled out a belt and removed two prongs from the buckle. 'Next best thing.' He returned and sat down beside her, picking up her hands and laying them across his leg. 'Any chance you can stop shivering for this part?'

A weak smile came and went. 'Apparently not.'

Their eyes met, and despite the jokes, his were full of concern. It took him a good few minutes to pick both locks.

'Is that a defender trick?' she asked when the second shackle popped open.

'I've picked plenty of locks over the years, but the double-pronged belt was a welcomed invention from Chadora.'

She rubbed the indented marks left on her skin. 'I should go before something bad happens.'

'Something bad already has.'

'I need to check on Simian and Trinka.'

His expression turned tense. 'And if they chain you up again?'

She tilted her head. 'Do you have a one-rescue limit?'

Some of that tension melted away.

'Do you mind if I lie down for a moment?' Her vision kept blurring, likely from fatigue. 'I'm seeing three of you right now.'

He rose and gestured to the cot. 'Go ahead. I'll organise that soup. It'll warm you up.'

Her eyes remained on him as she lay down. Her teeth had stopped chattering, but the rest of her was still shaking. 'You could lie beside me. Body heat is the fastest way to warm a person.'

At first, he did not move. He simply stared at her, then looked around the tent as though searching for the correct response. When he did not find it, he removed his boots and climbed onto the cot, lying on his side so they were face to face.

'Put your arm around me,' she said, eyes already closing.

Tolly did better than that. He gathered her close and wrapped both arms around her. Soon, she was swimming in warmth and drowning in his earthy scent.

'You might be the bravest man I know,' she said into his chest. 'I hope it doesn't kill you.'

She never heard his response because she drifted off to sleep.

CHAPTER 25

Tolly should have left the cot the moment Lina fell asleep, except she continued to shiver even while sleeping, so he decided to wait until it stopped. But then she nestled against him, all rosy-cheeked and comfortable. He could not bear to disturb her. She smelled like rain, and he found it oddly intoxicating. So instead of doing the hundred other things he should have done, he lay entirely committed to the moment, marvelling at the ease of it and knowing that at any moment, the tent flap would open and someone would announce that warriors were approaching the boundary.

'I told you body heat was the best,' she said, her voice croaky.

Tolly had not realised that she had woken. He moved back slightly so he could see her face. She had creases down one cheek from his uniform, and her crystal eyes were blinking like they wanted to close again.

'Feel better?' he asked.

She nodded. '*Now* I can feel the hunger.'

'I'll get something for you.' He went to move, but she grabbed the front of his uniform to stop him.

'Don't go.' She relaxed her grip. 'This is all we get. When I step back over that boundary, we're back to being enemies.'

'You're not my enemy.'

'Of course I am. Everything I belong to, that I'm a part of, is across that line.'

His eyes moved between hers. 'You sure you want to go back there?'

A smile spread across her face, and her eyes shone a little brighter as a result. 'What's the alternative? You want to keep me here? Have me as a bedmate while you kill my family? Put me to work in the kitchen?'

'That depends. How are your cooking skills?'

'Good enough for Sture to take me as his wife. If I'd known I was on trial when I cooked him dinner that time, I would have undercooked the mutton and burned the bread.'

He chuckled quietly.

She wet her dry lips, reminding him she was likely still thirsty after having water withheld. He reached back for the waterskin and handed it to her. Propping herself up on one elbow, she took a long drink, then handed it back.

'Thank you.'

He placed it down on the ground. 'I'm going to get that soup now.'

Her gaze fell to his lips before she nodded. 'All right.'

As he climbed off the cot, Tolly felt a familiar heaviness settle in his chest. He walked slowly to the entrance of the tent, his hand hovering in front of the flap. But he could not bring himself to walk through it just yet. That ache in his chest was really holding on.

After a moment of internal struggle, he turned and walked back to the cot. Lina's eyes followed his every movement as he knelt before her and took hold of her face. His thumb caressed her cheek as he looked at her. Her expression was a blend of curiosity and apprehension, and he felt a rush of emotion that he had never felt with a woman before. Leaning in, he brushed his lips against hers, trying it out. It was everything he could not put into words.

Lina slid forwards on the cot to deepen the kiss, and a surge of heat exploded inside Tolly, drowning every rational thought he ever had. The world outside the tent faded into insignificance, and when her fingers gripped the back of his head to pull him closer still, he lost himself to the experience entirely.

Just as the flames were threatening to consume them both, the tent flaps opened and Ryder stepped inside. He froze when he saw them, then looked behind him, as though deciding whether to leave.

Tolly got to his feet, the confusing combination of arousal and embarrassment resulting in awkward silence.

'Sorry to… interrupt,' Ryder began. 'There are two chieftains and twenty-plus warriors waiting for Lina at the boundary.'

Tolly and Lina exchanged a concerned look, even though they had both known it was coming.

'Have someone bring Lina some food,' Tolly said, walking over to Ryder. 'She's not leaving this tent until she's eaten.'

'And what should I tell the angry men waiting for her?'

Tolly stepped past him. 'Nothing. I'll speak with them myself.'

'Better I go alone,' Lina said, standing up. 'I can eat later.'

Tolly paused at the tent's entrance and looked back. 'Eat now, please. Don't go back to them weak.' There was a slight plea in his tone. If he was honest with himself, he was terrified that they would punish her for his actions.

Lina's shoulders fell an inch, and she nodded. 'All right.'

The two men left the tent together, walking ten yards before Tolly stopped and turned to Ryder. His brother met his gaze, waiting.

'I know what you're thinking,' Tolly said.

'I wish I could say the same.'

Tolly brought his hands to hips and shifted his weight. 'You once handed yourself over to an English guard in order to get into Harlech Castle, where Isabel was being held. I watched you leap from the embrasure into a moat before we were chased through the woods by armed men.'

Ryder looked heavenward, then exhaled. 'All right.' He nodded and repeated, 'All right.'

Catching the attention of a passing guard, he called him over. 'I need you to bring a tray of food to the general's tent straight away.'

The soldier appeared confused but did not question the order. 'Yes, sir.' He left at a jog.

'If you're going through your reckless-for-love era,' Ryder said, 'then I'm not leaving your side.' He nodded towards the boundary. 'Let's go talk with our new friends.'

Tolly swallowed hard and gave his brother's shoulder an appreciative squeeze before continuing towards the boundary.

As they approached the heavily guarded perimeter, Tolly could feel the tension in the air. The chieftains stood tall and imposing, their faces etched with determined lines and eyes narrowed on them. They were both heavily armed for the occasion.

The soldiers moved aside for Tolly and Ryder, weapons at the ready. Sture regarded Tolly with cold eyes and was the first to speak.

'Rather brave of you to come in person.'

Tolly looked at him with pure disdain before focusing on Farulf. 'What sort of father allows his daughter to be chained up, deprived of food and water, and left out in the cold?'

Farulf had the decency to look ashamed, even if the moment was brief.

'It was Lina's choice to remain there,' Sture said. 'She could have chosen freedom at any time.'

Tatum joined the already crowded gathering. 'Brock Tatum, Defender of Chadora and King Consort of Carmarthenshire.' He looked between Tolly and the chieftains and, picking up on the tension, raised his hands. 'However, no need for formalities or a fuss of any kind. Pretend I'm not here.'

'Where's my daughter?' Farulf asked, anger creeping into his tone.

Tolly's gaze returned to him. 'She's eating. I insisted on it, because there's no guarantee of food on your side of the boundary.'

Farulf's eyes narrowed. 'You dare—'

'Dare feed her? Give her water? Permit her to sleep?' He nodded towards Sture. 'Stop his men from beating her when she collapses from exhaustion?' He paused for effect. 'What were you going to say?'

Sture raised his chin. 'He was going to say *touch* her. It would not be the first time you have put your filthy waste-lander hands on my future wife.'

Tolly did not reply.

'Where's my daughter?' Farulf asked again.

'I'm here!' Lina called, coming at a clumsy jog despite being unable to walk a few hours earlier. She stopped beside Tolly, pale-faced and out of breath. 'I'm right here.'

Relief washed over Farulf's face. 'Did they hurt you?'

She shook her head, appearing confused. '*Hurt* me? General Tolly risked his own life to free me from the chains you left me in.'

Apparently, she was not holding back.

'He breached the agreed boundary and killed two Vargr warriors,' Sture said, his stare piercing. 'Then he abducted you.'

Lina looked offended by that suggestion.

'Come,' Farulf said. 'This is a family matter to be discussed in *private*.'

When Lina went to step forwards over the boundary, Tolly caught her arm. It was more of a reflex than anything else, but it had every warrior and soldier in a quarter-mile radius reaching for their weapons.

'Either you take your hand off her,' Sture seethed, 'or I do it.'

Farulf raised his hands in a calming gesture, moving forwards so he was positioned between the two sides.

Realising Lina's father was trying to prevent a massacre,

Tolly let go of her arm. 'If I see her chained up again, I won't wait a day to cross next time.'

Sture's gaze narrowed on Tolly. 'Do you really think you are in a position to make threats?' He gestured to Lina. 'Go to your father.'

The hesitation from her was brief, but Tolly felt it. With all eyes on her, she crossed the boundary and went to stand at her father's side. She did not look at Tolly again after that.

'Let's go,' Farulf said, gesturing for her to start walking.

Her throat bobbed as she turned away. Sture did not follow straight away, nor did the warriors behind him.

'Something else you wanted?' Tolly asked, hand resting on the hilt of his weapon.

The chieftain stared at him for a long time, then looked at Ryder before his gaze finally settled on Tatum. 'Which one are you? A defender of Chadora or the king consort of Carmarthenshire? You can only serve one master.'

An amused expression settled on Tatum's face. 'Warden or wife.' He pretended to think on the matter. 'Please don't make me choose.'

Sture clearly did not know what to make of Tatum's sense of humour. After a prolonged silence, he simply bowed his head and said in a dry tone, 'Your Majesty,' before turning and following the others.

The warriors remained in place until the chieftains were well out of shooting range, then slowly dispersed.

Tatum moved closer to Tolly and crossed his arms, staring after them. 'This is where you shot the arrow from? This spot right here?'

Exhaling, Tolly looked at him. 'Is that really what you want to discuss right now?'

'That and the way Sture had me questioning my love for the warden. Hasn't anyone ever told him love doesn't divide but multiplies?'

Tolly returned his attention to Lina's retreating back. 'Do you think she'll be punished?'

'All she needs to do is pander to Sture's ego and she'll be fine,' Tatum said. 'Terrible choice for a husband. He's a chieftain, sure, but he's also a bit of a knob.'

When Lina was gone from sight, Tolly turned to face his brother's disapproving stare.

Immediately picking up on the unspoken tension, Tatum said, 'Now what?'

Ryder raised an eyebrow, waiting for Tolly to speak.

'There's more?' Tatum asked in a lowered voice. 'Please tell me you didn't deflower the chieftain's betrothed.'

Tolly walked off. 'I need to check the perimeter.'

'It was just a joke,' Tatum called after him. 'But if I'm right, place your middle finger in the air.'

With a shake of his head, Tatum continued along the boundary.

CHAPTER 26

The atmosphere at the camp was tense. There seemed to be a clear division between the clans suddenly, likely because of the palpable tension between Sture and Farulf. Lina also noticed some tension within the clans. Many of the Wolfvanir were clearly unhappy about Sture's treatment of Lina and angry that Farulf had not stepped in. People were waking up to the changes happening. The divide within the Vargr was also noticeable. Friction between Sture and Toke, and their respective groups, was palpable. Though Lina suspected it had little to do with her and stemmed from a longer-term internal disagreement.

Simian burst from the tent when he heard Lina arrive, pulling her into a crushing embrace. 'I tried to come to you.'

'I know.' She wrapped her arms around him, knowing he stood no chance of taking on Sture and his men—or even their father, for that matter.

He drew back, eyes shiny. 'I wasn't allowed to leave the tent.'

'It's all right.' She glanced over at Olga, who was confined to her crate. 'I'm fine.'

Farulf stepped around them, pretending the moment between them was not happening, and disappeared inside the tent.

Simian glanced after him, then whispered, 'I heard him arguing with Sture. He's lost control. He demanded your release, but Sture basically ignored him. He sent men to watch our tent. There's no doubt in my mind that Father regrets inviting them here.'

While it was unsettling to hear that her father, one of the strongest men she knew, was powerless suddenly, it was not surprising. She stared at the tent, wondering if she should talk to him. Then she felt a flicker of anger that it fell on her to initiate the conversation. He had left her chained to a pole overnight. No, *he* could fix what he had broken.

'Have you seen Trinka?' she asked.

Concern flashed in his eyes. 'No, I haven't seen her.'

There was something he wasn't saying. 'Well, do you know where she is?'

His nose crinkled as he broke eye contact with her. 'She threatened Sture with an axe.'

Her eyes pressed closed. 'Where is she?'

'Last I heard, she was confined to her tent under her father's watch.'

Releasing him, Lina took off at a jog towards Trinka's tent.

'I don't think you're supposed to leave!' Simian called to her back.

Ignoring him, she continued, praying she would not run into Sture or any of his men on her way. Tension hung in the air like a storm about to break. People looked in her direction as she passed by but said nothing. Some were sympathetic, and others were hostile. Perhaps they blamed her for the conflict.

As she approached the tent Trinka shared with her sister and father, she heard the distinct sound of metal against stone coming from within. Frode was outside by the fire, making something from the hare skins. He looked relieved when he spotted her.

'Thank the gods,' he said, rising to his feet. 'She's been an absolute nightmare.' He was clearly traumatised from the experience of trying to keep his eldest daughter confined. 'I had to tie her up at one point, tether her like a horse. And do you know what she did?'

Lina pressed her lips together. 'Cut through the rope?'

'*Chewed* through the rope.' He shook his head and gestured behind him. 'She's inside.'

Stepping past him, Lina pushed through the flaps of the tent and found Trinka sitting cross-legged on the ground, expertly sharpening the blade of her axe. Her hands stilled and she looked up, a smile splitting her face. But what caught Lina's attention was the enormous bruise blossoming on Trinka's cheek, reaching all the way to her eye.

'Thank the gods,' Trinka said. 'I was just preparing for an epic battle between myself and the entire Vargr clan.'

'A battle you would have lost. What happened to your face?' Lina dropped down onto the ground to get a closer look. 'Who did that to you?'

Trinka stared at her blankly, then, as if remembering something, said, 'Oh, did he leave a mark?'

'Half your face resembles a pufferfish.'

She waved it off. 'One of Sture's arse-lickers didn't appreciate me swinging an axe at his chieftain. He lost two teeth after this, but then they got my father involved, and you know I stand no chance against him. He uses weapons I can't fight, like guilt and shame.' She shrugged. 'He doesn't want me to die like my mother. I can't hold that against him.'

Affection bubbled up inside Lina, and she threw her arms around Trinka. 'You're the bravest, most loyal insane person I know. I'm so lucky to have you on my side.' She let go. 'That way I get to keep all my teeth.'

Trinka's expression softened. 'I was worried when I heard the soldiers breached the boundary. Then I learned it was the *general* who came for you. How utterly heroic.' She fluttered her eyelashes before her expression turned curious. 'Did you hump him?'

Lina sat back. 'Well, that took a turn.'

'Hopefully he was better than that shy boy back in Trondheim who took your virginity. What was his name again?'

'Carlson. And he was kind.'

'*Carlson*. Even his name bores me.' She looked Lina over. 'So, what happened with the general?'

Lina got comfortable as she recalled the exact feel and temperature of his lips. 'We kissed.'

Trinka appeared impressed. 'A man who warms you up first. How rare. In my experience, most warriors lead with their little warriors, if you get my drift.'

Lina shook her head, fighting a smile.

'So, that's it? A kiss?'

'We were bracing for an attack.'

'A good fight can be an aphrodisiac for some. I'm not

ashamed to admit that when I knocked the teeth from that warrior, I was a little aroused.'

Lina's face twisted in disgust.

'So, now what?' Trinka asked. 'There's every chance Sture will retaliate. You could find yourself at war with General Foreplay.'

Lina rolled her eyes. 'Can we stick with Tolly, please?'

'Hopefully your father changes his mind about you marrying Sture, because I'm officially against the match.'

Lina suspected her father had also changed his mind, but he was too honourable to break an agreement. She also knew Sture was not the kind of man to remain humble in the face of rejection. 'I can't marry him. I can't even stand to look at him now.' Tolly pushed his way into her mind, his tortured expression as he returned to the cot. She had felt the same pull he had. 'Also… do you think it's possible for two souls to entangle in a single moment, one brief encounter, then remain attached years later?'

Trinka was staring at her like her head was upside down. 'Entangled souls? A brief encounter? Can you hear yourself?' She leaned closer. 'Did you hit your head on the pole you were chained to?'

'No—'

'Because you're making *me* sound like the sane one.'

It was entirely possible that her feelings for the man were starting to consume her from the inside out.

The tent flap opened and in stepped Simian, surveying the scene inside. Lina knew what he was about to say.

'You need to return to our tent,' he told Lina with a solemn look. 'Father wants to speak with you.'

It seemed he had finally figured out what he wanted to say to her.

She rose, nodding. 'Now that I know Trinka isn't chained up somewhere, I'm happy to return. But you need to help me with something first.'

Simian's eyebrows rose.

'I need your help in locating a willow tree,' she continued.

'Why?'

'I need its bark.'

Intrigued, Trinka got to her feet. 'Ooh, witchcraft. What do you need me to do?'

'Ah, no.' Lina cast a wary look in her direction. 'It's for Father, to reduce his inflammation.'

The intrigue on Trinka's face was replaced with boredom. 'I'm busy this afternoon. You two go ahead.' She sat back down and picked up her axe, inspecting the blade.

Lina glanced at her brother, who wore the same wary expression he always did around Trinka despite knowing her since birth.

'I believe there's a tree not too far from here,' he said, backing out of the tent.

Simian led the way through the bustling camp, weaving between tents and stepping over chickens scratching at the ground. As they exited the camp, the noise dimmed until all they could hear were leaves rustling above them.

'Here it is,' Simian said as they arrived at a solitary willow tree. Its graceful branches swayed in the breeze.

It started to rain, but Lina was undeterred, trailing her fingers over the smooth bark. 'Help me, would you?'

Simian drew his dagger. 'So, where did you learn about this magical remedy?'

'Tolly.'

'Ah.' He began carving. 'Is he as good a man as I suspect?'

She nodded. 'He is.'

Pausing, Simian looked at her. 'You know, it would be very inconvenient if you fell in love with him.'

'I know,' she said tiredly.

Simian cleared his throat.

'Oh maiden of the seas,
Brighter than dawn,
Behind my pleas,
Sits a warrior's scorn.
In battle, we fight for our own version of right,
For land, for life, as stories will tell,
It's thee, oh maiden, in my dreams at night,
Who leaves me torn between duty and love's spell.'

Lina tried very hard not to look at him. 'Did that just come to you in the moment?'

'Actually, I wrote it the night you told me you "respected" the general, when I was feeling rather inspired.'

Her hands stilled momentarily before resuming carving. 'I think we have enough.' She ran her thumb over the intricate patterns etched into the bark.

'Now what?' he asked.

'Now we boil it.'

The pair made their way back to their tent, the bark cradled carefully in Lina's palms. When they arrived, they found their father seated in front of the fire, staring at the flames.

'Fetch some wood,' he told Simian, barely looking up.

Simian exchanged a glance with his sister before leaving them.

'Where were you?' Farulf asked.

Lina went over to the crate to let a very vocal Olga out. 'With Trinka. One of Sture's men hurt her.' She observed him for a reaction but did not get one. 'Did you know that?'

He shook his head. 'Is she all right?'

'She will be.' Filling a small pot with some water, Lina dropped the bark into it and went to set it atop the flames.

Farulf eyed it suspiciously. 'What is that?'

'Something for your pain.'

He shook his head. 'I don't want it.'

'I know, but at least try it—for me.'

He leaned forwards, watching her. 'Don't worry, I'm not fool enough to sit you down in the hope of an apology.'

The defeat in his voice was hard to hear. She drew a long breath and released it. 'I *am* sorry.'

He cast a doubtful glance in her direction.

'I am. I'm sorry for being stubborn and for aggravating the situation. I'm sorry that you're in this terrible position where you have to choose between my happiness and what's best for the clan.' She paused. 'And I'm sorry you're afraid.'

He straightened. 'I'm not afraid.'

'Of course you are. You wouldn't be the chieftain you are without healthy fear.'

He pressed his eyes closed. 'I'd feel much better if I knew you could handle that man like your mother used to handle me.'

A faint smile came and went on her face before she focused on the fire. 'The two are incomparable. You loved her, so you *allowed* her to handle you. I'm just a means to grow Sture's clan.'

His eyes went shiny. 'I misjudged him, but that doesn't change the fact that we need him and the rest of the Vargr.'

Lina took the pot off the fire and poured some of the liquid into a cup, handing it to him. Farulf took the cup, smelled it, then made a face conveying his repulsion.

'It smells like dirt.'

She smiled. 'Probably tastes like it too.'

His expression turned serious again. 'I wish I could give you a union like the one I enjoyed for many years.'

Tolly appeared in her mind again, and she fought hard to push him out.

'Tell me nothing happened with that man,' Farulf said, his voice barely above a whisper.

She knew he was talking about Tolly. What was she supposed to say? Nothing had happened, really, and yet *so* much had happened. A new piece of herself had been unveiled.

'Nothing happened,' she lied.

Farulf searched her eyes for a long moment, then drank the tea.

CHAPTER 27

Her father retired early that night, and Lina prayed the tea would help him sleep with less pain than usual. She and Simian remained by the fire long after dinner, speaking in soft voices so as to not disturb him. Sture came by at one point, wanting to speak with Farulf. The siblings told him he had just retired for the evening, even though he had been asleep for some time.

'I am pleased to see you fed and back with your family,' Sture said, gaze falling to the goose eyeing him from her lap.

'Are you?' She felt only numbness in his presence now.

'Some lessons just need to be learned.'

Lina gave him a tight-lipped smile. 'Let us hope the lesson sticks.' Of course, the lesson she was referring to was that she would not be tortured into submission and false remorse.

'I have no doubt you will make smarter choices in the future.'

His arrogance almost knocked her backwards off her seat.

'Would you like to take a walk with me?' he asked.

Simian remained silent, eyes on the fire.

'Actually, I was about to retire for the evening,' she said. 'I'm exhausted after spending the night out in the freezing cold, forced to remain on my feet.'

Sture wet his lips. 'Lucky that General Tolly arrived to save the day.'

'Lucky for *me*. Less lucky for your men.'

His eyes remained locked with hers for a moment before he finally looked away. 'I should probably get some sleep myself. Who knows what the next few weeks will bring?'

He was being intentionally ambiguous, likely trying to spread fear.

'I'm sure our father will keep us well informed,' Lina said.

Sture bowed his head slightly. 'Goodnight, Lina.'

'Goodnight.'

After he had left, Simian let out a low whistle. 'That was intense.'

Lina relaxed her hold on the goose. 'He's a real piece of work. The fact that he thinks he achieved something last night shows how clueless he is.'

It took some time for the tension in the air to dissipate.

'I noticed you kept a firm grip on Olga,' Simian said.

'Because I don't trust that man one bit.'

With a sigh, Simian rose from his seat. 'I'm surprised you're able to keep your eyes open after last night. I'm exhausted just from worrying about you from the comfort of my warm bed.' He gave her a sad smile. 'I failed you.'

'No,' she said immediately. 'You read the situation and knew your limits.'

'Yes, I'm well aware of my limits.' He swallowed. 'You

deserve a brother who would walk through fire for you without weighing up the risks first.'

She shrugged. 'I have you to weigh up the risks and Trinka to leap blindly into the flames. How lucky am I?'

He gave her shoulder a gentle squeeze as he passed her on the way to the tent. 'Don't stay up too late.'

Lina watched him disappear between the folds of canvas, then sat alone by the dwindling fire, her mind turning to Tolly. She had struggled to think of much else that day. The best way to rid herself of him was sleep.

Leaving the fire to die out, she placed Olga in her crate, then scrubbed her face and hands. She cleaned her teeth with some salt and sage, then headed for the tent.

'Psst.'

Whipping her head around, Lina found Trinka standing by the dying fire. 'You scared me.' She walked over to her. 'What are you doing here so late?'

'I'm off to keep watch on the western border. I thought you might want to come.'

Lina looked over her shoulder. All was quiet. 'While I'd love to keep you company—'

'Not to keep *me* company. To sneak you across the border so you can go finish what you started with General Foreplay.'

Lina felt a pang of excitement and panic at the same time. 'Let's not call him that.'

'We'll send a message via one of his soldiers.'

It was an extremely bad, exceptionally dangerous suggestion. And yet Lina knew she would do it for the chance to see him.

'If you don't want to—'

'I'll get my cloak.'

A mischievous glint flashed in Trinka's eyes before Lina tiptoed into the tent to fetch her cloak, her heart pounding hard in her chest the whole time. Re-emerging, she tugged up the hood, and the pair melted into the darkness.

Neither of them spoke as they walked. Trinka moved with silent grace, her steps sure as she navigated her way through often thick undergrowth towards the western boundary.

As they approached their destination, Lina spotted the silhouette of the warrior stationed there. Trinka gestured for her to hide while she went to do the changeover. Every whisper of leaves and snap of a twig had Lina flinching. She kept bracing for Sture to pop out from behind a tree and drag her back to the pole.

After the warrior left, Trinka waited a few minutes before gesturing for Lina to join her. Lina made her way over, eyes on her surroundings.

'Now what?' she asked when she stepped up next to Trinka. 'I thought there would be more soldiers around the place.'

'Oh, they're around. The question is, how do we lure one over?' She took a few steps forwards, stopping just past the green flag.

Sure enough, a torch came into view, the flame growing bigger until a face was visible. A stern-faced soldier approached them. 'Move back,' he warned, stopping a few feet from them.

'Lina here would like to see General Tolly,' Trinka said, her feet anchored. 'And I'm confident the general wants to see her too.'

The soldier looked Lina over, then nodded. 'Do not move from this spot.' His expression made it clear he was not playing games. With a final warning glare, the torch whooshed past them, then began to grow small again.

The women waited as instructed, Lina feeling nervous. All it took was for one warrior to see her, and she risked getting Trinka into trouble as well.

A few minutes passed before the torch returned, this time illuminating a tense-faced Tolly. His eyes were fixed on Lina as he approached, and he walked straight up to her without hesitating. 'What happened? Are you all right?'

He was assuming the worst, and she could not blame him after what had taken place earlier. 'I'm fine.'

He flicked his gaze to Trinka. 'Do you need something?'

'Lina does,' Trinka replied. 'Hopefully you can help. I'm on watch until sunrise, but don't cut it too fine.' She turned away.

Finally understanding, Tolly looked at Lina. 'I don't want to get you in trouble.'

She took a large step over the boundary to stand in front of him. 'I'm already in trouble.'

He searched her eyes as he weighed up the risks. Then, reaching up, he adjusted the hood of her cloak so her face was covered before taking her hand. 'This way.'

Lina glanced back at Trinka, but she was still looking in the other direction, a smile on her face.

The grass was long and damp as Tolly led Lina through it. The skirt of her dress seemed to soak up every drop. When they reached the camp, he skilfully navigated his way between the tents, sticking to the shadows to avoid being noticed. The camp was still active, even at the late hour. Soldiers walked about or were gathered around fires playing cards and dice.

When they arrived at Tolly's tent, he guided her inside and quickly closed the flap behind them.

Lina looked around the small but tidy space before turning to face him. His expression was far from relaxed.

'Water?' he offered.

She shook her head.

'I could send for some food.'

'I've eaten.'

He nodded slowly. 'Want to tell me what happened when you returned?'

Lina could see how much he needed reassurance that she was all right after everything. 'Nothing happened. Sture kept his distance, mostly. And my father… he's backed into a corner, and I'm not sure he knows how to get out.' She did not know whether to say the next part aloud. 'As a leader, he's vulnerable. There's no one to fill his boots at present.' She felt like she was betraying her clan by saying those things, but the genuine sympathy on Tolly's face put her mind at ease. 'We have a lot of good men, great fighters, some sharp minds. What we're short on is leaders.'

Tolly was silent for a moment. 'I gather Sture knows all these things too.'

'Of course. Men like him can sniff out weakness from miles away.' She crinkled her nose when she felt it sting. 'A weak clan is a dead clan. My father's decision to have me marry Sture is smart. It ensures the Wolfvanir are protected after he… when he can no longer fight.' Her eyes met his. 'I'm certain the match will be a complete disaster on a personal level, but I'm hopeful the rest of the clan will enjoy the security that comes from it.'

A heavy silence hung between them. Tolly seemed lost in thought for a moment. 'If this marriage is what's needed, then why are you here?'

'That's a very reasonable question.' She lifted her shoulders in a shrug. 'I wish I could give you a reasonable answer.'

He stared at her. 'Are you afraid of him?'

She swallowed and looked around the tent once more. 'I think I'm more afraid of never experiencing what I felt with you earlier today ever again.'

'Look at me,' he said.

She did.

'Tell me what you experienced earlier today. Tell me so I can give it to you again.'

His words turned her insides to pulp. No one had ever asked her what she wanted or what she needed, let alone been prepared to give it to her. 'It was a feeling, like my stomach might fly away at any moment.' She shook her head. 'But it was also more than that. It was letting go of fear. It was safety despite being in the middle of an enemy camp.' She wet her lips. 'Being close to you makes me forget the danger.'

Tolly stepped up to her and took hold of her face, his thumbs brushing the curve of her jaw. 'I wish I could give you a world that's safe.'

The way she felt his touch, like his fingers were simultaneously running along her arms and hips… 'Simian helpfully pointed out earlier that it would be very inconvenient if I fell in love with you.'

Tolly dipped his head and kissed her lightly. 'Your brother's very smart.'

Her eyes closed at the sensation. 'Trinka said I would move on quickly after a disappointing experience.'

He laughed lightly, and his breath on her lips was delicious. 'Of course she did.'

'If she's right, we can both move on.'

He drew back a little. 'And if she's wrong?'

She opened her eyes to look at him. 'If she's wrong, we'll have this moment. My father and Sture have no control over my memories.'

Tolly ran his thumb over her lips. 'Pray for disappointment so that seeing you across the boundary, always out of reach, becomes bearable.'

Her eyes moved between his, noting the desire and uncertainty. The raw emotion she felt was literally choking her. His lips found hers again, the kiss firmer this time. She melted against him, and just like that, the uncertainty dissipated and the feeling of complete safety enveloped her. The world outside the tent could no longer touch her.

Their hands roamed each other's bodies, learning every curve, plane, and texture. Their kisses grew hungry, bordering on ravenous. His touch sent shivers up and down her spine. His breath made her own catch. When he picked her up, her legs instinctively went around him, tightening and drawing him closer until she was dizzy with the warmth of him. He carried her over to the cot and sat her down on it, kneeling between her legs and kissing her deeply.

'Ready to pray?' he whispered into her open mouth.

Her head fell back as his hand found its way beneath her sark. 'Gods have mercy…'

CHAPTER 28

The sound of the rain hitting the tent was oddly soothing in the aftermath. They lay facing each other, Tolly never looking away for fear he might miss a moment of her.

'I guess the gods didn't hear our prayer,' Lina said, looking down at his lips.

He had never experienced anything close to what he just had with her. 'They ignored us entirely.'

She touched the stubble on his cheek and jaw. 'I've no idea what we're supposed to do now. Should we pretend it didn't happen?'

'Impossible.' A few hours wrapped in a blanket with her had altered his brain chemistry.

Her hand fell away. 'I have to go.'

'I know.'

She propped herself up on one elbow. 'I could visit you again next time Trinka's on night watch.'

'It's too risky.'

'The risk is mine alone.'

He rose to a seated position, staring at her in the dark. 'Don't say that. It's not yours alone. We've crossed a line that means it will never be yours alone again. Your risk is my risk. Your suffering is my torture.'

She rolled onto her back. 'That was some line we crossed.'

'It was.' He pushed some hair away from her face. 'Get dressed. We need to get you safely over that boundary.'

Begrudgingly, she swung her legs over the side of the cot and picked up her clothes. 'I guess this is it, then.' She glanced over her shoulder at him. 'This will be the last time you see me naked or *feel* me naked. The last time—'

He tackled her playfully to the bed, catching her laughter with his mouth. After kissing her deeply, he said, 'Come back to me, but only if it's safe. If your family is asking questions or Sture's men are following you around, don't take risks. Promise me.'

'I promise.'

Tolly watched her dress, not ready to let her go but knowing he had to. Every minute he kept her there with him was one more minute that it could all go very wrong.

'Are you getting dressed, too, or are you going like that?' Lina asked as she secured her cloak pin.

He climbed off the cot and gathered his belongings, leaning over to kiss her as he stepped into his trousers.

Once dressed, Tolly took Lina's hand and led her out of the tent into the cool night air. Wet tents glistened like liquid diamonds under torchlight. Despite the camp being quiet, he still took her the long way through the shadows to reduce the chances of being seen. They did not speak but stole glances at each other. With each step closer to the boundary, the weight of the separation grew heavier.

They reached the edge of their worlds, where Trinka stood keeping watch. Her sharp eyes spotted them from far away, giving them a knowing look as they drew close. Her gaze fell to their joined hands. 'You took your time with her, I see.'

'Trinka,' Lina said.

'Would you say you have small hands or average?' Trinka continued, undeterred.

'Please ignore her.'

Tolly released his grip on her hand, the tips of his fingers lingering on hers for a moment before falling away. 'If you need me for any reason, let one of the boundary guards know.'

'And you'll come running into enemy territory?' Lina asked in a teasing tone.

He shifted his weight. 'I'll assess the situation.'

Trinka laughed lightly. 'You really have him by the balls now. Enjoy, because it won't last.'

Lina and Tolly stared at each other in the dark, their amusement mirrored in the other's eyes.

'I'll see you soon, General,' Lina said as she stepped away and crossed the boundary to Trinka.

Tolly nodded once. 'I'll see you soon.'

Lina adjusted the hood of her cloak, then ran off towards the camp. Tolly remained there, watching her until she disappeared.

'So much for getting you out of her system,' Trinka said. 'You're going to break her heart.'

Tolly's gaze went to her. 'Thank you.'

'Listen, whatever happened in your tent was all her.'

'No.' He blinked. 'Thank you for protecting her—or trying to. She told me what happened.'

Trinka frowned. 'Was that conversation at the beginning or end? Or perhaps in the middle?'

Tolly began backing away. 'You take care.'

'And *you* take a bath. I can smell her on you.'

It was one of those rare occasions when he was lost for words. With a shake of his head, he returned to the camp.

A peculiar dread gnawed at him as he neared his tent. When he entered, he discovered the source of that unease. His brother stood there waiting for him, his midnight eyes gleaming in Tolly's direction.

'You took a big fucking risk tonight,' he began immediately.

So he had not gotten away with it as he had hoped. 'Hello to you too.'

'If she's caught—'

'I know.'

Ryder stared at him for a long moment. 'You already have a target on your back. That chieftain will come for you.'

'He doesn't deserve her.'

Ryder nodded. 'I believe you. Are you going to see her again?'

'Given she'll be living across the boundary for the next few months—'

'You know what I mean.'

Tolly exhaled. 'You've been here. You know.'

'It will end badly.'

He did not reply.

Ryder looked around the tent. 'Tell me this isn't leftover

gratitude from when she saved your arse all those years ago.' His eyes returned to Tolly. 'It's real? This is the woman you would jump off a castle wall into a moat for?'

A smile flickered on Tolly's face. 'This is the one.'

His brother stood there nodding, as though deciding something. 'Then we jump together.'

Tolly could not speak after that.

'No secrets, though. Don't lead me into a fight blind. Understand?'

He nodded. 'No secrets.'

CHAPTER 29

'Are you ill?'

Lina's eyes sprang open, and she found Simian standing over her with a worried expression. 'What?'

He sat back on his heels. 'It's late. Are you ill?'

'No, I'm...' She sat up and looked around the well-lit tent. 'Tired.'

Simian relaxed at hearing that, then got to his feet and went to let Olga out of her crate.

'Where's Father?' Lina asked when he returned with the goose in tow.

'With Sture.'

She rolled her eyes. 'Of course he is.'

Walking to the corner, Simian pulled four eggs out of the egg basket. 'Hungry?'

Lina stretched her arms luxuriously above her head. 'Starving.'

Simian was halfway to the tent's exit when he glanced in

her direction and stopped suddenly. 'Are you sure you're well? Your cheeks look a little feverish.'

It had been several hours since she had left Tolly's tent, and she could still feel the heat from his mouth as if it were trapped inside her. 'I'm quite well. Don't fret.'

Content with her response, he left the tent, while Lina opened her blanket so Olga could snuggle with her. She lay there thinking about how not only had she gotten away with *seeing* him, but she had gotten away with *being* with him. It was so reckless, so dangerous, and yet all she could think about was how to do it again.

And she succeeded.

Over the next seven days, Lina managed to sneak across the boundary four more times. On the three days she could not get to him safely, they found other ways to see each other, even if it was just a glimpse from afar. During her third visit with him, he told her those glimpses were essential to his sanity. He needed to know that all was well, that she was safe.

The hours flew by when they were together. They would lie in a tangle of limbs and blankets, whispering to each other and smiling in the dark. Most of the time, she could not see his smile, only hear it in his voice. She had to imagine it and felt deeply saddened by the realisation that she might never see it in the light of day. Their daytime encounters were cold on the outside. Smiles had to remain buried. Exchanging a glance was dangerous enough.

'There's an entire world to explore, but we'll only ever see the inside of your tent,' she said to him during her fourth visit.

He was quiet for a long time. 'Where would you want to go?'

'To Ireland,' she replied without hesitation. 'I want to see where you grew up. Watch you remember things you may have forgotten. We could visit the graves of your family, and you could tell me stories.'

His arms tightened around her, and he buried his face in her shoulder. 'What about your home?'

'We could go there next and watch you freeze.'

'Would I travel on the same boat as your family and husband?'

The smile fell from her face. He had crossed an unspoken line by mentioning Sture. Or perhaps she had crossed it when she fantasised aloud. There was no future in which they would be together. The mention of one was forbidden within the canvas walls of the tent.

'I'm sorry,' he whispered.

She pressed her eyes closed. 'So am I. The inevitable separation is hard enough *without* having met your future wife.'

They were silent for a long time.

'What if he treats you poorly?' Tolly said into her shoulder.

She was not sure how to respond to that, because she already knew Sture would treat her like the rogue, disobedient woman she was. 'I can handle him. I'll have him trained in no time.'

Tolly lifted his head and kissed along her hairline. 'It's time for you to go.'

'I don't want to.' She felt him exhale.

'You could stay, but the cost would be enormous.'

She lay still as reality crashed in once more. 'Aside from the devastation my elopement would cause my family, I'd be more worried about the retaliation that would follow on your army. If the Vargr attack, you won't win.'

He propped himself up on one elbow. 'We outnumber the Vargr.'

'Yes, but we both know it won't be just the Vargr fighting. We would fight alongside them. They're here because of us, and we're safe because of them.'

'We've been ready for retaliation for the past week. What's taking you all so long?'

She touched his face. 'That's not funny.'

'Who's laughing?'

Her hand fell away. 'We shouldn't even be talking about this.'

'We shouldn't be doing a lot of things.'

They watched each other in the dark. The guilt Lina felt in that moment was crushing. Visions of dead warriors laid out in a line flashed in her mind, their men scattered along the river's edge with arrows protruding and stomachs cut open. Tolly had done that. He had crossed the river that day and slaughtered them with his own hands.

Nausea rolled over her.

'What are you thinking about?' he asked.

She sat up so they were at the same height. 'I'm thinking you should be ready for the worst.'

'What does that mean?' He combed his fingers through her hair, making her eyes sink shut. 'Do I need to worry about you killing me in my bed, daughter of the Wolfvanir?'

She wished she could see him better. 'You're safe for today.' Turning away from him, she reached for her clothes. 'I have to go.'

He did not stop her, even though they still had a little more time. He also did not ask her if something was the matter, likely because he knew the answer. They took the moments they could steal and did not look beyond them. Each visit could be her last. There was no point torturing each other by being openly sad about it.

Tolly stood and dressed, then waited for her by the entrance. The air was heavy with unspoken words as they made their way to the boundary.

When Trinka came into view, Lina stopped and turned to him. He waited for her to say something, but she did not know what to say. She stood with a stomach full of dread, knowing this goodbye might be their last because it should be.

'It's all right,' he said.

She enjoyed being outdoors with him because the moonlight helped her see him better. 'What's all right?'

'Everything you're thinking and feeling.'

Her eyes began to sting. 'I'll see you soon, General.' And she would. Across enemy lines.

Tolly checked his surroundings before stepping closer, fingers twisting her knotted hair as he dipped his head to kiss her. Lina's reaction to him had not changed. Heat still pooled in her belly the same way it had an hour earlier. Her body still melted against his involuntarily. Or perhaps voluntarily.

'See you soon,' Tolly said as he released her from the kiss.

She leaned in as he withdrew, then remembered they were not inside the tent, remembered all the things that could go wrong if they were spotted. Opening her eyes, Lina turned away from him before she could change her mind. She kept her gaze fixed on Trinka from that point on and did not look back.

~

'Get up—now.'

Lina's teeth all but rattled in her mouth when she was violently shaken awake by her brother. 'For the love of—'

'Get dressed. We have to go.' Simian leapt up, snatched up the first dress he saw, and threw it at her.

'Go where?' She could see he looked genuinely fearful.

'We can come back when he's calmed down.'

She sat up. 'When who's calm?' She looked around, his panic catching. 'Where's Father?'

He stilled and looked at her. 'Trying to talk Sture down from his rage.'

Lina instinctively began to dress, never taking her eyes off him. 'What happened?'

His eyes bored into hers. 'Sture knows. He knows, and now Father knows.'

A cold sensation crawled down her spine. 'Knows what?'

'About you and the general,' he whisper-shouted. 'And that Trinka has been aiding you. Toke told me they've been watching you all week. The entire *week*.'

Lina shot up and reached for her belt. 'I must go to Trinka before—'

'It's too late. He already has her.'

She froze. 'What do you mean? Who has her?'

'Sture. And his men are coming for you next. We need to leave. We'll hide until—'

'Where are they?' Lina asked, strapping on her sword.

The colour drained from Simian's face. 'You can't go anywhere near Sture right now. He's out of his mind.'

'I won't let Trinka pay for my mistakes.'

Simian crossed his arms. 'Well, it's nice to hear you use the word "mistake". What on earth were you thinking, sneaking across the perimeter to him? How else did you think this would end?' Registering the surprise on her face, he added, 'Yes, I knew.'

'Why didn't you say anything?'

'To what end? When have you ever listened to me? Would you have stopped going?'

She swallowed. 'Tell me where they are.' Her voice was quieter that time.

He pressed the corners of his eyes. 'I saw Bo drag Trinka into their camp. I told Father straight away, and he's gone to find them. Now I'm here, begging you to leave with me.'

Lina grabbed her bow and quiver and exited the tent, almost tripping over Olga at the door.

'You need to think this through,' Simian said, following her out. 'If you show up armed and start making demands, you'll only fuel the fire.' He fell into step with her. 'Are you listening to me?'

'I'm listening.'

'Then what's your plan?'

She glanced sideways at him. 'To protect Trinka at all costs and worry about the rest later.'

Simian blinked slowly. 'Of course that's your plan.'

As they entered the Vargr's camp, they could hear a crowd gathered near the kitchen area. They made their way towards the noise, and Lina spotted her father and Sture arguing. She looked around for Trinka, heart racing. Nausea hit her hard when she spotted her friend tied up to a post and stripped to the waist. Her face was a mask of defiance despite the vibrant red lines across her back.

The colour drained from Simian's face when he saw her.

The bow slipped through Lina's fingers as she took in the

scene. She dropped her quiver alongside it and marched forwards. 'What in God's name do you think you're doing?' She practically spat the words at Sture.

The chieftains fell silent and looked in her direction.

'Lina,' her father warned. 'Let me handle this.'

She drew her sword and continued towards Trinka. 'Thanks, but I've seen the way you handle his mistreatment of women. I'm quite capable of cutting a piece of rope.'

The defiance on Trinka's face melted away at the sight of Lina, her pain becoming more apparent.

'Touch that rope and see what happens,' Sture said, his voice too calm for her comfort.

Lina stopped walking and looked over at him. 'You are not my chieftain or my husband. You do not get to tell me what to do.' She took a moment to rein in her rage. 'How dare you?' Looking around at the other clan members, she added, 'And how dare all of you stand by in silence? If you think this is normal, acceptable punishment from a leader, then I pity all of you.' She continued towards Trinka.

It was clear from people's faces that no woman had ever spoken to their chieftain that way. She was more than happy to be the first.

Sture headed towards her, prompting Simian to curse quietly behind her.

'Sture!' Farulf called to him. 'If you lay a hand on my daughter, you will be finding yourself another wife.'

Lina reached Trinka in a few paces, preparing to cut the rope. Sture caught hold of her hand, squeezing until her fingers opened and her weapon fell to the ground. When her father moved to intervene, Bo and another Vargr warrior stepped in front of him.

Sture released Lina with a shove, then retrieved a leather strap off the ground. 'Feel free to stay and watch. This is what comes of those who whore out their friends.'

Trinka raised her chin and gritted her teeth, but as the strap was coming down, Lina stepped in front of it, taking the full brunt of the lashing. It struck her arm and the side of her face, but she held in the yelp despite feeling like her skin was on fire.

'Stop!' Farulf roared, pushing between the two warriors and drawing his weapon.

Before he reached them, Olga came flying into the scene, going straight for Sture's head. She somehow simultaneously beat him with her wings while biting his face. Sture grabbed hold of her neck and threw her so hard on the ground that she did not get up. When he drew his weapon to finish the job, Lina threw herself over Olga, covering her with her body.

'Step back from my sister!'

Lina looked up in surprise at the sound of her brother's voice. There he was, the bow she had dropped loaded in his hands, pointed at Sture. His face was set with grim determination. But the best sound of all was the faint honks of Olga beneath her. She was still alive.

'If you think I will stand by while you take out your bad mood on my family, and our goose, then you are sorely mistaken.'

Bo made a move towards him.

'I'm a nervous shooter,' he warned. 'Unless you want to see your chieftain accidentally shot in the face, then I suggest you stop right there.'

The warrior pulled up with a confused look.

'Well, look who found his balls,' Trinka said. 'Good for you.'

A very stressed-looking Frode arrived on the scene with Toke. His eyes widened when he saw his daughter tied up with a bleeding back. 'What the hell is going on?' he asked, rushing to Trinka's side.

'Oh, just airing my bosom,' she said through gritted teeth. The humour fell flat on account of her injuries.

Frode dragged her torn dress up to cover her, then drew his knife to cut the rope around her wrists. She slumped against him before straightening.

'You've proven yourself unworthy of my daughter's hand,' Farulf said, his eyes like slits as he addressed Sture.

Sture exhaled sharply through his nose in place of laughter. 'Your daughter proved herself unworthy of any man when she crawled into the bed of our enemy.'

Farulf's glare intensified. 'Inviting you here was a mistake.'

'You did not have a choice,' Sture growled. 'Look at you. You can barely keep hold of your sword.'

'We can test that theory if you like,' Farulf said calmly. 'Right now. Your youth against my experience.'

Lina scooped Olga up in her arms and sat back on her heels, waiting for Sture's reply.

'My father taught me to respect the elderly,' Sture said. 'I came here to honour his promise, old man. A fact you seem to have forgotten.' He gestured towards Lina. 'Take your used-up daughter with you when you leave.' Completely ignoring the arrow still pointed at him, he turned and retreated to his tent.

Lina got to her feet, clutching Olga close to her, and went

to Trinka. 'Are you all right?' She struggled to keep the wobble out of her voice.

'At least mine's on my back,' Trinka said, wincing as she adjusted her dress. 'He just missed your eye. Lucky, or we would have been forced to make you a patch and send you off to the pirates.'

Lina could not find any laughter within her.

'You're not going to waste that, are you?' Trinka said, gesturing to Olga.

Lina looked down. 'She's still alive.'

'Really? It sure looked like a roast dinner landing.'

Frode removed his shirt and wrapped it around his daughter. 'Let's go. Before I follow that man to his tent and start a war we weren't betting on.' He led Trinka away.

Farulf walked over to Simian, who was still standing with the bow nocked and drawn. A brief fatherly touch had him lowering it and looking around like he was coming out of a dream.

With Olga tucked against her, Lina followed the others, struggling to process all that had happened. Trinka's brutal lashing, an injured goose, her father finally rediscovering the chieftain within, Simian stepping up to defend her. But the lightness in her chest was for one reason only: she no longer had to marry Sture.

That nightmare was over.

Lina reached up to touch the weeping mark across her face and realised her lips were turned up in a faint smile.

Freedom had never felt so good.

CHAPTER 30

The best place for healing and cleansing was the sea. Not only for the body but also the mind. Lina and Trinka saddled a horse and rode the ten miles to the coastline, where they could let the saltwater do what it did best.

Upon arrival, they tethered the horse and removed their outer garments. The cool embrace of the sea enveloped Lina as she submerged herself in the water. Within minutes, her mind and body felt lighter as the stress of the morning washed away. The pair swam further out, knowing the key to fending off the cold was movement.

'How's the back?' Lina called to Trinka.

'I'd almost forgotten it happened,' she lied.

In the boundless expanse of the sea, Lina found a much-needed sense of peace. The sound of the waves drowned out her thoughts and the cold numbed her face so she could no longer feel it stinging. She emerged with renewed energy and a clear mind.

The women sat on the beach with a blanket around them, looking out to sea and not speaking for the longest time. Trinka was the first to break the silence.

'He turned out to be an even bigger arsehole than I originally thought.'

Lina did not have to ask who she was talking about. 'I knew it all along.'

'Having life-altering relations with our number one enemy might be the smartest thing you've ever done.'

'Do you think my father will agree with your assessment?'

She laughed. 'He would be within his rights to make your back look like mine.'

'I do love it when we accidentally match.'

Trinka fell silent. 'Can I tell you something that you're never to repeat or even acknowledge that I said?'

Lina looked at her. 'Of course you can.'

Wrinkling her nose, Trinka said, 'It hurt like hell, and it still does.'

Lina wanted to put her arm around her but did not want to cause her more pain. 'Of course it hurts. You don't have to be strong all the time.'

The wind picked up for a second, and Trinka closed her eyes. 'But I do. That was the last thing my mother said to me before she died, remember?'

'I remember.' She took hold of Trinka's hand and squeezed. 'She told you to be strong for your sister. Little did she know that your sister would be stronger than the two of us combined.'

'That girl's a feral animal. It's my favourite thing about her.'

Lina laughed softly, then sighed. 'We should head back. I'm sure my father is very keen to speak to me.'

'If he asks, I tried to talk you out of it.'

Lina laughed again.

The two friends dressed, then made their way over to the waiting horse. They headed back to the camp at a slow walk, neither in a rush to face the people waiting for them.

When they arrived, Lina could tell by the way people were staring that she had been the topic of conversation that day. The chieftain's daughter had breached the perimeter, slept with the enemy, and shattered her chance to wed the Vargr chieftain. It was the juiciest story she could have given them.

Farulf exited the tent when he heard the horse arrive, running his eyes over Lina as she dismounted. 'Your face is swollen.'

She touched two fingers to the wound. 'Hardly surprising given the size of the man holding the leather strap.' Her hand fell away. 'You saw Trinka's back.'

He broke eye contact with her and ambled away. 'Walk with me.'

Drawing a breath, she followed and fell into step with him.

'I went as soon as Simian told me,' he said. 'The damage was already done by the time I arrived. The Vargr's disciplinary methods are…'

'Brutal?'

He did not respond.

'And we still have two months of the summer left,' she said. 'What are the chances they'll leave early?'

'We would be in trouble if they did.' His tone was stern. 'They're the only reason we have these paths to walk and lands to hunt on. The Carmarthen Militia will push us back to Llangrannog the first chance they get—or perhaps out of Cardiganshire entirely.' Leaning his weight on one foot, he looked around. 'Sture would be within his rights to leave. Any goodwill between us was destroyed the moment you willingly stepped foot over that boundary.' He met her gaze as he added, 'I'm ashamed of what you did. I gave my word to Sture, and you betrayed it.'

She did not attempt to defend herself because her actions were indefensible.

'The sneaking around. The promiscuity…' he continued.

That last one stung because she hated having her deep connection with Tolly reduced to *promiscuity*. It would never have gone as far as it did with anyone else. She had not been merely scratching some itch.

It was at that moment that she realised they were heading towards the perimeter. 'Where are we going?'

'To lay eyes upon our enemy.'

Her feet slowed. 'Why?'

'Because you've forgotten who they are and what they've done to us since we arrived.'

She shook her head. 'No, I've not forgotten.'

Farulf continued walking, and Lina had no choice but to follow him.

'They murdered six of our people the first day we arrived,' he said. 'Then they used their corpses to mark their territory.'

She remembered. 'And we drove the entire population of Lampeter from their homes the next day, burning down their houses in the process.'

'But we've never set foot on Carmarthenshire soil.'

'They would likely disagree with that statement.'

He stopped in the middle of the grass, eyes on the

Carmarthen Militia's camp beyond the boundary. 'Even with Sture out of the picture, I've an obligation to defend your honour.'

Lina almost tripped over her own feet when he said that. 'What do you mean?'

He was staring so hard at the camp that she thought he might not have heard her, but then he said, 'General Tolly must pay for the disgrace he has brought upon my family.'

His words turned her blood cold. 'It's not his fault—'

'It has already been decided.'

'What has?' Her frustration was evident in her tone.

Farulf looked at her. 'Sture wants all the land between Llangrannog and River Teifi.' His expression hardened. 'And we're going to help him get it.'

Lina stared at her father, his intentions hitting her like a physical blow. Not seeing or being with Tolly was one thing, but coming face to face with him on the battlefield was something else entirely. She pictured her brother dying at the hands of her lover, imagined driving a sword through the stomachs of the men he had survived alongside in the wastelands for all those years—or perhaps even his brother.

'No,' she said plainly. 'No, I can't.' She tried to find reason in his eyes, but all she could see was sad resolve that chilled her bones.

'This is what Sture wants from our allegiance now. This is what we must give him to ensure peace between our clans.'

'If it's peace you want, then don't do this. So many people will die unnecessarily.'

'What did you think would happen afterwards? You humiliated him. You humiliated *me*.' His voice was devoid of emotion. 'In the absence of remorse, you will, at a minimum, accept the consequences of your actions without complaint. The entire clan will pay for your mistake. Your discomfort is the least of my worries right now.'

She swallowed the enormous lump in her throat. He was not done.

'You should be begging for forgiveness, not airing grievances.'

Tears brimmed in Lina's eyes as she struggled with the weight of the guilt and the gravity of the situation. Every word he had just spoken was the truth, and yet her loyalties remained conflicted. 'I can't control how I feel about him. If I could, if it were a choice, I would have chosen differently for your sake, for his sake, and for my own sanity's sake. It was going to end in heartbreak either way. I wanted to have something to show for it, even if that something was a memory to carry into a loveless marriage.'

He looked around the field they stood in. 'Soon you will have plenty of memories to take into your loveless marriage, assuming I can find a man willing to take you now.'

That last part stung—a lot. She did not care what other people thought of her, but she cared what her father thought. 'You can tell me not to love him, but you can't tell me to kill him.'

He did not answer for a long time. 'You will protect your brother, your clan, and yourself, as you've always done.' He paused. 'Do you hear me?'

Lina felt the tears on her face and quickly brushed them aside. She rarely cried, and never in front of her father. 'I hear you.'

Farulf left her standing there, his words hanging in the air like a suffocating fog. She watched him walk away, and then her gaze drifted to the boundary. She stilled when she caught sight of Tolly standing with one of the guards. He looked in her direction, and she felt the moment his eyes landed on her like it was physical contact. They stared at each other, too far away to see the other's expression but close enough to feel their thoughts. The pain, the longing, the knowing. The inability to offer any form of comfort to the other.

Leave now. Live.

To warn him about what was coming would only reduce her family's chances of living through it. The element of surprise had always been their greatest weapon. If their enemy had time to prepare, then more Wolfvanir would die.

She knew what she had to do: nothing. Be silent and ready to act when her father asked it of her. Behave. Be loyal. Stop *feeling* so much and just do. Expel all thoughts of him and wring out her heart.

With a heavy chest and pounding head, Lina squared her shoulders and looked away from Tolly, praying her feet could do what she needed them to—*walk*. Carry her obedient self all the way back to the centre of the camp.

Thankfully, they were up for the challenge.

As she left the clearing, she could feel eyes on her back, as warm as the sun. She made a special effort to keep those shoulders steady the whole way.

Once out of sight of him, she had to navigate the people located between her and the safety of her tent. She passed by familiar faces, every one of them now full of suspicion. Some people avoided her gaze entirely, while others whispered between themselves. They were judging her, and they had every right to.

When Lina finally reached her tent, she was relieved to

find it empty. She took Olga from the crate and curled up on the bed with her. It was clear Sture had hurt her. At the very least, he had broken the goose's spirit. He was that kind of man.

Lina fell asleep within minutes, even though that had not been her intention. When she woke, it was dark outside, and Olga was no longer there. Her gaze landed on Simian, who was seated on his bed, staring at the tent wall opposite. He was holding the goose like a baby.

'What's the matter?' Lina asked, sitting up. She instinctively knew something was wrong.

He flinched when she spoke, gaze snapping to her. 'Didn't you hear?'

'Hear what?'

'We're going to fight the Carmarthen Militia.'

Her shoulders slumped forwards. 'I know.'

His throat bobbed. 'Tomorrow. I'll be at the front. Sture's idea. He's giving me the honour and privilege of breaking through their defence line and clearing a path for the next line of warriors.'

She felt sick.

He nodded slowly, as though she had spoken. 'I'm going to die tomorrow.'

CHAPTER 31

'Something's going on,' Ryder said as he stepped inside Tolly's tent.

It was a few hours before sunrise, and Tolly had only just fallen asleep. He forced his eyelids open and sat up, swinging his legs over the side of his cot as he rubbed his eyes. 'What are you talking about?'

'Their fires are still burning bright. There's far too much activity for this time of night.'

Tolly blinked at him in the dark. 'You think they're planning something?'

'I think they've already planned something. I think they're about to implement that plan.'

Rising from his cot, Tolly put on his uniform. 'I saw Lina earlier. She was out in the field with her father.' He glanced at his brother. 'Something felt off. I assumed it had to do with me.'

Ryder's eyebrows drew together. 'Did she say anything?'

'No. She was far away and left soon after her father. The soldier on duty thought they might be arguing.'

'Perhaps he finally found out about the two of you.'

The thought had crossed Tolly's mind, but he had no way of accessing that part of her life. 'It's possible.'

They fell silent for a moment.

'What do you want me to do?' Ryder asked.

Tolly stepped past him and exited the tent, looking around. All was quiet in their camp. 'Let's wake the men who are rested and increase security around the camp.'

Ryder nodded, went to leave, then stopped. 'The plans and processes we have in place in case of invasion, has anything changed?'

Tolly met his brother's eyes in the dim light cast from a nearby tent. 'Nothing has changed. Our defences are set, our strategies in place. Now we trust our preparations and be vigilant.' His voice was surprisingly steady and full of resolve.

Ryder hesitated before saying, 'So, if Lina or another family member were to—'

'Nothing has changed,' Tolly repeated. 'It can't. There are too many people depending on me to keep them safe.' He raked a hand through his hair, feeling ill suddenly. 'Farulf wouldn't send her into battle.' That part was for his own benefit.

'She's a warrior. She would fight alongside the others.'

There was that nausea again.

Tolly strode off towards the boundary, eager to soothe himself by seeing and hearing something different from what his brother was claiming. He reached the perimeter within minutes, stopping beside one of the flags and looking down the hill. Cold moonlight illuminated the landscape, casting strange shadows across the ground. A moment later, Ryder slowly stepped up beside him, a hand resting on the hilt of his sword as he looked towards the trees at the bottom, lit up by the campfires. The hum of conversation drifted up to meet them.

'You're not technically allowed to fight alongside my army unless you receive explicit orders from your warden to do so,' Tolly said. 'Isn't that what Alveye said in his letter?'

'That's what he said.' Ryder nodded slowly. 'I can only act in self-defence or to protect other members of the unit.'

'A unit presently made up of you and Tatum, since Hadewaye and Alveye are being detained. I thought Shapur would have let them return to monitor the situation.'

'I don't pretend to understand the workings of Shapur's mind. Perhaps he misses Hadewaye and wants to keep him around.'

A ghost of a smile passed over Tolly's face.

'While I can't go charging across the border with you, I'll be ready if they cross.'

Tolly met his gaze. 'One is an act of war, the other an act of self-defence. Is that how that works?'

'Exactly.'

The trees on either side of them swayed in the wind, their branches reaching in the dark.

'What do you think?' Ryder asked, eyes ahead. 'Is there a storm brewing?'

Tolly swallowed down the acid rising up his throat. 'I think you should rouse Tatum. And send a messenger to Chadora.'

~

Farulf marched between the tents with a determined expression on his face as he delivered orders to his warriors. Lina watched him from Trinka's campfire, feeling more helpless than she ever had in her life. They were creeping towards sunrise. Soon, she would have to wake her brother, whom she had forced to sleep, and tell him it was time to take up arms.

'I'll be with him,' Trinka said across the flames. 'No soldier will get to him with me in the way.'

Lina looked over at her friend, who had finished sharpening her axe with a whetstone and was now working her way through her collection of knives.

'These soldiers have been trained by defenders,' Lina reminded her.

Trinka simply shrugged. 'And your brother was trained by the chieftain of the Wolfvanir. It always sounds so much more impressive than the reality.' She paused to test the blade. 'He'll be fine if he follows through with all that he's been taught.'

That made Lina feel slightly better, as Trinka rarely had faith in anybody.

'He has a keen eye,' Trinka continued, 'but, more importantly, the ability to think fast. It might be his first battle, but it's not his first time outsmarting people.'

The pure comfort in her words had Lina weeping on the inside. She was the one who was always telling him it took more than strength to be a great warrior. 'You're right.'

'Every warrior starts with their first battle. Simian is no different. Once he's out there genuinely fearing for his life, he will suddenly remember every technique and trick he's ever been taught.'

Lina gave her a grateful smile. 'And what about you? Will you be all right?'

Trinka held up her knife, inspecting it in the light from the fire. 'I'll be just fine, because I'll have the clan's best archer watching my back.' She gave Lina a pointed look.

'Maybe I should have made myself sleep too.'

'At the very least, go prepare.' Trinka looked up at the sky. 'The sun will be up in an hour.'

Lina rose and walked around the fire to Trinka, hugging her tightly from behind. 'I'll see you soon.'

Not one for emotional fusses, Trinka simply nodded, then picked up the next knife in line for sharpening. 'We'll go to the sea when this is over. Or perhaps the river by then.'

She was referring to the River Teifi. If they gained the territory they were fighting for, they would have access to it as well.

Tolly's face came to mind, his white teeth flashing in the dark at something she said. She could almost feel the whisper of his breath on her skin from his soft laugh. Shaking the image from her head, she went to leave.

'You'll take care of Aife, won't you?' Trinka said suddenly.

Lina stopped and looked back.

'If something happens to me?'

It almost sounded like fear, but Trinka did not know fear. That made her words even more unsettling.

'Nothing's going to happen to you,' Lina assured her. 'And never ask me a question like that again. Family always takes care of family.'

Trinka dropped her gaze and nodded. 'I'll see you soon.'

When Lina arrived at her tent, she found her father seated before the fire, preparing his weapons as well. Her gaze went to the cup of steaming liquid by his foot. He had made himself willow bark tea. Lina picked up her quiver and sat beside him, checking every arrow.

'It helps,' Farulf said without looking up. 'If that's what you're wondering.'

Lina looked over at him, then down at the cup. 'The tea?'

He nodded.

'Good. I'm pleased.'

He extended a hand in her direction, then opened and closed his fingers. 'It might not look too different, but I can feel it.'

The willow bark had been Tolly's suggestion, and now that tea meant her father would be a stronger fighter on the day he came for their land. She did not know whether to laugh or cry on his behalf.

The crackling of burning wood was the only sound from their campfire after that. The weight of the impending battle was enormous on both of them.

When the first signs of daylight appeared on the horizon, Farulf took some charcoal from the fire and ground it into a fine powder. He gestured for Lina to come closer and used it to darken her eyes. They had fought side by side over the years, but nothing like what they were about to undertake. The stakes were high and their enemy strong. A sad smile passed between them, a silent acknowledgement of what was ahead of them.

The peaceful moment was shattered by the sound of footsteps entering their camp.

The Vargr had arrived.

Farulf got to his feet and gestured towards the tent. 'Get Simian up. Tell him I've prepared his weapons.'

Lina dashed into the tent, where she found Simian already

up and dressed. He wore a long wool tunic with intricate patterns woven in gold thread. Over that, he had a leather chest plate. His legs were protected by leather and fur, his feet by heavy boots.

'I'm up,' he said.

Lina crossed the mat to him, taking a firm hold of his shoulders. 'Listen to me.' Her eyes locked on his. 'The time for self-pity and doubt has passed. You've had your moment and said your piece. Now it's time to connect with the warrior inside you, the fierce and skilled fighter. It's in your blood, you just have to reach for it.'

Simian's expression was a mix of surprise and uncertainty. 'I'm not like you—'

'Stop it.' She practically shook him. 'You've had the same training I did. You have the same knowledge and skills, even if they're not as refined as you would like. All that's missing is the *courage*.' She searched his eyes. 'Don't think of it as the courage to kill but rather the courage to endure what's coming and survive. If you've ever wondered what it's like to be one of the warriors you admire, then now's the time to find out. You rise the hell up and show everyone what your brilliant mind can achieve.'

Simian seemed taken aback by her unexpected little speech. When he opened his mouth to speak, she stopped him with a shake of her head. 'No more words. I want to see it.'

He gave her a confused look. 'What?'

She tapped on his chest with two sharp fingers. 'The warrior. Where is he? Show me.'

'I don't think—'

She pushed him. 'Where is he?'

'Lina—'

She pushed him again. 'Where?'

'Enough.' Lina went to push him again, but he caught hold of her wrist this time and shouted, 'I said enough!'

Her eyes moved between his as she witnessed the shift within him. 'Now let it consume you. Let it guide your hand and lend you strength.'

The flap of the tent was pulled back, and their father appeared as a silhouette against the grey light behind him. He looked between the two of them. 'It's time.'

CHAPTER 32

Tolly had not liked what he was hearing from the enemy camp, but he grew more unsettled when he could hear nothing at all. He walked the boundary with Ryder and Tatum. The sound of weapons being sharpened no longer rang out.

'I know you already have 50 percent of your men along this border,' Tatum said, 'but I think you should have the entire camp on alert.'

Tolly looked at Ryder, who gave a small nod of agreement. 'All right. Let's put the entire camp on full alert. Have the cavalry prepare their horses, just in case.'

The sun had almost reached the horizon, and shadows were forming around the camp. Tolly returned to the tents to give orders to each of the commanders. He remained in the centre of the activity, watching as his orders were repeated to the bleary-eyed soldiers coming out of their tents. The atmosphere was charged with a sense of urgency as the soldiers sprang into action. Soon, the rhythmic clanging of blacksmiths rang out across the camp while archers gathered to inspect their bows and restock their quivers. The infantry put on armour and strapped on their weapons. The absence of conversation added to the growing tension in the air.

Tolly shouted commands at different groups, ensuring their enemy could not invade from another direction. He had seen first-hand how capable they were of making themselves invisible. The decisions he made would determine the safety of the camp. They had been preparing for this possibility since their arrival. Every person knew their role. It was time for Tolly to trust their plans and the men in command and return to the boundary where he was needed most.

The sun emerged the same time he did, casting an eerie glow across the hill separating the two camps. Ryder stood in his black uniform, shoulders stiff with tension as he scanned the empty expanse beyond. There was not a single warrior in sight, and the silence was possibly the most unsettling thing he had ever heard.

'Where are the warriors who normally patrol the border?' Tolly asked, looking around.

Ryder glanced in his direction. 'Gone.'

'But where?'

'According to your men, they dispersed among the trees an hour ago and haven't been seen since.'

An uneasy feeling settled in Tolly's chest. It was the same feeling he got at the beach when the water suddenly disappeared, signalling an enormous wave was on its way. The absence of any opposition was more ominous than a fully armed clan in sight.

Ryder shifted his weight. 'We have the entire perimeter covered. If they come, we'll know about it.'

Nodding, Tolly fixed his gaze on the horizon.

'They have soldiers all along the perimeter,' Sture hissed at Farulf, approaching like a storm cloud. 'They know.'

Lina was a few feet away, eyes on Simian. It was her job to provide cover for the warriors going ahead. They were hidden in the trees to the east of the camp, preparing to cross the stream.

'They would have known the moment you pulled the warriors from the boundary,' Farulf pointed out.

Sture raised his shield in the camp's direction. 'Those soldiers arrived before we did. I withdrew them for their safety.' His gaze went to Lina, his expression darkening. 'You warned them.'

She was so taken aback by the accusation that it took her a moment to respond. 'What? No.'

'You sent word to your lover.'

She shook her head. 'That's not true. I haven't seen him.'

'Since you whored yourself out to him?'

'*Enough*,' Farulf growled, his voice low and dangerous. 'Your accusation is completely unfounded. I suggest you watch what you say.'

Somehow, Lina still felt guilty. Not because she had done anything wrong, but because she had been tempted to.

'We can't allow tension to escalate between our clans,' Farulf said, 'especially at such a critical time.'

Sture continued to stare at Lina. 'You are right. Now is not the time.' His distrust of her was evident in his eyes. 'We will uncover the truth later, when I have the general strung up from that tree over there.' He pointed.

Farulf did not indulge him any further. 'If we're moving in, we need to do it now, while their attention and numbers are still divided. They may be expecting us, but they don't yet know which direction we'll be coming from.'

Sture walked over to Lina, bringing his face close to hers. 'I am going to break both his legs so he cannot run from me. Then I am going to keep him alive until he begs me to kill him. You will have no choice but to watch.'

The sound of a sword being drawn made Lina flinch. The tip of her father's weapon was pointed at Sture's neck. 'From now on, you don't speak to her.'

Sture slowly turned his head to meet Farulf's gaze.

'I'll fight alongside you today,' her father said. 'I owe you that. I've given my word.' Every muscle in his face was tense. 'After we take Cardiganshire, our business will be done.'

Lina held her breath as the two chieftains stared each other down. As terrifying as those moments were, she also felt an enormous amount of relief that her father was more himself than he had been in a long time.

'We fight as family and depart as strangers,' Sture said, taking a step back.

The tension finally dissipated.

Sture returned to his men, his feet silent on the ground.

Lina exchanged a brief glance with her father. Anything they needed to say would be said later. They had more important things to focus on, like keeping Simian alive.

When Lina looked back at her brother, she found him still crouched safely behind his shield, alongside the other warriors. They were all focused on what was ahead of them, knowing better than to give in to distraction as they awaited the signal. Lina knew Trinka would be somewhere nearby, even if she could not see her.

Sture raised his hand, signalling to one of the warriors in the first line. The warrior rose to his feet and shouted, 'Tyr!'

The fighters leapt up and burst from the trees, charging into the water below.

A collective roar cut through the still air, drawing the attention of every soldier within hearing range.

'Eastern perimeter,' Ryder said, taking off at a run towards it.

A horn sounded, confirming it.

'Do not take your eyes off this boundary!' Tolly shouted to the men he passed. 'No matter what you hear, do not leave your post unless ordered to!'

The men responded with a resounding 'Yes, sir!'

Tolly heard the warriors before he saw them. They stampeded through the water, faces painted and axes beating against their shields, announcing their arrival. Then up the hill they charged, straight towards his men standing in a formation along the boundary.

'Oh shit,' Ryder muttered.

Tolly searched the faces below, then stilled. 'Is that Trinka?'

'Not just Trinka,' Ryder said. 'Simian.'

Heart racing, Tolly found Simian among the warriors climbing the hill, barely recognisable due to the fierce expression he was wearing. He immediately began searching for Lina.

'I can't see her,' Ryder said, putting his mind at ease.

Tolly reminded himself to breathe.

'The second they cross, I'm fighting,' Ryder said. 'Is that what you want?'

The protection of his men had to remain his priority. 'Nothing's changed.'

Ryder drew his sword. 'Kill them?'

The reply stuck in Tolly's throat. 'Yes.' He drew his weapon, eyes ahead. 'Hold the line! No one gets through!'

A chorus of affirmations echoed back at him as the first wave of warriors reached the boundary. Their collective battle cry resounded through the valley, shaking the very air he breathed. Their weapons met in a violent clash, a blur of glinting silver. The warriors' faces contorted in concentration, their movements as fluid and precise as the soldiers'.

Tatum arrived on horseback, having come from the south perimeter. He drew his weapon as he leapt from the horse straight into the fighting alongside Ryder.

'I was wondering where you were,' Ryder said, pulling his sword from a warrior's chest. Another replaced him.

Tatum disarmed a man coming at him with an axe. 'A horn *prior* to people dying would have been helpful.'

A shield flew overhead, and Ryder ducked to avoid it. 'We were at the northern boundary and still managed to beat you here.'

How the pair could carry out a conversation midfight, Tolly had no idea. It took every ounce of his concentration and energy to not die. As soon as he disarmed an opponent, another would replace him.

His rhythm was lost when a female warrior appeared before him, his own hesitation tripping him. She slammed her shield into his shoulder, and he responded by driving his boot into her stomach, sending her flying backwards into another warrior.

Tolly raised his sword as he turned, coming face to face with Simian. He was bleeding from the head, eyes wild. Tolly's weapon remained suspended in the air, and the fire in Simian's eyes dulled for a brief moment. It soon became clear that they were incapable of killing each other despite being equally duty-bound. It was as if Tolly had forgotten how to fight. Thankfully, another sword came his way, drawing him away from Simian and into a fight. But the relief was short-lived as he looked into the eyes of his new opponent.

'It's all right, General,' Trinka said, circling him. 'I'll make it quick.'

Lina was across the stream behind a line of warriors with shields, preparing to move forwards. Her father was in the group behind, axe in hand, ready to storm the hill if the warriors in front failed to break through the perimeter.

The nausea Lina felt grew more intense the longer she watched the fighting go on. She was desperate for another glimpse of her brother but kept losing sight of him. The deafening clash of weapons and agonised cries filled her ears, making it difficult to focus.

She almost gasped when her gaze landed on Tolly. She had known he would be there, that he would fight, but the visual still threw her. Her stomach dropped when she saw Trinka standing opposite him, weapon turning in her hands as she prepared to engage. Trinka was not one to hesitate on a battlefield, but she was hesitating in that moment. They were circling each other as though they had all the time in the world for a prelude, as if people were not bleeding out around them.

The bow shook slightly in Lina's hand as she searched for Simian again, and relief rolled over her when she spotted him. He was still on his feet, which was the key to remaining alive. But her relief was short-lived as she watched a soldier shove him to the ground. His shield splintered under the force of the assault that followed. She clutched her bow tightly, fighting the urge to run towards him. She could not do it, as she had her own part to play in this battle.

'Archers ready!' she heard her father shout behind her. 'Shields down!'

She was ready when the shields dropped, taking aim at the soldier standing over Simian. Her arrow sailed through the air with deadly precision, finding its mark in the soldier's chest. His body crumpled to the ground.

She had just killed one of Tolly's comrades.

A fresh wave of soldiers emerged, moving in synchrony like a menacing wave. Lina's heart pounded in her chest as she swiftly notched another arrow and took aim.

Hiss, hiss, hiss.

Their arrows targeted the new arrivals, trying to take them out before their own warriors got in the way. Her string went slack beneath her fingers as her gaze returned to the spot where her brother had been. The sounds faded into the background momentarily as she searched for him among the swirling mass of bodies. She could not remember seeing him get up.

Where are you?

Without thinking, Lina broke formation and ran towards the fighting. Her father's distant shouts were drowned out by the roaring rush of blood in her ears. He was telling her to stop, but to stop was to accept Simian's fate, and she could not bear it.

As she sprinted across the battlefield, arrows flew in all directions, stopping only when she reached the fighting. Lina leapt over a dead body, searching the ground as she did so. Every part of her screamed for her brother.

Then she was inside the fight, a legitimate target, like every other warrior around her. She slung her bow over her back and drew her sword, her gaze shifting between the soldiers fighting around her and the bodies on the ground. A sword came at her, and she raised hers in time to block it. An axe struck the soldier's back before he could try again.

Lina looked around at the trampled bodies, her chest tightening with dread. She was searching for anything familiar, trying to see past the mud and awkward angle of a neck or leg.

Amid the chaos and carnage of battle, Lina's gaze landed on a familiar figure in the mud. Simian's chest rose and fell rapidly, his face a mask of pain and exhaustion. She fought her way towards him, every step feeling like an eternity as the clash of weapons and screams of the dying pressed in on her. Then a deafening clang of steel stopped her in her tracks. She turned her head to see two swords locked together a few inches from her face. One belonged to a soldier, the other to Trinka. With an almighty groan, Trinka shoved the man back.

'Go,' she said. 'I'll cover you.'

Lina ducked down and ran the final three yards to her brother, dropping to her knees and taking in the sight of his battered body. Blood seeped from a wound on his side, his breaths now coming in panicked gasps. With no time to waste, she pulled him up into a seated position and drew his arm around her shoulders, blocking out his painful groans.

'I need you to stand up,' she said, her tone firm. 'I need you to get up and walk out of here, because I can't carry you.'

His eyes fixed on hers, full of fear now. 'Am I dying?'

'No.' Though she had no idea if that was true. 'If you're on your feet, you're fine, remember? So use those legs.'

'I can't feel them.'

'Walk anyway. Let's go.'

It took all her strength to get him to his feet, and every muscle in her body worked hard to keep him there. She knew she would not make it if he did not help her.

'Go!' Trinka shouted as she fought off a soldier. 'Get him out of here!'

Lina began dragging him along, but his feet seemed to catch on every lump of earth and broken limb. She could feel the wind created by the weapons flying around her. Safety was far away, and all she could think about was Simian getting shot in the back as they fled.

A warrior slammed into her, throwing her sideways. Her grip on Simian slipped as she struggled to remain upright. The injured warrior's eyes met hers as he collapsed to the ground, blocking their path. Terror gripped her mind. She knew that if she went down, the chances of getting back up again were slim. They would likely be trampled to death. Even Trinka could not help them then.

A firm hand shot out and grabbed her, pulling her upright. Lina found herself face to face with Tolly. His eyes were filled with a fierce determination, his face covered with scrapes. Flecks of blood spattered his cheeks and slicked one side of his hair. He dropped his forehead briefly to hers, a silent gesture, then called over his shoulder to Ryder, 'Cover me.'

With one swift motion, he lifted Simian and draped him over her back, positioning his arms around her shoulders.

'You hold on and do not let go,' he said into Simian's ear. 'Do it for your sister.'

Simian responded by tightening his arms around her.

'Fast as you can go,' Tolly told Lina, helping her over the now-dead warrior in her path.

She snuck a glance at Trinka, who was still fighting. 'They'll shoot us.' Her legs were already struggling beneath the weight.

'They won't. *Go*.'

It did not matter if they were midbattle and all the people he cared about were trying to kill all the people she cared about. If he said no one would shoot them in the back, then she would carry Simian down that hill until he was safely behind shields.

As terrifying as it was to step out into the open, her brother a slow-moving target on her back, that was what she did in order to save his life.

'Archers, hold!' Tolly shouted behind her.

She found the strength. With Simian's feet dragging through the mud behind her, she descended the hill. An arrow struck the earth beside her, making her flinch.

'I said *hold*!' she heard Tolly shout behind her.

They were a quarter of the way there. Then halfway. Her

father was shouting instructions ahead of her, and the wall of shields separated, creating space for them to pass through. Three-quarters of the way there.

'Simian?' Lina said, unable to feel his heart beating against her back and terrified by his silence.

'Mm.'

Her eyes sank shut with relief. 'We're almost there.'

Ahead, she could see her father through the gap, his eyes wide. The second she stepped through the gap, it closed behind her. Then her father was at her side, lifting Simian off her. She collapsed to her knees and thanked all the gods.

And Tolly.

CHAPTER 33

The sea warriors broke through the eastern boundary, claiming the hill and forcing the Carmarthen Militia to retreat to the tents. Tolly lost nearly a hundred men before making the decision to withdraw. It was better to give the warriors the hill than watch more of his soldiers die atop it.

They held the warriors off long enough to retrieve the injured, and the physicians got to work tending to the wounded. Tolly watched the warriors establish a new perimeter, his chest heavy with failure.

'They're not done,' Tatum said, stepping up beside him. 'They didn't do all this for a hill.'

Tolly nodded slowly. 'I know. I've taken some men from the other perimeters to see if we can deter them.'

'They're not fools. They know those soldiers have come from somewhere.'

'Well, anything we can do to slow things down is helpful at this point.'

Tatum nodded. 'I saw what you did earlier. That was quite the risk.'

Tolly did not reply.

'Your men saw it too.' Tatum kept his eyes ahead. 'They look to you, *their leader*. If you hesitate, they hesitate.'

'You saying this is my fault?'

'I'm saying it won't have helped. They can't be expected to know who the enemy is among the enemy.' He shook his head. 'There were at least three people on that battlefield spared due to personal attachments'—he raised his hand before he could be interrupted—'and I understand, but your men can't be expected to.'

A long silence stretched out between them.

'Any word from Chadora?' Tolly eventually asked.

Tatum shook his head. 'It kills me to say this, because my first instinct is to take back the hill from those bastards, but perhaps you should attempt a negotiation.'

'I agree,' Tolly said, his tone defeated.

'You do?'

If he did not try something, the bloodshed would simply continue. 'They wanted to make a point, and they've made it. Maybe now they'll listen.'

'Hope so.' Tatum looked over his shoulder. 'Let's send the messenger.'

'You need to control your daughter,' Sture said to Farulf, a finger pointed in her direction. 'Control her, or I will.'

Farulf tore his gaze from Simian and rounded on the chieftain. 'Worry about your own people. My family is no longer your concern.'

'Unless their actions put the lives of my warriors at risk.'

'She saved her brother's life!'

Lina was kneeling on the ground beside Simian, a bloodied cloth pressed to the open wound on his side as she tried to block out the fighting. Trinka paced nervously while Frida threaded a needle. Simian was staring straight up at the sky, his face white and slicked with sweat.

'See any interesting birds?' Lina asked, trying to keep him awake.

'A crow.' His eyes went to hers. 'Do you think that's a bad omen?'

'How many did you see?' Frida asked. 'Two is good luck.'

'Only one.'

Trinka stopped walking. 'What does one mean?'

Frida glanced at Lina before removing the cloth to inspect the wound. 'Just keep watching the sky. You don't want to miss the second one.'

Cursing quietly, Trinka resumed pacing.

'Ready your men,' Sture said to Farulf. 'We are going to take the camp.'

That had Lina looking up. 'We just lost over a hundred warriors between us, and many more are wounded.'

Sture's eyebrows came together in an angry line. 'A delay only benefits them. The Vargr are ready to fight.'

'The warriors need rest,' Toke said, walking over.

Bo was cleaning his weapons nearby and said, 'No, we don't. I'm ready.'

Lina got to her feet, eyes locked with his, but before she

had a chance to argue with him, Knud came jogging up. He stopped before Farulf, out of breath.

'What is it?' Farulf asked.

'It's General Tolly. He wants to speak with you.'

The mere mention of his name had Lina wanting to run to him. Simian was alive because of him. He had risked so much, and she was afraid she would never get the chance to thank him.

Farulf nodded. 'Very well.' He looked over at Simian.

'I will go,' Sture said. 'Let me handle the general, and you remain with your son.'

Lina's stomach fell as she watched Sture pick up his bow and check his weapons. 'He saved Simian's life.'

'And took many in the process,' Sture said without looking at her. 'Do not insult the dead and their families by requesting he be spared. He will die like his soldiers.'

Lina looked at her father, eyes pleading.

'He asked to speak to *me*,' Farulf said. 'I will show him the respect of—'

'Respect?' Sture said, his voice raised. 'Look around you. There are families grieving all around us, and you speak to me of respect.' He walked off.

'We attacked their camp,' Lina said, following him. 'There was a clear border, and we crossed it. What was he supposed to do? Lie down and die?'

'He could have surrendered.'

She ran in front of him, forcing him to pull up. 'Everyone knows the Vargr don't take prisoners. You would have slaughtered him and every person standing with him.'

He brought his face close to hers. '*Move*.'

'Lina,' her father warned. 'I'll go with Sture.'

She stepped aside. 'I'm coming too.' Looking over at her brother, she said, 'Keep looking for that second crow. I'll be back soon.'

When Toke went to follow, Sture said, 'You wait here.'

With a shake of his head, the warrior went to join the other Vargr warriors resting nearby.

Farulf and Sture set off, and Bo and Lina followed. The wind helped carry them up the hill to the new boundary, where a line of warriors stood guard. When they reached the top, the warriors split apart to let the chieftains through, and waiting on the other side was Tolly.

Tolly struggled to look away from her. Her appearance painted a clear picture of what she had endured. The entire left side of her overdress was red, most likely from carrying her brother, as she did not appear to be injured. He did not know if her brother was alive, but that she was standing dry-eyed before him indicated he was. His gaze narrowed on the bloodied line across Lina's face. The already-formed scab meant the injury was at least a day old. He had not noticed it earlier with everything that had been going on.

Her concerned expression suggested she was equally alarmed by his appearance. While he had splashed some water over his face and washed his hands for the meeting, his uniform told a different story.

He tore his gaze from Lina when the chieftains stopped in front of him. Farulf greeted him with a respectful nod, while Sture made no gesture of any kind. His stare was ice cold.

'I'll get straight to the point,' Tolly said. 'Both sides have suffered large losses this morning. You set out to prove a point, and you proved it. Now we need to figure out a better way forwards.'

Sture appeared amused. 'You think we came for that patch of bloodstained grass behind me?'

Tolly glanced over at Tatum and Ryder, who were listening in on the conversation, hands wrapping the hilts of their weapons. 'I think it's no accident that we find ourselves cut off from the only water supply in this region.'

The chieftain gave a satisfied nod. 'While that is good news indeed, it is only the beginning.'

He had been afraid of that. 'You want more land, is that it?'

Farulf cut it. 'You called us here, General. What is it you wanted to say?'

'I'd hoped we could end the senseless killing.'

Nothing changed on Sture's face. 'We would agree to that if you were willing to pack up your fancy tents and march your army back to the River Teifi.'

Tolly's gaze flicked to Lina, who was standing completely still. 'You know I can't do that.'

'Then this conversation is over,' Sture said.

Tolly looked at Farulf. 'Is the conversation over for you also?'

It was clear from the way Sture's entire body stiffened that he did not like that. 'If you mean to turn us against each other, General, it will not work. Our clans have a long history.'

'It must be one hell of a history if you're prepared to let so many die for it.' He met Farulf's gaze once more. 'Even if you succeed in this grab for land, who will be left to feed?'

'We are done here,' Sture said. 'Take your guard dogs and move back.'

The temptation to kill him right there on the spot, even knowing he would likely die moments later, was so very tempting. 'I have one more question.'

'What?' Sture hissed, his patience running thin.

Tolly looked at Lina. 'What happened to your face?'

She did not have to say one word. The answer was there in her ashen face and averted gaze.

He drew a calming breath. 'I see.'

'I watched Lina shoot dead one of your soldiers earlier,' Sture said, attempting to poke the bear. 'She is quite the little archer, do you agree?'

Lina pressed her eyes closed.

'We've all said our part,' Farulf said. 'We're done here.'

Sture looked over at the defenders. 'I will see you all very soon.' With that, he turned and disappeared between the warriors.

Farulf remained there for a moment, not saying anything. It might have been that he did not know what to say or could not say it with all the Vargr within earshot.

'Are you going to let your daughter end up like your son?' Tolly asked, trying one last time to appeal to Farulf's common sense. But his words had no effect, as the chieftain walked off, stopping at the warriors to wait for Lina to follow.

Lina looked at Tolly, her eyes full of tears. 'Simian's alive because of you.' She sniffed. 'When do you think this debt of ours will be settled?'

He might have smiled if the situation had not been so dire and tragic. 'Perhaps never.'

She nodded. 'Well, I owe you.'

'Lina,' her father called.

She slowly made her way over to him, then turned

suddenly. 'I'm not marrying him. Not anymore. I realise that changes nothing, but I wanted you to know.'

The relief he felt was enormous. 'Good.' That was all he could manage.

'It turns out we're not very suited,' she said. 'Who knew?'

A weak smile came and went on his face. He would have given anything to go to her in that moment, to comfort and protect her. But he remained where he was.

'Come, Lina,' her father said, his tone firmer that time.

Her feet obeyed, but her eyes remained on Tolly. He took a step after her, but a simple clearing of Ryder's throat stopped him from taking another one. The warriors closed the gap, and Lina was gone from his sight.

CHAPTER 34

'I want all but a handful of watchers here and ready to fight,' Tolly told a commander as he hurried between the tents.

The commander frowned up at him. 'You think they'll strike today?'

'I think they'll do whatever they want.'

'Surely they need time to tend their wounded and feed their warriors as well.'

Tolly looked west. 'I'm sure they do, but I don't think Sture is prioritising the wellbeing of his fighters right now. Get them ready.'

The commander saluted before striding away.

Over the next half hour, soldiers began arriving from other parts of the camp, their heavy footsteps building to a chorus as they formed precise lines in front of the tents. Their weapons gleamed beneath the sun as it made its way overhead. Tolly stood at the forefront, his gaze sweeping over the ranks of men.

'That's all of them?' Ryder asked, stepping up beside him.

'All but a handful.'

They watched as the soldiers adjusted their armour and weapons while exchanging quiet words with one another. Occasionally, the distant sounds of clanging metal carried on the wind, a reminder of the looming threat that could strike at any moment. The two brothers walked the length of the front line, eyeing the warriors in the distance.

'I'm going to ask you again,' Ryder said, 'if any part of the strategy has changed.' He stopped walking and turned to Tolly. 'Because clearly it had by the time you stepped onto that battlefield.'

Tolly could not pretend anymore. He had exposed himself earlier when he not only spared Lina and Simian from certain death but Trinka too.

'You were never going to fight Lina,' Ryder said. 'Never could. Never will.'

Tolly squinted in the direction of the warriors. 'Tatum's right in what he said to me earlier. I'm supposed to be leading these men, but I'm too weak to—'

'You're not weak,' Ryder said. 'I won't stand here and listen to you beat yourself up because you can't *kill* the woman you love, or her brother, or her closest friend.' He paused. 'You can be tragically in love and still lead these men just fine.'

The weight of his brother's words settled over him like a comforting cloak. He knew how to squash doubt and fear.

A rumble of thunder sounded, and Tolly looked up at the dark storm clouds gathering overhead. 'At least the rain will wash the blood away.'

'That's the spirit,' Ryder said.

Tolly turned back to the soldiers, who stood ready for the imminent clash. Drawing his sword, he raised it high. 'Today we face an enemy who seeks to take everything we have fought to build.' His voice carried across the assembled soldiers. 'They won't take an inch more of the land we stand on. They've not earned that right. We're the ones who starved and suffered through the famine for the right to stand here. We don't seek to claim it. We fight to protect it and the people who've earned the right to live here peacefully.' He pointed towards the warriors. 'Like the English, they wish only to exploit the land. They want to take whatever they can fit into their longships at the end of the summer, then leave the land for us to replenish.' He walked slowly along the line of men, eye to eye. 'This fight isn't just about borders. It's about showing the world, once and for all, that we belong here. This land was ours when there was nothing here, and it will be ours when it's flourishing, because we'll care for it through every season. We turned the wastelands into a thriving kingdom built from mud and bone.'

A resounding cheer erupted from the soldiers, their hunger forgotten and spirits renewed. But the mood was dampened by the arrival of Commander Ithon. He walked up to Ryder and said something in his ear before jogging away. Tolly turned to his brother, waiting. Waiting and knowing.

'Great speech,' Ryder said. 'And well timed.' His expression was almost apologetic. 'They're preparing their warriors.'

Tolly nodded. 'Here we go again.'

~

Rain had just begun to fall when Sture went to tell Farulf to ready his fighters. 'Archers at the front,' he said. Then he looked over at Simian. 'Can he hold a sword?'

Even Trinka was taken aback by that question. 'He can't even *stand.*'

Frida, who was still tending to Simian, stepped in front of him. 'He won't be fighting for some time. Nor will any of the other injured men and women before you.'

She was including the many Vargr warriors in that statement.

Sture looked around, nodding. 'We will do just fine without them.' His gaze went to Lina. 'Fetch your bow and replenish your quiver. You will be in the first line.'

Lina felt hot and cold all at once. It was not that she was afraid to die but afraid to kill.

'Lina will remain here and take care of her brother,' Farulf said. 'She will not be fighting.'

The Vargr chieftain squared his shoulders. 'She is able-bodied and therefore must do her part like every other warrior.'

The two men stared each other down.

'I can shoot a bow,' Trinka said. 'I'll take her place.'

Sture was not having it. 'You will fight alongside her, not instead of her.'

'It's too soon,' Farulf said. 'We should be letting our people rest and putting together a proper plan.'

'While the Carmarthen Militia work on theirs? Are you so intent on dying? The Vargr are here, in this godforsaken place, because *you* wanted our help. You brought us here, and now you expect us to starve alongside you?'

Heat climbed Farulf's neck.

'It's fine,' Lina said, attempting to defuse the situation. They were dealing with enough conflict. 'I'll get my bow.'

Satisfied, Sture turned away.

Lina returned to Simian's side and took hold of his hand, squeezing it. 'Rest. I'll see you when this is over.'

Tears filled Simian's eyes. 'Make sure you don't miss. I couldn't bear it if I was here at the end and you weren't.'

'Even if she does miss,' Trinka said, picking up her bow, 'I sure as hell won't.'

Lina forced a smile for her brother's benefit. 'Keep your eyes on the sky. I'll be back before you know it.'

He grabbed her hand when she moved to leave. Looking down at his whitening knuckles, she covered his hand with her own. Neither of them spoke. She simply waited for his grip to ease, then rose.

'See you soon,' he said.

Somehow, she smiled through the burn in her throat as she went to get her bow. Trinka waited for her, and then the two of them climbed the hill to where two hundred archers were gathered beneath a wall of warriors. Knud was among them. He greeted Lina with a nod as she stepped up beside him. The rain was getting heavier, making their bows slippery.

'This fucking rain will be the end of us,' Knud grunted beside her.

Lina looked over her shoulder, surprised to find her father coming towards her, bow in hand. 'What are you doing up here?'

He stepped between Lina and Knud. 'You're not fighting without me by your side.' His eyes met hers briefly.

Lina swallowed. It was the most fatherly thing he had

done in some time, and it took all her strength not to fall to pieces because of it.

A horn signal pierced the air, making everyone look around.

'A little late for a warning, isn't it?' Knud said. 'Both sides are ready to engage.'

Lina raised a hand. 'Quiet.' She listened, hearing a faint sound in the distance. It seemed to be growing louder with each passing second. The ground beneath her boots began to vibrate, sending tremors up her legs. Her father was immediately on alert.

'What is that?' Trinka asked.

Farulf exchanged a concerned look with Knud. 'Marching.'

An army was approaching. An army so large, their footsteps reverberated through the ground they stood on.

The archers shifted nervously, exchanging uneasy glances. Farulf's grip tightened on his bow when he saw the warriors in front back up a few steps, their gazes fixed on the horizon.

Sture arrived, pushing through the archers and heading for the crest of the hill. Farulf and Knud followed, prompting Lina to do the same.

'You can't leave me behind,' Trinka said, running to catch up to her.

When Lina reached the top of the hill, her eyes widened at the sight before her. A wave of soldiers and horses was pouring over the hill behind the camp. Their black armour made them look like an ominous cloud under the dark sky. Their red banners waved defiantly.

'Chadorian defenders,' her father said, standing tall beside her.

Lina looked over at Sture, whose face was tense as he

watched their approach. The atmosphere felt suffocating as fear gripped everyone around her. Trinka swore aloud, multiple times. No one seemed to notice or care. They were too busy bracing for what was coming their way.

'We're all going to die,' Knud said, sounding perfectly calm.

'We're not going to die,' Lina replied, 'because we're not going to fight an army of defenders.' She looked to her father for confirmation. 'Right?'

Before he could answer, Sture shouted, 'Archers forward! We hold this line!'

Lina and Trinka exchanged a look of disbelief.

'We'll be dead within minutes,' Knud said.

Lina reached for her father. 'You need to stop this madness.'

He did not respond.

'Back in formation!' Sture shouted at Lina.

Trinka pulled her back, fingers entwining with hers in a silent gesture of comfort.

Knud began backing up. 'May the gods have mercy on our souls.'

'You may want to have a word with your men about their signals,' Tatum said, joining Tolly and Ryder. 'That warning was about an hour too late.'

'It came from the other side of the camp,' Ryder said. 'Perhaps there's a second threat.'

Tatum glanced in that direction. 'I just completed a full

check of the perimeter, and no one has seen a warrior on that side all day.'

Tolly rubbed his forehead, which was pounding. 'There's no cover for them along the eastern perimeter. They're unlikely to attack from that side.'

Ryder was no longer listening, his focus elsewhere. 'Can you hear that?'

They all fell silent. Tolly heard it then, the sound of horses and many boots on the ground. The three men exchanged concerned looks when they felt the ground tremble slightly beneath their feet. The soldiers in formation no longer appeared confident as they realised the magnitude of the incoming threat.

'We need horses!' Tolly shouted, running towards the mounted soldiers at the back. Ryder and Tatum followed.

The three of them were handed horses and were galloping between the tents a moment later, kicking up mud in their wake. They dodged startled soldiers and skidded to a halt as they reached the edge of the camp.

'Well, that's a sight I thought I'd never see,' Tatum said.

Ryder released a long breath. 'Defenders.'

From the east, a sea of soldiers in black uniforms descended the hill in perfect formation. Their presence brought a renewed sense of hope. Every prayer Tolly had uttered that day was being answered. The Chadorian army had left their walls behind to come and fight alongside them.

His thoughts went to Lina. He reminded himself that defenders were the most disciplined army in the world. Their presence was enough. It was unlikely they would even need to draw their weapons.

As the army drew closer, Tolly spotted Alveye and Hadewaye at the front with two commanders. 'Who are the men riding alongside Alveye and Hadewaye?'

Tatum relaxed the reins of his horse. 'On the left is Harlan Wright.'

'The warden's son?'

He nodded.

'And on the right is Roul Thornton,' Ryder said. 'The man who trained us.'

Tolly had heard plenty of stories about Roul over the years but never met him.

Hadewaye broke away from the group when he spotted them and cantered towards them. Tolly had never been so happy to see his grinning face.

'Did we miss it?' he asked, pulling his horse up.

'If by "it", you're referring to our death on the battlefield, then no,' Tatum said. 'Your timing is spot-on.'

Ryder steadied his excited horse. 'Could have used your help earlier, though.'

'Hopefully, the one thousand soldiers we brought back with us will make up for the inconvenience,' Hadewaye replied. He looked past them. 'I can smell the blood. How bad was it?'

'Bad,' replied all three of them.

'And they're preparing to attack again,' Tatum added.

'I suspect they're rethinking that plan at present,' Hadewaye said. Then his expression turned serious. 'Queen Charlotte is worried about you, by the way. She was going to accompany us here, but we convinced her to wait for you in Lampeter.'

Tatum appeared relieved. 'I'm pleased she listens to one of us.'

Hadewaye gestured behind him. 'It took an army of defenders, mind you.'

The four men watched as the thousand-strong army split down the middle to bypass the tents. Tolly thought about how terrified Lina would be, watching from behind enemy lines.

'Let's go,' Tolly said, digging his heels into his horse's sides. Perhaps the clans would be fleeing into the trees by the time they got there, or maybe even their longboats. He had to remind himself that watching her leave was better than watching her die.

When they reached the other side of the camp, the Chadorian defenders and Carmarthen Militia merged into one unified force. The defenders filled in the spaces around the soldiers, as if they had rehearsed it all prior to coming.

Tolly made his way to the front, unsettled by the silence. The defenders did not speak. Their commanders did not utter a word. They simply held their position and watched the warriors lined up before them.

Tolly searched for Lina but did not see her. He hoped she was far away from the conflict this time, safe with her brother.

That hope burst when a gap opened in the line of warriors and Sture stepped through, gaze sweeping the length of the two armies. Before the line closed, Tolly spotted Lina a few yards back, bow in hand. Her eyes locked with his, her broken expression morphing into one of slight panic before the gap closed again and she was gone from sight.

It was unsettling the way the defenders arrived in silence, filling up every inch of space and siphoning all the air until there was nothing left for the warriors to breathe. It was not only the sheer number of them that was intimidating, nor the quantity of weapons strapped to their bodies, but their matching expressions and the way they spaced themselves exactly two feet apart. The intimidation came from the disciplined way in which they conducted themselves.

'Assure them we'll advance no further.' That had been the last thing Farulf had said to Sture before the chieftain stepped forwards.

The chieftains had been arguing right up to that moment. Sture was behaving like the arrival of the Chadorian defenders changed nothing, when every person there knew their presence changed *everything*.

'Your father learned this lesson the hard way,' Farulf had said, his voice low. 'Don't repeat his mistakes.'

Sture's expression had changed upon hearing that, but Lina could not tell if the change was good or bad.

Now she held her breath as he stepped forwards to address the enemy. Whatever he said next would affect them all.

As the warriors separated to let Sture through, Lina saw Tolly through the gap. Their eyes met. They had a habit of finding each other at the most desperate times. The intensity of his gaze made her panic a little. It was as if he knew something of her fate she did not. Then he was gone from sight, and the panic only increased when she realised it might be the last time that happened.

'The silence is making my skin crawl,' Trinka whispered beside her.

Lina took a small step forwards so she could peer through a gap.

Sture's gaze swept the length of the army. 'It is a long walk from Chadora to stand silent before me.'

Lina expected one of the commanders on horseback, identifiable by their gold pins, to reply. Instead, it was Tolly's voice she heard.

'There's little to say and plenty for you to do, like turn around and collect your families from the camp on your way to Llangrannog.'

'Once there,' Tatum said, 'you can climb into your boats and sail away.'

Sture stared across the mud at him.

Farulf walked forwards, stepping between the warriors and going to stand beside Sture. 'Will we have safe passage to Llangrannog?' he asked when Sture did not speak.

Lina crept closer to get a better view.

'You will,' Tolly replied.

It was the best outcome they could have hoped for in that situation. No more death. No more fighting. Just her shattered heart scattered across the mud as a result of the separation.

She kept telling herself she was grateful. Everyone she loved most in the world was still alive. Including Tolly.

'Warriors ready!'

It took Lina a moment to register those two words from Sture's mouth. *Warriors... ready?* It sounded like a war cry instead of a retreat.

'Wolfvanir, stand down!' Those words came from her father's mouth at the same time the Vargr drew their weapons, creating one of the most confusing scenes she had ever been a part of. Knud and Trinka also drew their weapons amid the confusion.

'Stand down!' Farulf shouted. 'Warriors, stand down!'

Trinka was looking around, her breaths coming fast.

'Weapons on the ground!' her father instructed.

The bow slipped from Lina's fingers as the collective sound of a thousand swords being drawn rang out across the battlefield.

'Are we fighting or retreating?' Knud shouted, turning his axe in his hand.

Sture raised his own axe. 'Vargr with me!'

Toke came running to the front. 'Have you lost your mind? You're going to get us all killed.' He looked around. 'Put your weapons down!'

Some of the Vargr listened to him, but many did not. The Wolfvanir warriors were looking around with panicked expressions.

'Cowards!' Sture shouted at Farulf, eyes glinting with anger. He signalled to his warriors. 'Vargr with me!'

Those who had not laid down their weapons emitted an almighty roar as they foolishly charged forwards. They did not stand a chance against the army calmly waiting to receive them. Sture was sending his clan to their death.

When she looked back at Trinka, she saw that her friend was still holding on to her weapon. Lina ran over and tore it from her hand, throwing it on the ground. 'If you're armed, they'll kill you. We need to get out of h—'

A warrior running uphill slammed into her, knocking her six feet before she hit the ground. Trinka ran to her, pulling her to her feet.

'We need to go—now.'

A line of defenders was now moving forwards to face the Vargr.

'Wolfvanir!' Farulf was shouting. 'Retreat!'

Their clan members tried but were swept towards the battle by the incoming Vargr. Some could not even hear Farulf's instructions and were still holding on to their weapons.

'Keep going,' Trinka said, pushing Lina forwards. 'I'll be right behind you.'

Panic filled Lina's chest as she watched Trinka run off to help some clan members who were being crushed. She was quickly swallowed up by the crowd.

Lina flinched when the first clash of steel reverberated around her. The scene was dissolving into a whirlwind of chaos and violence. She looked around for her father but could not see him, feeling vulnerable without a weapon.

Fixing her gaze on the trees at the base of the hill, she began weaving through the madness. She had barely made it a few paces when she was knocked backwards to the ground and trampled. She knew all too well what happened to people who stayed down, so she clawed and pushed, trying to get back on her feet, ignoring the pain each time she was stepped on.

As she got to her knees, a horse appeared beside her. She looked and saw Tolly seated upon it. He reached a hand towards her, and she took it immediately, knowing any delay would risk his life too. He took off with her still dangling from the side of the horse, pushing through the remaining warriors making their way to slaughter. The moment they were free of them, Tolly swung her onto the horse behind him. She held on, pressing her eyes shut as cries of agony and desperation faded into the background.

CHAPTER 35

'Stop,' Lina pleaded behind him. 'Stop. They'll kill you.'

Tolly slowed his horse and took in their surroundings. They were halfway between the battleground where she had almost died and the camp where he would most certainly be killed on sight. They were standing on the closest thing to neutral territory they had.

Lina slid off the back of the horse and looked towards the fighting, which could be heard clearly from where they stood. 'I shouldn't have left them.'

'You had to get out there.'

She turned in a circle, her breathing shallow. 'Trinka went back to help. I should have gone with her.'

Tolly dismounted and went to her, taking a firm hold of her shoulders. 'Breathe.'

'They'll kill him.'

'Your father?'

'Yes, my father!'

'He laid his weapons down. He told his clan to retreat. They won't kill him.'

She pulled free of his grip. 'The defenders wouldn't have heard that. No one could hear him over the sound of my people dying gruesome deaths.'

He reached for her again, and she stepped back.

'You knew what would happen when you sent for them,' she said, eyes brimming with tears.

'Do you honestly think I have any say over what the Chadorian army does? They brought *themselves* here.'

Her hands went over her face. 'Please take me back.'

'Not a chance in hell. You're going to return to your brother. You can wait for them there.'

Whereas he *had* to go back. He was the general of the Carmarthen Militia, for God's sake. A general who had disappeared in the middle of a battle to save the woman he refused to let die. All while his soldiers remained there at risk. Not that his men were doing much at that time. They could not even get to the front line. The defenders were an efficient killing machine, and the most helpful thing the Carmarthen Militia could do was protect the rear and stay out of their way.

'Then what?' Lina asked him.

'Then you'll be safe.'

'And then what?' she repeated.

He understood what she was asking then. 'Then we celebrate the fact that you're alive, and I get to love you from afar, for years to come, comforted by the fact that I got to save you one more time.'

She started to cry. 'It's all such a mess.'

Stepping up to her, he wrapped his arms around her, cradling her head to his chest while the sounds of battle drifted down to them—the scrape of metal, the screams of the wounded and dying. Lina's tears mixed with the mud and blood on his uniform as he held her tightly, trying to shield her from the noise. They had fought fate to be together, and they had lost. Even though they had both known they would, it was still crushing.

When Lina lifted her red-rimmed eyes to his, he kissed her, stealing a brief respite from the violence and grief. She tasted of blood and salt, and it fit them perfectly.

Breaking the kiss, he steadied his breathing. 'I have to go.' He pressed his forehead to hers. 'Promise me you'll go to your brother.'

Her face contorted as fresh tears arrived, but she nodded.

Movement in Tolly's peripheral vision had him pulling Lina behind him. Barely ten yards away, Queen Charlotte and her guards sat atop their horses, staring at them. The queen's expression was unreadable, while Ita was visibly shocked. The rest of the queen's guards simply appeared confused. A sea warrior in the arms of a soldier was not something one saw often—or ever.

Charlotte's gaze was fixed on Lina as she continued to process what she was seeing. 'I gather the defenders have everything under control, General Tolly?'

Lina slowly stepped out from behind him, eyes widening as she realised who it was. She wiped at her tear-streaked face. 'General Tolly was just leaving, Your Majesty.'

Charlotte blinked. 'I see.'

'What are you doing in a war zone?' Tolly asked, looking accusingly at Ita. 'It's not safe for you to be here.'

'Ensuring my husband does not die,' the queen replied. 'I am well guarded.'

'She refused to wait in Lampeter any longer,' Ita said, telling on her.

Charlotte glanced in her direction. 'Thank you for that unnecessary explanation.'

'Go,' Lina said, attempting to appear brave. 'Do what you need to do, and make sure they come back to me.'

Leaving her was difficult, but it was also necessary. He needed to get the queen somewhere safe. 'I'll take you to the eastern perimeter of the camp,' he said, mounting his horse. 'It's the safest place for you. Then I'll return to the front line.'

He led the queen and her party away from the conflict, directing Ita to a safe zone.

By the time he arrived back at the western boundary, the fight was over. The scene before him was as devastating as it had sounded. Their enemy had been defeated, and the Vargr warriors lay twisted and bloodied on the hill. Only those who had laid down their weapons survived.

As Tolly walked his horse through the aftermath, the air was heavy with the foul scent of blood. He stopped when he came across a large figure facedown in the mud. Dismounting, he used his foot to roll the body onto its back.

It was Sture.

'He deserves a thousand more deaths just like it' came Ryder's voice behind him.

Tolly glanced back. 'All this death for the sake of his pride. Who had the honour?'

'Commander Wright. The chieftain went straight for him. He knew exactly who he was targeting.'

That made sense. 'What better way to avenge his father's death than to kill the warden's only son.'

Ryder nodded. 'My thoughts exactly.'

'Where's Farulf?'

The defender gestured down the hill.

Tolly looked in that direction and spotted the chieftain and Trinka leaving with a limping warrior between them. The instant relief Tolly felt, knowing Lina would only have to experience one heartbreak that day, was immense.

'He knew it was hopeless,' Ryder said. 'Most of the Wolf-vanir are alive because of his decision. It's not an easy thing to lay your weapons down before an army that size.'

'No.'

Ryder looked him over before asking, 'Is she safe?'

He licked his lips, tasting her still, then nodded.

The three Chadorian commanders approached, Alveye at the front, with Harlan and Roul following closely behind. Their expressions were suitably grim for the setting they found themselves in.

'This is Commander Wright and Commander Thornton,' Alveye said as the two commanders came to a stop before Tolly. 'They were an integral part of convincing the warden to send defenders beyond the wall.'

Tolly bowed his head. 'I'm grateful to you both, and I'm sorry the outcome wasn't what we all expected.'

'We were definitely expecting to win,' Roul said, brushing a hand over his shorn head.

Harlan's gaze fell to the dead chieftain. 'And I'm always expecting sea warriors to kill me.'

'Then it sounds like all expectations were met,' Alveye said cheerfully.

Ryder looked around. 'Where's Tatum?'

'With the queen,' Alveye said.

'She's *here*?'

Roul frowned. 'Your queen is not one to shy away from danger, is she?'

'No,' they all replied in unison.

Harlan looked back at his men, who had returned to their careful lines to guard the camp. 'I've informed the Wolfvanir chieftain that every warrior is to be back in the water by sunset, no exceptions. Our men will do a full sweep of the region before we return to Chadora.'

'I appreciate that,' Tolly said, hoping the gratitude was present in his voice and not the devastation. It would all be over soon. That was great news for everyone.

Almost everyone.

Lina would be gone in a matter of hours, likely never to return to their shores again.

'Is there a problem?' Roul asked.

Tolly shook his head. 'Not at all. It's a relief for everyone.'

Ryder and Alveye exchanged a look as they all dispersed.

CHAPTER 36

The warriors shouted to each other as they loaded heavy barrels and crates into the longships. Their efforts could be heard from across the beach, where Lina sat with Simian. It was a chorus of clanging metal, creaking ropes, and waves lapping against the hulls. Soon, the sun would disappear. Soon, they would set sail.

'You look ready to burst into tears,' Simian said. He was pale and exhausted from the effort of sitting up. 'I'm sorry I couldn't be there for you today.'

'Don't say that. You were busy trying not to die.' She was watching Olga, who was clearly feeling much better judging by the way she was running about the beach.

'Never did spot that second crow,' Simian said, eyes on the sky.

'Keep searching. It has to be around.'

'I still can't believe Sture's *dead*. What's even more

surprising is that the remaining Vargr warriors are taking orders from Father at present. I hear they're going to sail south with us.' He looked around at the large men passing with crates perched on their shoulders. 'Father will have his pick of chieftain replacements if they stick around.'

'Mm.'

Simian looked at her. 'Talk to me.'

'About what?'

'Your broken heart.'

She averted her gaze. 'The less I talk about it, the better. I need to be practical from now on. I'll likely never cross paths with the general again, so there's no point dragging out the pain.'

He blinked up at her. 'The great poets may disagree with you.'

She side-eyed him. 'Oh, really?'

'They predict you'll be roaming the earth, in this life and the next, forever searching for each other.'

'That sounds sad and exhausting. I think I'll just move on as planned.'

The faintest smile came and went on his face. 'He's a good man, and clearly in love with you. I suspect the poets know better.'

They sat in exhausted silence while the warriors finished loading the boats. When they were done, Farulf signalled to Lina that it was time to depart. Nausea hit her as she rose. They were really leaving.

Helping Simian to his feet, she asked, 'Can you walk?'

'I can if I'm being chased or the alternative is certain death.'

She held on to his arm.

The sun was getting closer to the horizon now, painting the waves with fiery streaks of light. As they walked, Lina could not ignore the thoughts and feelings crashing in on her.

Simian cleared his throat. 'Oh maiden of the seas—'

'Please don't.'

He fell silent. They were halfway to their boat when he glanced east. 'Ever get the feeling you're being watched?'

She followed his gaze, her breath catching when she saw the entire horizon covered in defenders. 'They really want to make sure we leave, don't they?'

Trinka came jogging across the beach with far too much energy for the occasion. She took hold of Simian's other arm. 'I just had this vivid image of you falling overboard while attempting to relieve yourself. Hopefully it's not a vision.'

'You don't have visions.'

'Just in case this is my first one, be sure to hold on to something.'

Somehow Simian grew more pale. 'Thank you for that.'

'I can hold on to you if you like,' Trinka offered.

He scowled at her. 'That's very kind, but I'd prefer to drown.'

'Can you help him into the boat?' Lina asked. 'I have to catch Olga.'

Trinka nodded, then called to her sister. 'Aife! Grab that plank we use for the elderly!'

Simian's cheeks flushed pink. 'A little louder. I don't think the defenders on the hill heard you.'

A smile flickered on Lina's face as she headed back up the beach to fetch Olga.

'Lina,' her father called. 'We're leaving!'

She broke into a run. 'I'll be right there!'

As if sensing the urgency of the situation, Olga decided to run in the opposite direction. Cursing, Lina took off after her. 'Olga, stop!'

The goose honked in response but did not slow down.

Ahead, Lina saw a group of people step out onto the beach. Her feet stopped when she saw Tolly. With swift movements, the general caught hold of Olga, cradling her expertly in his arms as he walked over to an out-of-breath Lina.

'Thank you,' she said, taking her from him. She could barely meet his gaze.

'You can take it straight down to the chieftain,' said a familiar voice behind him.

Lina peered around Tolly and saw the queen standing with a handful of guards, each with a sack balanced on their shoulder. 'What is that?'

'Grain,' Tolly replied. 'For your clan.'

Lina stared after the guards marching across the beach. 'We can't pay for that.' Then to the queen, she shouted, 'Everything on that boat is essential for our survival! We've nothing to trade!'

Her guard took a step towards Lina, fingers brushing the hilt of her sword.

Queen Charlotte looked in her direction, then down at the goose in her arms. 'It is a gift.'

Lina's eyebrows rose. 'A *gift?*'

'To ensure your clan does not have cause to stop here again when you return north.' Charlotte paused for emphasis. 'I suggest you explain that to your chieftain, who is behaving less than graciously with my guards.'

When Lina looked towards her longship, she saw her

father animatedly conversing with the soldiers. She glanced at Tolly briefly before heading off down the beach at a jog.

'Father, take the grain,' she called to him. 'They just want us gone. Take it.'

Farulf's brow was deeply furrowed. 'Likely poisoned.' He looked at the guards when he said that.

'Simian can test it for us,' Trinka said from the ship. 'That way, we don't lose anyone of use.'

Her brother glared in Trinka's direction. 'Is there another boat you can travel on?'

'Yes, but then I'd miss the sound of you complaining for hours on end.'

'You're sure about this?' Farulf asked Lina.

'Yes, I'm sure.'

Looking over at the queen, Farulf nodded in a gesture of gratitude, then signalled to the warriors behind him to load the grain into the longships. 'Somewhere *dry*.'

'Look at all these soldiers,' Aife said to her sister. 'I should have dug a hole.'

A horn rang out just as the sun touched the horizon, and they all looked towards the Chadorian army.

'I believe that's our cue to leave,' Trinka said. 'Everyone aboard!'

The soldiers retreated up the beach, back to their queen, and it hit Lina that she never said goodbye to Tolly. She told herself that it was for the best. What could they possibly have left to say to each other without making things worse?

'Give that damn goose to Aife,' Trinka called to her. 'We need to get these ships into the water.'

Lina passed Olga up to Aife and remained in the water with the other warriors, taking hold of the rope. Her father climbed in and made his way to the front. As they dragged their longship into the sea, the horn sounded again, hurrying them along. The cold sea spray hit Lina's face as the boat slid into the water. Farulf shouted orders, and a few seconds later, they were all climbing in.

Lina took up her oar and looked back at the beach, eyes meeting Tolly's across the sand. He stood very still beside the queen, his expression unreadable, yet there was an understanding that transcended words.

A familiar ache began in her throat as she gripped the oar and rowed in time with the others, propelling the longship into the crashing waves.

All the muscles in Tolly's body were tense as he fought every instinct to go after her. Everything he felt was impractical, but he felt it anyway. Even if he had run after her, what would he say? She already knew how he felt. They both understood the impossibility of their situation. More words would help no one. All that was left to do was watch her leave.

'I am disappointed in you, General,' Queen Charlotte said beside him.

He had been expecting a speech at some point after he was discovered kissing Lina earlier in the day. 'It won't happen again.'

She frowned in his direction. 'What will not happen again?'

So, she was going to make him say it. 'The incident earlier, when I was… distracted.'

'Oh, that.' She looked forwards again. 'I think it is safe to say the defenders had that matter in hand. And I have no doubt you would have been front and centre if they had not.'

Her response confused him. 'Then what are you disappointed about?'

She gestured towards the boat. 'This tragic separation of two people clearly in love.'

Of all the responses he was expecting, that had not been one of them.

'Brock filled me in on your long and interesting history with the chieftain's daughter. Clearly, fate brought the two of you back together for a reason.'

He kept his eyes fixed ahead. 'And what would you have me do in such a situation? Everything she cares about is packed onto those ships. Everything I care about is *here*.'

'Not everything,' she replied casually.

He drew a slow breath. 'This is the best outcome for everyone.'

'No, this is the *easiest* outcome. It could also prove the loneliest. The best outcome would require some serious thought and compromise.'

He remained silent.

'I am sad on your behalf,' Charlotte continued. 'You have been fighting since you arrived here on these shores. Fighting to stay alive, fighting to protect the people you care about, fighting for the right to remain here.' She paused. 'You must be exhausted.'

The air felt unbreathable suddenly.

'But you refuse to fight for your own happiness,' she finished.

Ita, who was doing a good job of pretending she was not

listening, glanced in his direction when the queen said that last part. There was truth in what Charlotte had said. Somewhere along the way, he had convinced himself that remaining alive was enough. That Ryder surviving was *more* than enough.

As he watched Lina grow smaller against the vast expanse of the sea, the hollow feeling in his chest grew bigger.

Before he could completely indulge in his own pity party, there was a commotion on board. Olga flew out of the boat, disappearing into the foamy waves. Lina moved to go after her but was stopped by her father. An argument proceeded as she searched for the goose amid the waves.

Removing his sword, Tolly took off at a run towards the water. He waded straight in, boots and all, diving under the surface as soon as the water was deep enough. As he swam towards the boat, he searched for Olga.

'Over there!' Aife cried out, pointing.

Tolly followed her direction and spotted Olga struggling to get to shore on account of the retreating water. He swam towards her, arms burning from his efforts. As soon as she was within reach, he grabbed her by her legs, bracing for a bite to the face. Instead, the goose simply honked in protest. Perhaps she understood that Tolly was there to help. Tucking her in one arm, he used his other one for the tedious swim to the longship.

Because the ship was designed to cut through the waves, not loiter in them, the warriors were wrestling with their oars, trying to keep the thing straight. Lina was leaning over the edge, her eyes wide with worry. Her relief was palpable when she spotted Tolly approaching with Olga in hand. She extended an oar towards him, reaching it as far as she could. Tolly grasped hold of it, allowing himself to be pulled the rest of the way. He passed the complaining bird up to her.

'I'm sorry,' Aife said to Lina, close to tears as she took hold of the goose once more.

Lina gave her a reassuring smile before looking back to Tolly, eyes full of gratitude. There was a deep sadness in them too.

A wave came, and he ducked his head as it smashed into him. The boat seemed to groan in protest.

'We can't hold it any longer!' Knud shouted.

Lina's expression turned to one of pain.

Farulf approached the edge, peering down at Tolly. 'Lina, we have to go.'

Suddenly, Tolly was fifteen again, gripping the oar for dear life. 'Stay,' he said, right before another wave crashed into him. Lina struggled to hold his weight. 'We'll figure it out. Just stay.'

Her face went slack at his words, her eyes hollow.

'Get that oar up,' Farulf said, moving to take it from her.

'I can't,' she said, holding on tight. Her eyes filled with tears.

Frustrated, Farulf turned in a circle. 'I should have let him drown the first time.'

'I'm sorry,' Lina said to Tolly, her face contorting with emotion.

For once, Trinka was quiet. Simian looked like he was about to pass out from the pain, wincing every time the boat swayed.

Of course she could not stay.

Without saying another word, Tolly let go of the oar. The

water instantly swept him away from the boat, then came another wave. He let it drag him under, let it throw him towards the shore. When he resurfaced, he could no longer see Lina, only the oars working to guide the longship through the last of the surf.

Turning away, he swam towards the shore.

CHAPTER 37

The warriors went to Ireland, where they spent the rest of the summer sailing along the coast south of New Ross. Lina lost herself in the rugged beauty of the place, gazing out at the cliffs that seemed to reach all the way to the sky and the green hills dotted with grazing sheep. Some of those sheep ended up on their boats, traded for fish and trinkets they made on their journey. They did not raid or steal, because no one had any fight left in them—not even the remaining Vargr.

Simian's wounds healed after a brief infection that left him fevered and bedridden for a few days. He slowly got his strength back, the endless fatigue finally releasing its grip on him. Farulf was also doing well, all things considered. Lina noticed he drank the willow bark tea daily, and when he ran out, he sent Simian in search of more. Despite doing much better, no one knew how long it would last.

Farulf spent a lot of time with the Vargr warriors that

summer, getting to know each one. They fished, hunted, sparred. He spent evenings by the fire with different individuals, eating and talking, sometimes well into the night. Lina and Simian knew what he was doing but said nothing of it.

By the time summer came to an end, Farulf had a clear favourite, and no one was surprised that it was Toke. The man was patient, had an even temperament, and was highly skilled with weapons of all kinds. Children from both clans loved him, which helped when mentoring the next generation of warriors.

'Are you jealous?' Trinka asked Simian when they were discussing it. They had stopped at an inlet north of Youghal to hunt. 'Your father is besotted.'

Simian's bow was still on his back. He had collected a pile of leaves and was examining each one closely. 'No jealousy whatsoever. I'm relieved, truly.'

Seabirds soared overhead, their cries cutting through the salty air.

Trinka jogged a few paces to catch up to Lina. 'Safe to say your father has his next chieftain.'

'Looks that way. I wonder at what point they stop being Vargr and start being Wolfvanir.'

Lina smiled. 'I think we're already there. I'm glad they remained with us. They can't survive on their own, and we're safer together. I think the worst of the Vargr died alongside Sture that day and the best survived.'

'Agreed,' Simian said. 'Those remaining are the ones capable of listening to reason.'

Trinka watched Lina for a few paces. 'So, your father is doing well. Simian is back to being *semi*-useful. The future of the clan has never looked brighter.'

Her tone had Lina giving her a suspicious sideways glance. 'Why does it feel as though you're trying to make a point?'

'Just making some observations.'

Simian caught up to them. 'I suspect she's pointing out that you may not be as essential to the clan as you were when we departed Cardiganshire.'

'Thank you for that,' Lina said, frowning over her shoulder.

'And that's a good thing,' Trinka said. 'It affords you certain… freedoms.'

It dawned on Lina then what she was getting at. She had nudged the floodgates in Lina's mind open, and now Tolly poured back in. It had been that way all summer. Just when she had contained him to a small part of her mind, something or someone would remind her that he existed in another part of the world, and she would struggle to breathe through the memory of him.

'Everything's as it should be,' she said. 'Father's happy. The clan's thriving. I don't want any part in ruining that.'

Trinka and Simian exchanged a knowing look.

'What?' she asked, annoyed that they were siding against her.

Simian dropped a leaf and watched it float to the ground. 'I think you give yourself too much credit. The clan won't fall apart in your absence.'

'Why would I be absent?'

'I might fall apart temporarily,' Trinka said, 'but it would be a small price to pay to see you properly satisfied by a man again.'

Simian covered his ears.

'You should at least speak to your father,' Trinka said.

'To see if he's keen on me abandoning my family and returning to the place where many of our warriors were slaughtered to fornicate with the man responsible?'

Wincing, Simian said, 'I'm going hunting with the men next time.'

'So you can show them your leaf collection?' Trinka said, giving him a doubtful look.

He stopped and raised his hand. The women stopped also, looking around. Lina was about to ask what he had heard when he signalled to a section of grass next to the beach. Raising her bow, Trinka drew her arm back and released an arrow, striking a hare.

'You would have missed that if not for me,' Simian said. 'You're welcome.'

Trinka ruffled his hair. 'You're a dog trying to please its master. Now, go fetch that rabbit.'

'If you're carrying it,' Lina called to him, 'Father might believe you caught it.'

Trinka screwed up her face. 'Doubtful.' She watched Simian walk off to collect her kill. 'Can't believe we start our journey home tomorrow.'

Lina was not looking forward to it. She had enjoyed being in Ireland, perhaps because of Tolly's connection with the place. Leaving Ireland would mean leaving him behind entirely.

'Are you really not going to talk to your father?' Trinka asked.

'About what?'

Trinka gave her a tired look.

'No,' Lina said, shaking her head. 'And you shouldn't be encouraging it.'

'Encouraging you to be happy?'

'I am happy.' Or at least a version of it.

'Fine.' Trinka waved a hand. 'Just don't be surprised when your father announces that you're to marry Toke.' She went to join Simian.

Lina remained where she was, anchored by reality.

'You coming?' Simian called to her after a minute.

She found a smile. 'Yes, coming.'

The Carmarthen Militia received word from Chadora that a fleet of longships had been spotted a few miles off the coast, northbound. Tolly had soldiers dispatched along the coast but decided to travel there himself and ensure the ships passed without incident. Ryder insisted on going with him, and when Alveye and Hadewaye found out Ryder was going, they went along also, sending word to Dinefwr Castle prior to departing.

The four men made their way from the barracks to Llangrannog, timing their arrival with the passing of the ships. The air was cooling considerably, a reminder that summer had come to an end. Leaves had begun their transformation, turning shades of red and orange.

When they arrived in Llangrannog, they headed to the clifftop overlooking the sea. Below, Tolly could see Carmarthenshire banners snapping in the wind. The sound of waves crashing against the shore reached the group. A pair of soldiers rode up to meet them, confirming that there had been no sightings of any ships so far.

Tolly surveyed the horizon, the breeze tousling his hair. 'They can't be too far.'

'Unless they've passed further out to sea,' Hadewaye said.

'At least then we won't have to think about them again until spring,' Alveye said.

Ryder turned his horse towards the track that led down to the beach, and the others followed. They were halfway down when a horn sounded above them, warning of approaching ships.

'At least we didn't have to wait long,' Ryder mumbled.

The four men trotted their horses down to the bottom and rode out onto the sand, eyes on the water. They stopped clear of the waves and watched as a fleet of longships came into view, their sleek wooden forms cutting gracefully through the water. Tolly's chest tightened when he recognised the vessels.

'They look like Wolfvanir longships,' Hadewaye said.

Alveye squinted against the glare. 'Likely heading home after terrorising the south.'

'I see the Vargr ships are still among them,' Ryder noted. 'Rather brave of them to sail so close to the shorelines, given your history.'

The three defenders looked at Tolly, waiting for him to say something. But he had no words, only a feeling of suffocation. Memories bubbled to the surface, vivid ones. Lina was out there on one of those boats, likely watching the shore. Perhaps suffocating too.

The rest of his soldiers arrived, weapons at the ready. There was no reason for panic, as the fleet appeared to be continuing north with no signs of slowing. But then one ship broke away from the fleet, curving towards the beach. Its bright sails billowed before them. Tolly's hand instinctively moved to the hilt of his sword. The soldiers loaded their bows and took aim, ready to unleash a volley of arrows if need be.

Hadewaye looked at Alveye. 'Do you think they realise there's a *beach* in front of them?'

'I'd say so. On the plus side, *one* ship coming at us is better than *all* ships.'

'Agreed,' Ryder said, retrieving his bow and taking aim.

As the ship drew closer, Tolly tried to make out the faces aboard it. Then, just as the tension on the beach had reached its peak, a figure stepped up to the front of the ship, one arm raised and holding some sort of white fabric in a gesture of peaceful intent.

It was Lina.

Tolly drank in the sight of her. Her face was full and sun-kissed, her hair braided but windswept. She searched every face before her, and he could tell the moment she recognised him by the instant change in her expression. He felt it to his core.

Tolly signalled to the soldiers as he moved closer to the shoreline, shouting back at them, 'Hold your fire!'

Hadewaye brought a hand to his forehead, blocking out the sun so he could see better. 'It's Lina.'

'Yes, but not *only* Lina,' Alveye pointed out. 'Should we be worried about the rest of the passengers *not* waving white flags?'

Tolly was barely listening anymore. His full attention was on Lina.

'I'm more worried about the ship not showing any signs of slowing,' Ryder said. 'Everyone back!'

The wind and water carried the ship right up onto the

beach, lodging it in the sand. The wooden hull creaked as it settled, the waves continuing to roll around it.

Tolly approached slowly, his gaze flicking to Farulf, whose expression was painfully serious. Simian and Trinka were also on board, along with the rest of Trinka's family and a dozen other warriors. No one moved or spoke.

'Are you trying to get yourself shot?' Tolly asked, eyes settling back on Lina.

Her eyes went to the soldiers whose bows were nocked and drawn. 'I have a question.'

Tolly looked around at all the faces, watching and listening. 'Ask away.'

'You said we could figure it out,' she began, bringing volume to her voice. 'I was wondering what you meant by that.'

His eyebrows lifted slightly. 'I hoped we could come up with a way to remain together without sacrificing everything we care about.'

Her expression was as serious as her father's. 'Such as remaining in Carmarthenshire from autumn through to spring and spending summers sailing the Irish Sea with the Wolfvanir?'

Out of the corner of his eye, Tolly saw Ryder lower his weapon. 'That's one possibility.'

'What of marriage?' Farulf asked in English, rising and walking over to the edge of the boat.

'What of it?'

'Do I look like I'm in the mood for games, General?'

Tolly had never seen him in any mood other than the one he was currently in. 'I would marry your daughter in a heartbeat, if that's what she wanted.'

Simian came to stand on the other side of his sister. He was looking much healthier than the last time Tolly had seen him.

'What if we wished to see Lina at other times during the year?' he asked.

'I would be her husband, not her keeper. She would be free to see you whenever she liked. The security of Carmarthenshire is a separate matter.'

Trinka spoke up at that. 'He just wants to know if you'll shoot us if we arrive on your shores in autumn.'

'It's autumn now,' Tolly said. 'No arrows have been fired.'

'Yet,' Alveye muttered behind him.

Hadewaye threw his elbow into Alveye's side.

Farulf lowered himself over the edge of the boat, boots splashing in the shallows. He walked towards Tolly, making every soldier on the beach nervous. Ryder took a step closer to Tolly, and Farulf heeded the warning and stopped. The chieftain spent a few moments looking Tolly up and down, as though trying to decide something.

'You made a mistake the day you asked my daughter to stay with you,' he said.

Tolly nodded. 'I've been trying to convince myself of the same thing for months, but I can't bring myself to regret it.'

'Your mistake was not asking her to stay,' Farulf said. 'Your mistake was not asking *me* first. There's a proper way of doing things.'

Tolly looked past him to Lina, who was completely still. 'There was quite a lot going on that day.'

Farulf crossed his arms. 'Well, that excuse doesn't apply to today.'

'You want me to ask you *now*?'

Farulf grew taller before him. 'Tell me now what you would have that day.'

Everyone fell to a new level of silence, waiting for him to speak.

Tolly cleared his throat. 'I would have reminded you that your daughter once found me on the brink of death. She saved me that day. There's no question that I'm standing here on this beach because of her. And for that, I owe her my life.' He paused. 'But I don't owe her my heart. That I gave to her freely and completely. Not because of anything she's done in the past but because of who she is now.' His eyes found Lina's. 'Your daughter is kind and brave. She cares deeply about the people in her life and loves fiercely. I've witnessed it first-hand, and I've been lucky enough to experience it too.' His gaze returned to Farulf. 'We can keep finding and saving each other in this life. I'm sure of it.'

Lina jumped over the side of the boat, landing in a crouch before taking off at a run towards Tolly. She leapt at him, and he caught her, arms going around her. The instant comfort from having her close had his throat thickening.

Farulf made an exasperated gesture with his hands. 'I've not even given my answer yet.'

Simian chuckled. 'Even you couldn't tell him no after that.'

The sound of a horse approaching had everyone looking towards the trees. Tatum appeared on horseback, cantering across the sand towards them. His horse came to a skidding halt a few feet away from the other defenders. 'Sorry I'm late. What did I miss?' He looked from the armed soldiers to Tolly and Lina, then at Farulf. 'What's happening here? We have bows ready to go and some people hugging. Friend or foe? I genuinely can't tell.'

'None of us know yet,' Alveye said.

'I think they're going to get married,' Hadewaye said, sniffing.

'The general's speech was a little much,' Trinka added, 'but we're all still hopeful.'

Tolly placed Lina down on the ground, eyes searching hers. 'Are you sure about this?'

'*I'm* still not sure about this,' Farulf said, drawing everyone's attention to him. He looked around at the faces of the soldiers, then at his own warriors. 'Fine,' he renounced. 'However, I insist Simian remain here for the first year.'

Simian straightened. 'That's a wonderful idea. It would be the perfect opportunity to complete my study of the local bird life.' Then, seeing his father's expression, he added, 'And protect my sister.'

'As hard as this is for me to admit,' Trinka said, placing a hand on his shoulder, 'I'll miss you.'

Simian turned to look at her. 'You will?'

She gestured to the crate. 'I was talking to the goose.'

Slowly, one by one, the bows were lowered, and the tension dissipated. They were a long way from anything resembling amicable, but the reduced desire to kill one another was a start.

'I'm so happy,' Lina said quietly while Simian and Trinka's banter continued. 'And so afraid.'

His expression turned serious. 'From now on, you never have to be afraid if I'm standing at your side. Understand?'

She nodded slowly, her fingers entwining with his. 'I understand.'

'Well, will you look at that,' Simian said, pointing.

They all looked to see a crow perched on the side of the boat, watching the scene unfold.

'My second crow,' Simian said, pressing a hand to his chest. 'I'm going to be all right, everyone.'

Tolly gave Lina a questioning look.

'I'll explain later.' She let go of his hand. 'First, I need to get through the goodbyes.'

'I'll be right here.'

Her eyes searched his. 'I know.'

EPILOGUE

It had been the most difficult thing in the world to watch her clan sail away, knowing she would not see them until the following summer. Lina had stood on the beach with her heart lodged in her throat and hand wrapped firmly in Tolly's. She had siphoned all of her bravery from him. Surprisingly, Simian had been unafraid—perhaps even excited. He might not have been the bravest of men holding an axe on a battlefield, but he was stoic in the face of change.

The eyes of every soldier and defender had been upon her as she stood on that beach, wondering what to do next. Thankfully, Tolly had the answer. It was almost as if he had been planning for that exact scenario. And maybe he had. She had played out imaginary scenarios in her own mind enough times, imagining life in a foreign land with strangers. Imagining a life with Tolly, where they were free to love each other out in the open.

Tolly took Lina and Simian to Maddock House in

Llanelieu. There they met Ryder's wife, Lady Isabel. From that moment on, Lina knew they were going to be all right. Isabel was one of the warmest and kindest people Lina had ever met, instantly accepting the pair of them as family. Her brother and mother also lived there, along with their one-year-old son, Dom, who had the same thick black hair as his father and uncle. Seeing Tolly in a relaxed family setting was heart-warming. He was a different person outside of an army setting—relaxed, affectionate with his nephew, making jokes. Lina had trouble looking away.

Isabel's brother, Everard, was the same age as Simian, and the pair became instant friends despite being opposites in many ways. Simian taught Everard Scandinavian history and interesting facts from all over the world. Everard liked to spar and ride horses. They both talked incessantly, sometimes over the top of each other, much to the disapproval of Isabel's mother.

Lina and Tolly were wed in a church in the village, the union blessed by a god she did not know. But it was legally binding, and that was all Lina cared about. Tolly Blackmane was her husband. Hers for life. Never again would a border separate them.

'Behold my oath that I will take no one as my wife except you,' Tolly had said before witnesses.

'Here I take you as my husband,' she had said in reply, 'to have and to hold until the end of my life.'

The wedding celebration would take place in the summer once reunited with her clan.

As autumn settled over Carmarthenshire, Lina adjusted to the rhythm of their new life. The Blackmane brothers decided to build a small cottage for the newlyweds within walking distance from the main house. It was nestled among the golden trees that painted the landscape. Everyone helped, Lina enjoying the physical labour and the thrill of watching their new home take shape.

There was still plenty of work to be done outside the building. With Tolly travelling frequently between the barracks and Maddock House, Lina and Simian took care of the hunting and gathered firewood in preparation for winter. When Tolly saw the pile of wood they had accumulated, he almost fell over.

'What?' Lina asked, worried she had accidentally mutilated a sacred family tree or something.

Tolly pulled her into his arms and pressed his lips to her forehead. 'This isn't Scandinavia. We're not going to be snowed in fighting the elements.'

'I tried to tell her,' Simian said.

The cottage went up quickly with the help of the family, along with Alveye and Hadewaye, and even Tatum occasionally. With each log stacked neatly, and each nail hammered into place, Lina felt a sense of belonging grow inside her. Their new home was completed by the end of the autumn and became their cosy refuge from winter. The nights grew longer and the days colder, yet the warmth of their new life seemed to defy the icy grip of the season.

They invited Tatum and Queen Charlotte to dinner. Their carriage pulled up in front of the cottage on a frosty evening, wheels crunching on the gravel path. Lina watched from the doorway as Queen Charlotte climbed down and looked around.

'Should I be nervous?' Lina whispered to Tolly when he joined her at the door.

He kissed her cheek. 'No.'

And he had been right. Conversation flowed easily throughout the night, with Queen Charlotte taking a genuine interest in Lina's life and culture. They talked about Charlotte's heartbreaking and fascinating rise to the throne.

'There is a lot to learn from each other,' Charlotte said, 'and perhaps lots to gain, eventually.' She smiled. 'Your marriage might prove to be the first step towards the impossible—a constructive and mutually beneficial relationship between this kingdom and your people.'

Olga chose that moment to come honking into the room. Tolly rose from the table and went to deal with her.

'She spends more time inside than she should on account of Lady Isabel's pet eagle, who likes to watch Olga from the trees,' Simian explained. 'Golden eagles can carry prey up to eight pounds.'

'And Olga is a little over six,' Lina said.

Tolly returned to the room. 'We have a perfectly good chicken pen out back, but apparently that's beneath her.'

Tatum picked up his drink. 'I share my bed with a 132-pound dog that drools, so you'll get no sympathy from me.'

Their laughter warmed the room.

Spring crept in, painting the countryside in colour. With far less rain than the previous year, flowers bloomed in abundance. The trees that had stood bare through winter budded. But Lina was most excited for the summer. Not for the lazy afternoons spent by the river watching dragonflies flit about but for the long-awaited reunion with her clan.

Queen Charlotte wrote to Tolly, giving permission for the Wolfvanir to come ashore for the wedding celebration so the two families could come together for the occasion. Afterwards, Lina would be at sea for a few months. Even though the separation from Tolly would be difficult, she knew she could never remain on land too long. She would never let that part of her go. Tolly knew their children would also spend summers at sea one day.

They waited for the longships to arrive. Finally, a report came that a fleet had been spotted along the coast in the north. Lina, Tolly, and Simian made their way to Llangrannog. Ryder, Isabel, and the defenders joined them as well. They gathered on the beach, and when the silhouette of longships appeared in the distance, Lina began to cry. Tolly wrapped an arm around her, saying nothing. There was no need for words, because he understood.

Trinka leapt from the boat before it had even made it ashore. Laughing, Lina ran straight into the foamy water, knocking her friend backwards with the force of her embrace. They tried to get up, fell, lost the ability to breathe from laughing too hard, then finally managed to stand.

'I brought mead,' Trinka said, holding Lina's hands as the waves smashed them.

'I brought *wine*.'

When the last of the longships had been dragged ashore, Lina went to her father. His eyes filled with tears when they met hers, and he hugged her so tightly that she expected a rib to snap at any moment.

'At least they're feeding you well,' Farulf said, drawing back to look at her. 'Where's your brother?'

'Here,' Simian said, coming at a jog.

Farulf clapped him on the back. 'I see you finally have some muscle on you.'

'We had to build a cottage to live in,' Simian said. 'I wasn't given a choice.'

Farulf steered his son towards the boat. 'Good. You can put that muscle to use and carry our things ashore.'

A few hours after the boats arrived, the entire beach was alive with laughter and music. The smell of meat roasting over open flames took over the air. They feasted on boar, bread, and honeyed fruits. Mead and ale flowed freely. Bonfires blazed brightly against the darkening sky. Lina danced with her family and friends, inviting Isabel to join in the chaos too. Tolly watched her from the other side of the fire, eyes smiling. He was seated with her father, and they were seemingly relaxed in each other's presence. The music stopped, and everyone raised their flagons in a toast, their collective voices blowing across the sand.

'Did you hear the exciting news?' Isabel said, joining Lina and Trinka by the fire at the end of the evening. Dom was asleep in her arms, his little face pressed to her neck.

Trinka stifled a yawn. 'What news would that be?'

'Farulf has agreed to take us all across the channel to Ireland.' She smiled. 'It will be the first time Tolly and Ryder have been home since…' The smile faltered. 'Since they left.'

Lina looked over to where Tolly was speaking with Toke. Ryder was on the other side of him, listening to Erik drunk-talk at him. Tolly looked in her direction, eyes creasing at the corners when he found her watching him. They *always* found each other.

'That *is* exciting news,' Lina said.

The following day, the Wolfvanir set sail, careful not to overstay their welcome. The rest of them returned to Maddock House to pack their belongings. Tolly sent word to

Dinefwr Castle requesting an immediate replacement for the time he would be gone. Tatum showed up at Maddock House a few hours after receiving the message, announcing that he would be commanding the Carmarthen Militia in Tolly's absence.

'I had a feeling you wouldn't mind stepping in,' Tolly said as he loaded the last of their things into the wagon.

Tatum took a bag from Isabel and loaded it. 'As their king—'

'Consort,' Ryder corrected.

'The soldiers will have no problem taking orders from me,' Tatum continued, ignoring Ryder, 'even if my uniform does look a little different.'

They said their farewells and began the long journey back to Llangrannog. When they arrived, they found the longships already in the bay, waiting for them under the watchful eyes of Carmarthen Militia soldiers. Lina's heart quickened with excitement as they made their way across the sand. When she looked at Tolly, she thought he seemed nervous.

'You sure about this?' she asked. 'It's not too late to change your mind.'

'Yes, it is,' Ryder said, his son perched on one arm. 'I sat through a one-hour address from my very worried mother-in-law, then travelled all night to be here. We're getting on that boat.'

Isabel guided her husband away, giving them some privacy. Simian followed them.

'You haven't been back on a ship since that day,' Lina pointed out. 'You're allowed to be wary.'

'I'll be fine.' He squinted in the direction of the waiting longship. 'So long as no one sets fire to our boat.'

'We're sea warriors. Some of the most hated and feared people on the planet. I can't make any promises.'

His mouth turned up.

Farulf had brought the boat up to the shoreline to load the additional passengers. When they reached it, Trinka stepped up to the side and gestured for the baby. 'Pass him to me.'

Ryder hesitated.

'It's tradition for the little ones to ride on the mast,' Trinka said. 'Teaches them early the importance of holding on.'

The defender's eyebrows drew together in an angry line.

'She is clearly joking,' Isabel said. 'Pass Dom up before we all get soaked.'

Reluctantly, Ryder passed the smiling infant to Trinka before helping his wife into the longship.

A few chaotic minutes later, the boat pulled away from the shore and headed towards the waiting fleet. They were ready to set sail to Ireland.

Tolly and Lina went to the front of the ship, looking out at the vast sea ahead of them.

'Do you remember the night we were inside your tent?' Lina said, keeping her voice low so her father would not hear. 'And you asked where I would want to go if we had the freedom?'

He entwined his fingers with hers. 'I remember.'

'I told you I wanted to go to Ireland and see where you grew up. Watch you remember things that you've likely forgotten.'

'I remember everything from that time, every conversation. I used to replay them in my mind when you would return to your side of the boundary.'

She leaned her head on his arm. 'We did it. We're actually going.'

'And it barely matters that your father's glare is currently burning a hole in my back.'

Lina peeked behind her, then faced forwards again. 'He's just getting used to you being on *his* territory for once.' She looked up at him. 'We're here because of you. Thank you for being brave enough to suggest it.'

'Thank you for thinking it over, then returning.'

'That's thanks to you not killing me and my family.'

His gaze met hers. 'Due to the fact that you saved my life all those years ago.'

They watched each other for a long moment.

'Perhaps you could both grab an oar and help,' Trinka suggested. 'We're going against the wind, you know.'

'Fair point,' Lina said, turning around.

'It's definitely time to teach your land-mammal husband how to row a ship,' Simian said.

'This isn't a fishing boat,' Farulf cut in. 'You'll need to listen to directions.'

'He knows, Father.' Lina gestured to an empty space between two oarsmen. 'Take a seat.'

Tolly did as instructed.

Ryder rose from his seat beside Isabel and went to fill one of the other spaces. When Tolly gave him a questioning look, he said, 'I can't watch you fail alone.'

Lina repositioned Tolly's hands on the oar.

'Now what?' he asked, looking up at her.

A memory surfaced as she looked back at him. Tolly, blue-lipped, watching her from the water as he gripped the end of her oar.

Lina brought her face closer to his and covered his hand with hers. 'Now hold on properly, and don't let go.'

ACKNOWLEDGMENTS

I would like to express my gratitude to the many people who contributed to this book. My biggest thanks goes to my readers—without you, I wouldn't get to do what I love. Next, a huge thank you to my rock star husband, who supports and encourages me even though my writing takes time away from him. I love you to bits. A big thank you to McKinley, Kristin, and the team at Hot Tree Editing for polishing the manuscript into something beautiful. A shout-out to my proofreader, Rebecca, for catching everything I missed. A round of applause for my cover designer, Stuart Bache, for another gorgeous cover. And finally, a huge thank you to my Launch Team for your encouragement, honest reviews, and being the final set of eyes on my work. You're all amazing.

ALSO BY TANYA BIRD

You can find a complete list of published works at

tanyabird.com/books

www.ingramcontent.com/pod-product-compliance
Lightning Source LLC
Chambersburg PA
CBHW030625310726
48979CB00003B/884

* 9 7 8 1 7 6 4 1 2 1 9 3 4 *